*"Why didn't
when you go.*

Hannah asked huskily, trying to ignore the tingles Race was causing as he touched her shoulder blades with a feather-light touch.

"Haven't had time. Couldn't get to a phone. Afraid you'd run if you knew I was coming. Take your pick."

"Run from what?"

"From me. From all the things about me that you can't accept."

"Oh, Race, please don't think I'm some kind of judgmental Puritan. I'm not. Just because I don't approve of certain kinds of entertainment doesn't mean I don't accept you."

Moving away quickly, she fluttered unproductively by the electric percolator, feeling the air practically sizzle between them. "Uh, how about something to eat? Are you hungry?"

There was hunger in the eyes that riveted her as Race slowly nodded his head, but it wasn't for food....

Dear Reader,

There's so much to talk about this month that I hardly know where to begin, so I guess I'll start off with this month's American Hero, Race Latimer, in Kathleen Eagle's *Black Tree Moon*. Race is a smoke jumper, an elite fire fighter who attacks the flames from above. He's also a cocky, hell-raising kind of guy who meets his match in social worker Hannah Quinn. You won't want to miss their story.

We're also highlighting new author Kate Carlton this month, as part of Silhouette's PREMIERE program. In *Kidnapped!*, Kate has created characters you won't soon forget. Talk about on-the-run romance . . . ! Be sure to come along for the ride.

Emilie Richards's *From a Distance* is memorable not just for the way this talented author reunites Stefan and Lindsey Daniels, whose marriage had foundered on the rocky shores of discontent, but for the secondary character she introduces. Alden Fitzpatrick is more than he seems, but in ways most people are not yet ready to deal with. Are you? Read this book—and then look for Alden's story, coming in 1993.

The month continues with Marion Smith Collins's *Baby Magic,* a deeply emotional story of loving, of giving, of the miracles of science and the unpredictability of fate. Two people who'd never expected to share the ups and downs of parenting find themselves in just that position. Join Frances Williams in *Shadows on Satin,* as heroine Lori Castleton returns to the brooding mansion that was once almost her undoing. There she has to confront the specters of her past as well as hero Keith McKinnon, a man who can't bring himself to trust her—even though he loves her. Finally, join Desire author Beverly Barton as she makes her Intimate Moments debut with *This Side of Heaven,* a potent mix of the here and now with the shadowy forces of the past.

In coming months, look for books by such favorite authors as Kathleen Korbel, Dallas Schulze, Rachel Lee and Marilyn Pappano. Here at Silhouette Intimate Moments, we try to make all your reading experiences happy ones.

Yours,

Leslie J. Wainger
Senior Editor and Editorial Coordinator

AMERICAN HERO

BLACK TREE

MOON

Kathleen Eagle

Silhouette®
INTIMATE MOMENTS®
Published by Silhouette Books New York
America's Publisher of Contemporary Romance

SILHOUETTE BOOKS
300 East 42nd St., New York, N.Y. 10017

BLACK TREE MOON

ISBN: 0-373-07451-4

First Silhouette Books printing October 1992

Books by Kathleen Eagle

Silhouette Intimate Moments

For Old Times' Sake #148
More Than a Miracle #242
But That Was Yesterday #257
Paintbox Morning #284
Bad Moon Rising #412
To Each His Own #428
Black Tree Moon #451

Silhouette Special Edition

Someday Soon #204
A Class Act #274
Georgia Nights #304
Something Worth Keeping #359
Carved in Stone #396
Candles in the Night #437
'Til There Was You #576

Silhouette Books

Silhouette Christmas Stories 1988
"The Twelfth Moon"
Silhouette Summer Sizzlers 1991
"Sentimental Journey"

KATHLEEN EAGLE

is a transplant from New England to Minnesota, where she and her husband, Clyde, make their home with two of their three children. She has considered writing to be her "best talent" since she was about nine years old, and English and history were her "best subjects." After fourteen years of teaching high school students about writing, she saw her own first novel in print in 1984. Since then, she's published many more novels with Silhouette Books and Harlequin Historicals that have become favorites for readers worldwide. She has received awards from Romance Writers of America, *Romantic Times* and *Affaire de Coeur.*

To Sue Geike-Lyon,
with affection and gratitude

The author wishes to thank Rose and Frances Cree
for keeping traditional willow basket weaving alive
and for showing me their technique.

Thanks also to Al Braddock, fire management
officer for the Black Hills National Forest.
His information, recollections, suggestions and
generous sharing of resource materials helped make
this story plausible, although he is in no way
responsible for any technical blunders or any literary
license I may have taken.

Prologue

Deadwood was Race Latimer's kind of town. In the past year, since the South Dakota legislature had loosened up on its gambling laws, the town once known as Deadwood Gulch had recaptured its bold and bawdy reputation. The infamous whorehouses were gone—had been since the early 1980s—but there was no keeping a good boomtown down. A perennial restlessness seemed to hang in the air.

Maybe it was the smell of gold still rising from the mines that made a man feel like playing fast and loose with his money. Or maybe the place really was haunted by the spirits of Wild Bill Hickok, Calamity Jane and the other rowdy characters whose graves had been carved into the steep side of Mount Moriah, overlooking the town. Whatever it was, with the new gambling laws in place, Deadwood's ghosts were probably feeling right at home. But for Race, who had no idea what *home* meant, Deadwood was one hell of a good party.

The Plugged Nickel was made for Race's kind of party.

Anybody who had a problem with smoke was welcome to turn right around and head back out the front door. There wasn't a circle-slash-cigarette sign in sight, and the air was perpetually blue. Race thrived on smoke. The acrid odor went down especially well with the bite of a good draft beer, and he was thinking of getting himself one in just a few minutes. No designated driver stickers were handed out at the Plugged Nickel, and if a guy wanted to chew, there were plenty of spittoons handy. In deference to the lost art of precision spitting, the floor was covered with sawdust. But, then, there'd always been sawdust. In the old days it had been a way for the barkeep to collect spilled gold dust.

So there was a nineteenth century feel to the place, even though there were some twentieth century conveniences. Indoor plumbing was one. Electricity, slot machines, prerecorded steel guitars—all the good stuff—were the others. That plus a leather-vested bouncer on duty right next to the big, heavy, rough-hewn door, carding everybody who walked in. The Plugged Nickel was not a place to take the kids.

Race didn't miss having kids around. As he remembered it, being a kid hadn't been much fun, so he couldn't imagine that being around them would be any better. Kids had little to do with the pleasures of life as long as a man made sure he kept his wits about him. And Race did. He was well-versed in all manner of precautionary measures. He believed in safety first.

These last few months he'd even been required to sermonize on the "safety first" principle. When new recruits came to him for training, he'd start out by asking what precautionary measures meant. "Yeah," he'd say, "it means keeping your wits about you while pursuing life's pleasures." And after he had entertained a few other suggestions, he'd always end up with his favorite warning.

"Take your chances at the poker table. Don't take any chances with fire. You're liable to get burned."

It was a worn out saw, but what the hell, it made his point to the rookies. He was a man who practiced better than he preached, anyway. He was a good fire fighter. Training new teams had only recently become part of his job, and far from his favorite. He'd rather be fighting a fire than talking about it.

And when he wasn't fighting fire, he wanted to be pursuing those proverbial pleasures, which were so abundantly available in Deadwood. Beer, women and cards, although not necessarily in that order, and generally one at a time. Tonight he'd decided to indulge in the cards. Since he was never in town for very long, he enjoyed the occasional chance to deal blackjack at the Plugged Nickel. It was one of the skills he'd cultivated after he'd moved out of his father's house, and after he was sure he'd seen South Dakota in his rearview mirror for the last time. In those days he'd been dealing for "the house," moonlighting in the casinos in Vegas before hiring on with the Forest Service.

Nowadays, he *was* the house. At least, he was half of it. His partner, Vicki Potter, was playing hostess up front while Race was tapping his toe to a Willie Nelson tune and giving people all the cards they wanted. He got a real kick out of the way they kept throwing chips on the table. *His* tables in his house. This was as close to home as Race Latimer figured he'd ever get.

The place was hopping tonight. Like old Wild Bill, Race preferred to keep his back to the wall, but he only got an occasional glimpse of the front door. Generally there was a whole slew of bodies in the way. All kinds of bodies jostled for a turn at the slots, but it was the pretty female variety that caught Race's eye. He thought it was kind of cute when the short, shapely ones had to put a little extra effort into getting themselves up on the bar stools. If they were wearing skirts, so much the better. He was a leg man. And he had a head for cards, so he could manage to spare a glance without losing count.

There were plenty of other distractions. Bells jingled and lights blinked on the slot machines to his left, while poker pots were accumulating in the centers of the four green tables on his right. Meanwhile, the faces of the players at his table were a pretty easy read. Nobody was losing his whole shirt, but a couple of guys were getting a little anxious about winning their buttons back. Race was taking their money and having a damn good time doing it. He was almost sorry to see Lester, one of the regular dealers, arrive for his shift.

But after he'd turned the high stool over to his replacement, there was time for that long-awaited draft beer. Race lit a cigarette and rolled it to the corner of his mouth while he helped himself at the spigot behind the bar.

"We've got some sharp cardplayers here tonight," he told bartender Billy Sutter. Billy glanced up from the well drinks he was pouring at the far end of the bar and smiled knowingly. The comment would soon send some would-be cardsharp from the bar to the tables.

Everybody who worked at the Plugged Nickel wore a black Stetson, which looked especially good on Billy. It covered the premature bald spot that was wreaking havoc with his ego. It also looked good on Vicki. In her scoop-necked, fitted Western blouse and tight denim skirt, she complemented the decor, which was not surprising, since she'd done all of the decorating. Race had secured the loan. They'd gotten in on the ground floor of the town's latest boom, investing before the state constitution had been amended to allow Deadwood to become a gambling mecca once again. No one had expected the kind of profits that had been turned almost immediately, but hardly anybody was complaining. It was the luckiest risk Race had ever taken. He could quit fighting wildland fires anytime now. Anytime he really wanted to.

He sipped his beer and imagined telling Al Stockert, his boss, that he didn't really want to jump anymore. Stockert would say, "Get the hell going, then," knowing there wasn't much chance Race would take him up on it. Smoke-jumping wasn't a job a man like Race would walk away from easily. Money, after all wasn't everything.

Money was nice. So were good beer, good music and good-looking women. Sweet-smelling women were nice, too, but Vicki, who was sidling up on the bar stool next to his, had overdone it on the perfume. When she laid a key next to his glass he had to sneeze before he could hike a questioning eyebrow her way.

"You need a place to stay while you're in town, don't you?" she asked with a smile. "I happen to know there isn't a vacancy within fifty miles."

He picked up the key and examined it. "Does this fit the cabin or your apartment?"

"The cabin. I've sublet the apartment, and I'm staying upstairs now. I've hardly used the cabin lately."

Race glanced up. The wistful look in her eyes made him uncomfortable, and she knew it. She touched the back of his hand and told him quietly, "You can relax. I know you don't want a roommate."

"I thought I was supposed to get the room upstairs when we fixed it up." He glanced over his shoulder at the stairway that led to the loft and remembered how they'd agreed that every Western saloon had to have an upstairs. Theirs had started out as a dimly lit landing with a red door, behind which had been an office and storage space. "I take it you fixed it up," he said.

"I added a shower, some bedroom furniture and a microwave. It's more convenient this way."

He braced his elbow on the bar, turning another few degrees so he could actually see the upstairs door. She'd added black trim to the red. "But it kinda looks like—"

"Exactly what it's designed to look like." Vicki nudged his knee with hers. "It's kind of a kick having a bed up there."

"You're somethin' else, Miss Vicki," he drawled, ignoring the nudge. "I've been meaning to look for a place of my own." He stuck his cigarette in the corner of his mouth, leaned back and pocketed the key in his tight jeans. "You wanna sell the cabin?"

"I'd sell it in a minute if it was here in town, the way property's going these days. But since it's up in God's country, where it's not worth as much . . ." Vicki straightened her shoulders as she followed the motion of Race's hand from his pocket to the cigarette he was puffing on. "Isn't that a hoot? God's country isn't worth nearly as much as a piece of real estate in Sin City." She laughed and shook her head. Her bottled blond hair brushed her shoulders. "Anyway, keep your money and use the cabin whenever you want. The way you breeze in and out, you just need a place to crash whenever the wind shifts."

"Yeah, well, they've got me training teams now. And fire seasons are pretty fickle, so I never know. That's why everything I own fits into my pickup."

"Except your half of this place."

"That's right." He nodded and lifted his glass toward the steer horns above the bar, silently toasting a fine business arrangement.

Vicki touched his knee, drawing his attention back to her ever-wistful smile. "Keep it simple," she repeated. "Use the cabin whenever you want."

He knew what she wanted, but they'd already tried it that way. Playing house together hadn't worked, and he still wasn't sure why. Vicki was beautiful. She was good in bed. She made no demands. She was a hell of a business-woman—uncompromising, unsentimental and unrepentant—which made them two of a kind. Living with Vicki was like living with his emotional clone. Totally unsatisfactory, even though Vicki had made it clear that he could move back in with her at any time.

The way she smiled at him now was a clear reminder of a standing invitation that was best left just standing, for the business's sake. At this point she was putting more into the Plugged Nickel than he was. She'd said she didn't mind. In fact, she enjoyed teasing him on the fact that he'd found a way to make a career of "dropping in," and he knew that it was a habit that fascinated women like Vicki. That was fine. Being fascinating had its advantages.

"Oh, and don't mind my new neighbor," Vicki added. Race glanced beyond the fading foam of his beer and gave her a quizzical look. "Kind of a sweet young thing," she explained with a mock smile and a fluttering of eyelashes. "Moved into old man Tappen's cabin, along with a dog. Her dog doesn't bite. Far as I know, neither does she, which means she isn't your type."

"Who says I like getting bit?"

Vicki raised her eyebrows, a gesture intended to remind him of God knew what. He indulged her with a throaty chuckle as he smashed his cigarette butt on the bar's logo—a silver nickel with a hole in it—at the bottom of a black plastic ashtray. "How young a thing?" he asked absently.

"Actually, she's got to be older than she looks. She makes you think Alice took a wrong turn on her way to Wonderland." Vicki sighed disgustedly. "So we've got Alice in Deadwood, and I don't mean Poker Alice."

"Is that her name? Alice?"

"I don't remember what her name is," Vicki claimed. Race wondered at the memory lapse, since she remembered almost any repeat customer by name. "She's not exactly memorable," Vicki went on. "Do you remember any of the Goody Two Shoes you went to school with? You know, the ones who got straight A's and wouldn't put out?"

Race laughed and shook his head. "Not a one."

"See what I mean?"

He wondered if Vicki's fair cheeks ever blushed with any kind of modesty. Probably they had, once upon a time. Innocence was as dim and foolish a memory for her as it was for him. And two of a kind was fine for business, which was the only kind of relationship Race Latimer was inclined to bet on anyway.

Chapter 1

"What is it, Critter? What's out there, boy?"

Hannah Quinn trusted her dog's instincts. The deep furrows he'd plowed into the molding that framed her back door wasn't damage, but a testimony to Critter's vigilance. She patted his big square head as she flicked the light off and peered through the window. All she could see beyond her backyard pines was a glittering trail of moonlight arrowing toward the opposite lakeshore.

"If it's a skunk, I think we should let it go this time, huh, boy?"

The yellow Labrador whined and worked his front paws furiously over his preliminary carvings.

"Please don't tear the door down over this," Hannah begged, hauling on the dog's collar. He came away whining. As soon as she let him go, he was back at it.

She gave in and opened the door. "Have at it, then. Chase it out of your territory, whatever it is."

The dog's wild barking echoed in the stillness beyond the back step. Hannah had chosen her rustic home by the lake for its quiet seclusion. Deep in the pine forest of the Black Hills, she had only a few neighbors, and their distant cabins were screened by trees, packed row on row like a book of matches. Most of the owners were seasonal residents, so Hannah had enjoyed the lake and the woods almost exclusively since she'd decided to move out of town in late winter, when the cabin had become available. After a day of working with the clients at the New Moon Center, she appreciated her own private retreat, and the isolation didn't bother her at all with Critter to protect her.

She watched the dog plunge into the darkness, heading straight for the lake. Laughing, she called out, "Don't be out too late!" She hoped there was enough tomato juice to bathe him if he got sprayed. She had just about decided to change his name to Stinker when she realized Critter wasn't doing his usual skunk-chaser bark. She made a face—the kind her mother had once warned would cause permanent wrinkles—as she lapped the front of her poodle-plush robe over her granny nightgown, cinched the belt and slipped out onto the back step. Critter was yapping joyfully on his way to the lake, the same way he always did when she came home from work.

A shrill whistle pierced the darkness. Hannah's eyes widened. That was no night bird's call.

Splash!

Hannah stopped short of calling out to her dog when she heard the quiet echo of a human voice. She shook off the sensible urge to go back inside and lock the door. Instead she followed where curiosity led. Critter was no fickle friend, and he wasn't the kind to take to strangers.

She trod lightly on the sloping path, the toes of her bootie slippers inching cautiously over the pine needle carpet. Hesitating at the snap of a dry twig, she tried to sort out the sounds that floated in the darkness all around her, but she kept the sound of her own breathing under wraps.

Deep, melodious male laughter reverberated across the lake like the gentle song of an oboe.

"Race you to it, boy. Ready?"

Critter answered the challenge with a single bark, and the laughter sounded again. Hannah hugged herself tightly around the middle and crept closer. Her eyes, straining against the shroud of night, were beginning to adjust to the dark. As she peered between two pines she saw a figure rising from the white pool of moonlight that drifted across the black lake. A man. A stranger to her, maybe, but apparently not to her dog. Critter was treading water a few feet away, waiting like a pup for a chance to play.

The man pushed his wet hair back with both hands while the water lapped at the base of his long back. He must have awfully thick skin, Hannah thought. She knew how cold the water was. She'd tested it with her own toes a few times and decided that swimming was not yet in season. But it didn't seem to bother the man at all. He took a couple of steps, wading deeper, and pointed toward the middle of the lake.

"See it?" he asked. Critter yapped wildly. Hannah searched the strip of moonlight and nodded absently when she, too, saw the bobbing stick. "Okay, that's what we're after," the man said. His quick surface dive, as fluid as an otter's, plunged his head below and popped his buttocks above the water.

Good Lord, the man was naked!

Dutifully, Hannah looked away, but a human yelp and a canine yap became a pair of invisible reins, drawing her head around. Either Critter had won the race, or his friend had declined to carry the stick in his mouth. The man was coasting through the water on his back now, with Critter paddling alongside, bearing the stick like a trophy. Once he reached shallow water, the man stopped and spoke quietly as he took the proffered stick. Then, with a sudden whoosh, they both shot out of the water, the dog anticipating the man's move. The man pulled his arm back and sent the stick sailing. Critter paddled after it while the man stood there watching, the water washing up against his thighs.

His body was sleek and powerful. His wet shoulders glistened in the moonlight. His hair appeared to be thick and dark, and his long back tapered to a small, tight...

Heat flared in Hannah's cheeks and she turned away, swallowing hard. She'd seen bare male buttocks before. In the village near the mission in Kenya, she'd seen them. No big deal. Of course, they'd been innocent boys, just playing. These two were playing, too, though. Except that this was no boy. This was a man, most primal. She'd happened upon a scene that might have come straight from Genesis.

Be still, heart, this is no cause for alarm.

About-face, body. Just slip back into the house as if nothing were amiss.

But her feet weren't moving. And with God as her only witness, she was peeking again.

The lake lapped at his shoulders now. He had hunkered down to wait for Critter, who was churning back to him with the prized stick. Hannah wondered a little jealously whether her dog had been lacking for human attention, the way he was turning himself inside out for this naked stranger.

"Hey, hey, that's my leg!" the man scolded. Critter was about to swim right over him, but the man laughed as he held the dog at arm's length. "You've got yourself some claws there, boy. The leg is one thing, but I don't want you shakin' the ol' maracas with those, if you catch my drift."

Critter yapped as though he did. Hannah decided that male bonding had some mysterious way of crossing the species barrier.

"Okay, one more time," the man said, "and then I've got to get going before your mama comes out looking for you."

This time he faked a toss from a crouched position. Critter barked, and the man laughed again.

Your mama? How did he know that Critter belonged to a woman? Hannah hoped he wasn't putting on an exhibition for her benefit. If he *wanted* her to see him this way, then he had a problem.

Then again, if she watched, *she* had a problem.

He shot out of the water and hurled the stick again. Hannah was mesmerized. In the moonlit water, under the star-studded sky, the man was as naturally beautiful as the dog. He was also just as lithe, just as agile. Romping together, wet and sleek, they made a glorious pair.

The outrageous impression turned Hannah on her heel and sent her scurrying into the cabin. She sat in the dark for what seemed to be a very long time, feeling foolish about what she was thinking, but thinking it nonetheless. If the man saw her turn on the light, he'd know right away she'd been spying on him.

And he'd think, that woman must have a problem.

Her problem, she decided when her good sense finally returned, was that she was forgetting to leave this kind of behavior analysis at the Center. A late-night swimmer was no big deal. Very soon he'd swim back to where he came from, and neither would ever see the other by the light of day.

When Critter came scratching at the door, Hannah reached for the light switch, hesitated, then boldly flipped it on before letting him in.

The New Moon Center was an austere standout from the business establishments on Sherman Street in downtown Deadwood. Most of the other signs offered More Chances To Win. New Moon promised A Chance To Turn Your Life Around. A simple white cross was affixed to the storefront above the Center's name, and the sign in the window advertised Gifts. Not a single slot machine was mentioned. These days such artlessness smacked of downright impudence. *Everybody* had at least one slot machine.

The gift store was an outlet for a variety of crafts made by women in the New Moon program, not only locally, but throughout the region. The church-sponsored program helped women who were starting over in their lives. Their stories were as varied as their circumstances and the vital statistics printed on their driver's licenses. Some had been deserted. Others had run away. Some suffered from addiction, others from abuse. Most of them had few marketable skills.

In years past Deadwood might have been a last resort for those who had only salable bodies, but the town had recently cleaned up its act in that respect. In the few short years since the closing of the brothels and the opening of the gambling halls, Deadwood had become a tourist town. Sodom reformed. The perfect place to sell handmade gifts and, ironically, a good home for a women's self-help center.

But now, suddenly, Deadwood was a gambler's haven once again, and New Moon was most noted for the fact that the Center had a year remaining on its lease—the lease to a piece of property that had skyrocketed in value since the gambling laws had been liberalized. The church board had considered some tempting subleasing offers, but it was the nature of the temptation that made the board shy away. So much money. So much sin. The church's challenge was clear. It was hard to keep up with the requests for meeting space. Attendance at Gambler's Anonymous meetings was outstripping A.A. So far, the board had opted to beef up its program rather than give up its lease, but the offers still poured in.

The gift shop was doing a brisk trade. For some of the Center's clients, sale of their handicrafts was a major source of income. Luckily there were many "gamblers" in the market for something to take home to the family. The Center sponsored craft classes and self-help group meetings daily. As the staff social worker Hannah had all the group facilitating and individual counseling she could handle.

She had been hired to run the counseling program less than a year ago, when Pastor Mike Murphy found that the project had become a full-time job. She was glad to be back in South Dakota, where she'd been born. Glad to be home. She called it home, even though she had spent much of her childhood living in the world's remotest pockets with her parents. College had brought Hannah back to the States, followed by a two-year stint with an urban social services program. When the chance to return to her South Dakota roots had surfaced, Hannah had jumped at it.

New Moon was still a fledgling program, but it was already chalking up success stories. Group member Tasha Baird coordinated the shop and the craft co-op, which had been started by clients in the program. Some of them now offered classes, some clerked in the shop.

The idea was to pitch in and find a new identity, and Hannah believed it was working for her almost as well as it was for her clients. She felt as though her roots were finally forming—sinking into South Dakota sod—and she was getting to know South Dakota people. The program was good for getting to know people. And like everyone who'd become a part of it, Hannah always headed for the craft room first when she arrived for work. That was where the coffeepot was, and it was where clients and co-op members gathered each morning.

The best artisan in the program was Nettie Couteau, who made the first pot of coffee and kept it from running dry throughout the day. She liked it strong and sweet. A quiet woman of Chippewa Indian descent, Nettie came to the Center every day and worked tirelessly on her prize-winning willow baskets. She offered classes in basketry and beading. She was always the first to arrive and the last to leave after all the sessions were over and the shop was closed.

In some ways, she reminded Hannah of her own mother, who had died three years ago in Guatemala. Like Marie Quinn, Nettie wasn't one to boss or fuss around. She offered her insight sparingly, and there it was, take it or leave it. When Hannah was hungry for a little subtle mothering, it seemed to come naturally from Nettie.

The funny thing was, Hannah's mother had been a missionary, while Nettie had spent six years in prison.

The small woman with the long, gray-streaked hair kept mostly to herself. She had spoken of that part of her past only once in group. There had been no embellishments, no justifications and few details. Nettie had related the cold, bare facts of her life as though they were dead things, all but one. She'd had a child who had not been touched by her misdoings.

It was hard for Hannah to imagine a young, wild Nettie. It was like trying to imagine her own parents as teenagers. The "misdoings" couldn't have been done by the Nettie that Hannah knew. And while she knew she ought to maintain a more professional distance from the older woman, this morning Hannah found herself telling Nettie about the naked man swimming in her lake and, worse, confessing that the burdensome part of it all was in the fact that she hadn't quite been able to take her eyes off him. Hannah was grateful to Nettie for not laughing, even when she added the single mitigating circumstance she thought she had to her credit.

"Of course, I only saw him from the *back*."

"Men are very nice to look at from the back," Nettie allowed as she took Hannah's mouse cartoon mug from her hand and filled it with coffee. "And he was the one who was trespassing, not you."

"I hope he doesn't come back. It's pretty awkward." Hannah sipped black coffee as she watched Nettie add sugar to hers. "It's actually a little scary. Do you think I ought to call the police?

"That's up to you," Nettie said stiffly. Hannah knew that if it were up to Nettie, she wouldn't. At the mention of police, Nettie always withdrew. End of conversation. Back to work.

No, she hadn't said the wrong thing, Hannah told herself as she watched Nettie busy herself in the corner of the room with a bundle of willow branches. Nettie was just going to have to get over her aversion to anything that had to do with the law.

And Hannah was going to have to get to her desk and take care of paperwork. The three women settling in at one of the long tables would probably have a quilt top pieced together by noon. Hannah would have loved to participate, but she had a new group meeting in an hour. By that time there would be children in the playroom and half a dozen women working in the craft room. The Center was a busy place.

"Look at this, Hannah," Tasha Baird said. She waited until Hannah reached her side of the table, then handed her a wooden pistol. "A friend of mine sent this to my son. Now that we've got the new jigsaw, we could probably make our own version. Isn't it cute?"

Hannah turned the painted toy over in her hand. "This looks real." She wondered what the little spring clip was for. They were always looking for new ideas, and right now children's gifts were in short supply. But a gun? She clicked the clothespin-like hammer a couple of times, then gave the toy back to Tasha. "Almost too real."

"But all it shoots is rubber bands." Tasha stretched a rubber band from the clip to the tip of the barrel, pointed it at the ceiling and let the ammunition fly. "See? Souvenir of wild, dangerous Deadwood."

"The town guaranteed to part a man from his money," grumbled Celia Darby, who was sitting at the end of the table and tearing into strips of fabric with a fury. "Especially one as dumb as my Jack."

"Celia's husband lost most of his paycheck at the blackjack tables last night," Tasha explained as she set the toy pistol in the center of the table, where it would eventually receive due consideration.

"Oh, dear." In a gesture of sympathy, Hannah took a seat next to the sullen woman. "What are you going to do, Celia?"

"I don't know." Celia snipped a notch into the last of a swatch of yellow cotton, yanked it in two and looked up with a thin smile. "Cut off his fingers, maybe?" She dropped her hands to her lap. "What can I do? He said he thought he could make up for what he lost last month. He was feeling just so-oo-o lucky." Bitterness was poking holes in her attempt to lighten up. "We've been married eighteen years, and I thought I knew every one of his weaknesses by now, but this is a brand new one."

"Well, Celia, he's just going to have to get help." It was the answer Hannah knew best, the one she truly believed in, as simple as it sounded. "He can't go on—"

"We've got a great idea, Hannah," Tasha announced, interrupting Hannah easily. She looked at Celia, who raised her brow, apparently not altogether convinced. Tasha ignored her and glanced across the table at Marta Turnbull, who offered a tentative nod. Then she switched her gaze back to Hannah. "Check it out," she said with a mischievous glint in her eye. "A sit-in at the Plugged Nickel, which is the particular den of thieves where Jack lost his wad."

Hannah's jaw dropped. "A sit-in? Are you serious? Who's going to—"

"All of us." Tasha's gesture seemed to embrace the world.

"*All* of us?" Hannah glanced toward the corner of the room, where Nettie was methodically sorting through the willow branches she'd unbundled. Apparently not all of them. "We wouldn't last long. The owner would just call the police."

"Right," Tasha said. "And where the police go, the news people follow. They ask us why in the world we'd be doing this, and we tell them."

Hannah laughed. "Before or after we go to jail?"

"I don't know. Which way do you think would be the best?" Tasha squeezed Hannah's shoulder in response to the incredulous look on her face. "Hey, somebody has to get the ball rolling. Somebody has to rally the concerned citizens. *Somebody* has to take the heat."

"And a lot of people are opposed to what's going on here," Marta put in.

"But a lot of people favor it," Celia countered. "You know, the town used to be flat broke, and it's not anymore. Just people like my stupid husband are broke. But look at all the new jobs."

"Dealing poker," Tasha supplied disgustedly. "And it's not our town anymore. Outsiders are buying up all the property. You know, gangsters and movie stars." She made the two sound as though they were practically the same thing.

"You could move," Nettie suggested, turning the heads at the table in perfect unison. The challenge surprised everyone but Hannah, who had to remind herself to keep to the sidelines.

Tasha bristled. "I was born here. I'm not moving. Why should I?" Then her indignation gave way to the more pressing need to enlist all the support she could get. "Do you like what's going on here, Nettie? The gaming and all the shady stuff that goes with it?"

"I don't go to the bars or play the machines," Nettie said flatly. She selected a willow stick and examined its lines from fat end to skinny tip. "It doesn't bother me."

"If you were trying to raise a family in this town, it would bother you, Nettie," Tasha insisted. "Just look at all the great choices we've got for entertainment. You can take your kids to Bessie's Soda Fountain and Casino, or the Carousel Taffy Shop and Gambling Parlor. I mean, how wholesome is that?"

Nettie said nothing, nor did she look up from the slender stick balanced across her palms. For all anyone could tell, she might have been cherishing the object or thinking of brandishing it.

Hannah hurried to fill the cavernous silence. "How do you plan to stage this sit-in? They won't let you block the door. It's a fire hazard."

"We're going to make our way to the bar stools and the chairs where people sit when they're waiting for a turn to play." As she spoke, Tasha turned her back on Nettie, as if she were dismissing a distraction. "We'll get a big bunch together. I've been talking to people, and the thing is, we have to call the media. Once we're in, if we've got enough people, we can occupy space, make a scene and make our statement."

"Who's going to care whether people are gambling big-time in a tiny little town in South Dakota?" Celia muttered as she tore into a length of blue calico. Her errant elbow sent her scissors clattering to the floor, and Hannah leaned down to retrieve them.

As she straightened, she glanced back at the corner. Nettie was busy stripping the bark from a branch. Not once looking up from her task, she tugged at Hannah's concern like an unanswered cry in the night. Something was bothering her, and Hannah wanted to hear about it.

Tell her off, Nettie. Don't let her sweep your comment under the table, she urged silently.

But Nettie had said all she had to say, and it was no good trying to coax her for more.

"Women," Tasha was saying. "Women are going to care. Look at us. We've all been through some particular kind of hell, and we're pretty damned tired of wading through all the muck."

Marta had some news for them. "Agnes Lundquist just sold out to some rich guy from Florida."

"There went our only women's clothing store," Tasha said. She rapped the table with her fist. "See? *Women's* clothing. Don't you think women are going to care?"

"I suppose there's going to be another bar," Hannah said, knowing full well that it would have to be. That was the only kind of business any rich guy from Florida would have reason to invest in in Deadwood.

"Well, of course." Tasha flashed a self-satisfied smile. "And pretty soon we'll have to drive to Sturgis to buy a carton of milk, even. They don't like to sell milk in saloons."

"We'll have to go all the way to Rapid City for tennis shoes," Celia said.

Hannah had been encouraging these women to be more assertive. If this scheme was the result of all those stand-up-for-yourself discussions, she guessed she had only herself to blame, but picketing wasn't quite what she'd had in mind. She tried to picture herself carrying a sign and chanting some kind of slogan. The very idea made her feel ridiculous. "We're not going to close down the casinos with a demonstration."

"Carrie Nation did it," Tasha pointed out.

"And look what she got for her trouble," Hannah argued. "A bar in Deadwood called Carrie Nation's Temperance Saloon and Gaming Hall."

Tasha snapped her fingers as she shot out of her chair. "Just for that, we ought to demonstrate. I say let's win one for Carrie Nation." She punched the air like the cheerleader she once was, then turned to Celia. "All we have to do is make the evening news and we've won, right? It's our move. It's up to us to make the rules."

"Then let's say we've won if we make *any* news," Celia said, swinging into the spirit. "Make it easy on ourselves since we're new at this."

"Okay," Tasha agreed. "Any news. And if one goes to jail, we all go to jail. Are you in, Hannah?"

"I guess I can't let you all go to jail without me." Hannah glanced up at the fluorescent ceiling fixture and sighed. She couldn't believe she was saying this. "Lord, if you don't want us to do this, now's the time to speak up."

The bulb flickered and hummed.

"Come on, Nettie," Tasha said. "All for one and one for all."

Nettie shook her head as she picked up her coffee mug and headed across the room for a refill. She had removed herself even further from the group than she usually did. The discussion continued as Hannah quietly left her chair and followed the older woman to the far corner of the room.

"Okay," she said, for Nettie's ears only. "Tell me what you really think."

Without looking up, Nettie held out her hand for Hannah's cup. As she filled it, she said, "I don't think you're going to like jail too much."

Careless wind pushed clouds across the face of the moon, then wiped them away and started over again. The treetops rustled in the breeze overhead, but the lake was calm. A horned owl called to his mate. It was the soft, hollow echo, not the chilly water, that made Race shiver. There was something spooky about an owl's call on a night like this. He hoped his neighbor would let her dog out again. Maybe that would chase the spookiness away. Not that he minded keeping company with owls—the eerie shivers gave him a perverse kind of ghost-story thrill—but he liked dogs, too, and his job left him in no position to keep one of his own.

The lake's ripples lapped softly at its banks. The witching hour was the best time for swimming. Once you got used to it, the water felt warmer than the air. There was peace and privacy for the taking and enjoying until chattering teeth sent you back inside. Then a warm fire, a shot of whiskey and a clean bed became life's finest pleasures.

Powerful strokes propelled Race into his neighbor's waters. If the yellow Lab was loose, he'd come running. Race flipped over and coasted on his back until he heard the familiar bark. He let his feet touch the lake's rocky bottom, pushed his hair out of his face and called out, "Come on in, boy, the water's fine."

A woman's voice answered. "I'd appreciate it if you wouldn't swim here at this time of night."

"Hey." Race peered past the little boat dock, but all he could see were shadows. He flexed his knees, and the water line crept up his chest. "What happened to your voice, big fella? I could have sworn that first bark was friendly."

"I keep Critter inside at night," the soft voice said. "But he goes crazy when he knows there's someone out here."

"That's because he's my friend." He watched a small shadow separate itself from the trees, then split into two. All he could tell from the dark silhouettes was that the dog was almost as big as the woman. "So, uh, can Critter come out and play?"

"I'm asking you very nicely. It's very late."

"You're not asking me if it's late. You're telling me it's..." He watched her take a step closer, shifting the shadows as she lifted her arm. "What's that you've got in your hand?"

"It's a defensive weapon, which I would prefer not to..."

Defensive weapon? He swallowed a wild urge to laugh at the way she'd said it, sort of nervous but prim. "Lady, are you actually pointing a gun at me?"

"Please understand, it's unnerving. This is my backyard, you see, and I have no idea who you are. So if you would please just—"

"No, that's not it. You're supposed to say, 'Come out with your hands up.'"

"I'm quite serious."

"I believe you." The trouble was, he couldn't be. If he hadn't let go of the laugh he'd have choked on it. He raised his hands chest high, palms out. "I surrender. You caught me without my white flag, but I've got my hands up. See? I'm coming out."

"No!" She retraced the one step she'd taken. "Just stay where you are."

"I think that's supposed to be, 'Stay *right* where you are,' and the truth is, I'm gettin' pretty damn cold where I am."

"Well, just...swim away, then, back where you came from. And in the future, don't come around—hush, Critter—at this hour. It just isn't decent of you to come..." Her voice trailed off as he surged ahead. The water sloshed as it sank to his waist. "What are you doing?"

"Comin' out, ready or not."

"You can't do that...oh!"

He figured when the water level slipped another inch, he was going to shrivel a notch smaller than prunes, and she was going to faint.

But she made the next move. With a shriek, she dropped both her gun and her leash and beat a hasty retreat through the trees, calling out over her shoulder, "I'm going to call the police, so you'd better leave!" The door slammed, but in a moment Race heard its hinges creak again. "Critter?"

The dog sniffed at the ground.

"Critter, will you listen for once?"

Laughter bubbled in Race's throat. Critter picked up the gun and headed for the lake. By the time the dog jumped into the water, Race had dismissed any concern that the gun might go off. Critter handled it as though it were made of Styrofoam. Back in the trees, the door slammed shut.

"Give it to me, Critter." A chunk of wood. He patted the dog between the ears. "They don't call you man's best friend for nothing, do they, boy? Couldn't see much of her in the dark. Nice voice, though. Is she pretty good-looking?" Critter yapped. "Yeah, well, you probably have to say that if you want to get back in the house. You have to admit, she's kinda crazy, pulling a stunt like that."

With another yap, Critter lunged for the toy gun.

"No, you can't have this. She might want it back." Holding the gun out of the dog's reach, he chuckled as he thought about the soft voice trying so hard to sound threatening. He had to have some kind of glass slipper if he was going to find out who the voice belonged to. Well, maybe he didn't *have* to, but it sure was going to make it a lot more fun.

"I'm sure she'll want it back." Race smiled. "She might even offer me a nice reward."

Hannah pressed her back against the door and struggled to bring her breathing under control. Close call. Heaven only knew what the man might have done. Stupid move on her part. What had she been thinking?

She hadn't. Not clearly, anyway. She should have known better than to try to scare a man like that away with a toy gun.

A man like what?

A man like . . . *naked.*

The character of this community was sliding downhill fast, and gambling and gangsters weren't the worst of it. Things were getting pretty bad when a decent woman had to worry about stepping outside her back door and finding naked men in her lake.

Maybe Tasha's protest wasn't such a bad idea after all.

Chapter 2

In order to "sit in," the newly formed Daughters of the New Moon had to lay claim to some seats, which were not easy to come by in the always crowded Plugged Nickel. They decided against trying to take the saloon by storm. Instead they planned to infiltrate, like a fifth column. They would occupy subtly at first, and when they were all in place, perhaps next in line to use the machines, they would unveil their message. Tasha was in charge, leading the point team—herself and Hannah—down Main Street's narrow sidewalk.

As far as Hannah was concerned, the whole thing was beginning to feel more like a caper than a demonstration. Her nerve had outmaneuvered her better judgment at the outset, but the closer they came to the weathered wooden portico of the Plugged Nickel, the less sure she was that she could actually go through with the plan. Tasha elbowed her and nodded toward the KWST News car parked across the street. Hannah grimaced, and Tasha grinned.

They passed one thriving enterprise after another with big plate-glass windows displaying well-lit spaces filled with slot machines. Slot machines and jewelry. Slot machines and doughnuts. Slot machines and T-shirts. The one-armed bandits were getting their usual workout. Hannah clipped along quickly, not because she was in a hurry to reach her destination, but because she felt as though she were walking past a long row of unshaded bedroom windows. It was embarrassing to catch the eye of someone on the other side of the window who was losing his or her money. Hannah wished she'd brought along a good pair of blinders to help her get through the coming ordeal. A brown paper bag would have done nicely.

"I thought we'd decided to try to dress to blend in," Tasha said. She was competing with the honky-tonk music that was piped out to the street, but Hannah heard her. She glanced down at her own sleeveless shirtwaist, then at Tasha's pink ruffled Western blouse and jeans. "You look too much like someone who works for a church," Tasha judged. "At least take the barrette out of your hair and let it hang loose and pretty. You've got beautiful hair."

The compliment was lost on Hannah. Her interest in what she wore centered around function rather than form. She touched the beaded barrette that Nettie had specially designed to anchor her long blond hair high up off her temples. "It serves a purpose. It keeps my hair from falling in my eyes."

"That's the problem." Tasha made a point of looking her straight in the face. "It's those eyes that give you away. If anybody asks before we make our move, you're a tourist from Kansas."

"I'm a social worker from South Dakota and proud of it. Do you think this will take—"

"Hey, Paula," a woman across the street called out. Two women walking ahead of them stopped in their tracks on the crowded sidewalk, stacking Hannah, Tasha and whoever was behind them up like dominoes. "Jim just got a hundred," came the announcement.

"Tell him he's buying the next round," Paula answered.

"Yeah, after we find our husbands," Paula's companion supplied. "Creeps got away from us again. Didn't leave us two damn nickels to rub together."

Hannah and Tasha exchanged glances. "Sounds like a real fun group," Tasha muttered as the traffic got moving again.

The two women hustled into the Plugged Nickel ahead of them. "Maybe I should slip a New Moon flyer into Paula's purse," Hannah said, and then she wondered whether she had any with her as she stepped aside to let Tasha go through the door first. Coward, she chided herself. The gaping maw of hell, and she was letting Tasha take the lead. Fine counselor she was.

The sign in the tiny window next to the door read Unlawful To Carry Firearms, Knives Or Other Dangerous Weapons In This Establishment. It brought meager comfort as Hannah stepped from early evening daylight into manmade night. She nearly gagged on the smoke. One boozy woman shouldered past her, headed for the door, and another bumped her from the other direction, headed for an open slot machine. She whirled on the next person to bump into her from behind.

It was Celia.

"I'm not too late, am I? About the only place left to park in this town is right on top of ol' Wild Bill."

Tasha laughed. "Next thing, somebody'll be offering to lease his space for a slot machine."

"He'd probably get a kick out of that," Hannah said as she surveyed the crowded room and tried to edge away from the door.

"All we want is the ground floor, some casino owner will say. You can stay right where you are, no problem, long as you don't scare the customers." Tasha showed her driver's license to a bearded man with a black cowboy hat, who gave her a look that said she'd better not be talking about him.

Hannah managed to locate her identification and maintain her balance while a buxom woman in a leopard print T-shirt squeezed past her without so much as a "pardon me." She hoped the bearded man would tell her the picture didn't look like her and that she would have to leave.

No such luck.

"There's a place at the bar," Tasha said. "You take that one, Hannah."

"No, you go ahead. I'll take the next—"

"Somebody's going to bowl you over like a spare pin, you keep standing here all eyes and ears like this." Tasha gave her a little nudge, but the deciding factor was the chance to get to the stool ahead of the woman in the leopard print T-shirt. Hannah won out, and as a reward she got to perch herself atop a bar stool for the very first time in her life.

It was pretty high. She was grateful for the rustic style of the place, particularly the lack of large windows. She didn't especially want to be seen by the throngs of people on the sidewalk. She felt as though she'd just crawled out of the sea and onto a rock.

Marta Turnbull came through the door with Cindy Statler, and Hannah gave them a discreet thumbs-up sign. Things were looking better. She had her rock now, and she was gaining strength in their growing numbers. Tasha claimed one of the chairs lined up against the front wall. Satisfied that she wasn't about to be left high and dry on this rock of hers, Hannah turned toward the man behind the bar. He was mixing several glasses of something out of a hose with something from a bottle.

Without looking up, he set the bottle down and extended his hand. "Lemme see some ID and then I'll take your order, ma'am."

"But I showed it to the man at the door." The open hand proclaimed him unconvinced. Hannah produced proof of her age once again, adding, "Anyway, all I want is mineral water, please."

"All the more reason to double-check." He scrutinized the license, front and back, then handed it to her with a smile that stretched his mustache into something resembling a caterpillar on the move. "Honey, you could pass for seventeen, easy. You want flavored?"

"Plain is fine."

His smile made her feel uncomfortable. She glanced past him. Above a double row of liquor bottles hung a painting of a nude woman lying on her belly and waving her feet like two white flags behind her head. It was not her nudity but her naughty smile that drew the eye. The nudity sent Hannah's away again.

"You meeting someone?" the bartender asked as he dropped a printed cocktail napkin in front of her on the only polished surface in the place.

"Yes. Thank you. I'm expecting several friends."

"For your sake, I hope one's a man." He centered her drink on the napkin, between the smoking six-shooter and the nickel it had plugged. "But if any of these cowboys start hittin' on you before your man gets here, give me a holler. It's the lobos you gotta look out for."

It was a thoughtful offer, Hannah realized. She glanced left and right as she sipped her water, wondering what a lobo looked like. Lean and hungry, maybe? Being hit upon, as the kind bartender put it, was not a pleasant prospect, especially in a place like this. But three other women from New Moon had just arrived, and Celia snatched up a seat four stools down from her. With a champion behind the bar and friends all around her, Hannah was feeling more secure all the time. She sipped and surveyed and tapped her fingers in time to the lively fiddle music supplied by the speaker that was sitting on the wall above a stuffed antelope head.

Race was dealing blackjack at his favorite table when the ruckus started up front. He couldn't tell what it was—maybe somebody hit a big jackpot or started a fight—but the players were rubbernecking, and the crowd was flocking up front like flies on a puddle of lemonade. He signaled for Lester to take over for him, and he made his way closer to the action.

Somebody near the door was holding up a sign that read ALL BETS ARE OFF. All he could see of the culprit was her hands. The crowd was all abuzz and packed tight around some kind of spectacle. Billy was watching from behind the bar, but when Race managed to get his attention and give the "What's going on?" look, Billy replied with a shrug and a half-amused grin.

"Cut the music," Race told Billy, but the bartender didn't seem to want to chance missing the show, whatever it was. There was no cheering, so it wasn't a fight. No shouting, either. Just a lot of commotion.

Then a familiar voice. Soft. Firm. Scared, but covering nicely.

"We are staying right where we are."

He wanted to bust out laughing. He couldn't see her yet—one of the bouncers with his black Stetson blocked his view—but he knew the voice, and he'd given her the line. *Stay right where you are.* She had it down much better this time. He reached over the bar and fished around underneath until he found her "defensive weapon," which he'd used twice already, jokingly catching a dealer and a bouncer off guard.

The plug was pulled on the jukebox, abruptly choking off the steel guitar that had been loudly twanging from a soundtrack. The Stetson moved.

The Lady of the Lake had finally come out of the shadows. She was perched prettily on a stool like a small bird on a fence, and the long hair that lay between her shoulder blades reminded Race of a sheaf of wheat. She was explaining to anyone who wanted to listen—and there were plenty of people standing around—just how much grief his gambling establishment was causing the women of Deadwood. It was the kind of talk he'd heard before, so he turned off the message and just listened to the tone of her voice.

Brave little bird, you're in my neck of the woods now.

He loaded up a rubber band and drew a bead on the flowered barrette near the top of her head. Bad choice. If she turned around, she'd get it in the face, and he didn't want to hurt her. He just wanted to ruffle her feathers a little. He lowered his aim and let the rubber band fly. It nested in the sheaf of yellow hair. A few laughs rippled among the onlookers.

When she whirled to face him, he felt a surge of long-forgotten schoolboy glee. Ah, she was indignant, but she sure was pretty. Then she noticed the toy pistol, and she rewarded his slow smile with completely artless, wide-eyed surprise. A delicate pink blush rose from her neck to her cheeks to her blond hairline as the moment of reckoning absorbed them both. She wanted to fly. He could see that. And he wanted, suddenly and inexplicably, to rise to the occasion and safeguard her flight.

On the other hand, he had her dead to rights, and he couldn't resist getting closer to her and wagging the wooden gun the moment she moved.

"Careful, ma'am. I've got you covered."

"According to the sign out front, firearms are not permitted," she reminded him, making him admire her quick recovery.

He felt a tug on his arm, and he turned to discover Vicki's outraged expression staring him in the face. "Race, they've got TV cameras going in here, for God's sake," she quipped menacingly between clenched teeth. "What the hell are you doing with—"

"No problem. This is just a simple little defensive weapon." He looked down at the wooden toy, noting once again how real it looked at first glance, especially in the dim light. He grinned, then turned to the blonde again, whose stunned expression was almost as amusing as Vicki's. "You'd better keep it handy," he suggested as he handed it to her. "I think you're going to need it."

A woman with a poofy red hairdo shoved a microphone at him. "Are you the owner of the Plugged Nickel?"

"Yeah." He glanced past the red beehive and noted that the aforementioned camera was now pointed at him. And it was rolling, damn it. He cleared his throat and added, "One of them."

"Apparently your place has been singled out by the women staging this protest. Any comment on that?"

"Protest?" With a chuckle, he turned back to the blonde. "Jeez, lady, all I did was go for a swim."

"What does that mean, go for a swim?" the reporter asked, then thrust the microphone under the blonde's pert little nose.

"I...um..." She reached into her purse, pulled out another ALL BETS ARE OFF sign and held it under her chin. "This establishment and the others like it are selling a nice town and its residents right down the river. That's what it means." Race laughed, but she only squared her shoulders and raised her voice. "Gambling is already demoralizing the community, causing—"

Moe Bartok, one of the town's two full-time police officers, shouldered his way into the picture. The cameraman stepped back for a wider angle, and the crowd accommodated him with a bigger circle.

"I'm afraid we'll have to arrest you ladies if you don't leave peacefully." The wiry policeman surveyed the crowd for familiar faces. "Come on, Tasha. Marta. Go home to your kids."

The reporter spoke into her microphone as she led the way for the cameraman, jostling for better access to the growing number of principles involved. "Eleven women, occupying various seats in this establishment, face arrest by local police unless—"

"Hey, wait a minute, let's get serious here," Race suggested, figuring the joke was about over, now that the police were here. "Why don't you just put these signs away and have another drink on me?"

Vicki had been edged out by the red-haired reporter, but she was working her way back in behind Moe. "Let the police do their job, Race."

"This is crazy." The cameraman wanted a shot of his response. What he got on tape was the palm of Race's hand. "Will you get that thing out of my face!"

The blonde hadn't moved from the bar stool, but she looked a little confounded when Moe held out his hand. "I'll take the gun now, lady."

"It's just a…" She looked at it for a moment, as though she wasn't sure anymore just what it was, but then she simply sighed and slapped it into his palm, ridding herself of the annoyance. "Here, take it. But I'm not budging. We want people to realize that we don't have to put up with this. A few bar owners pushed this thing through the state legislature, and people expected a little more gambling in the bars. No big deal." She squared her shoulders and looked directly into the camera. "Do you realize that we have more slot machines in this town than we have people?"

"I'm gonna have to take you in unless you—"

One of the protesters elbowed her way past the camera crew. "This wasn't Hannah's idea. It was mine."

Moe ignored her. He was still dealing with the blonde on the bar stool. "Listen, I'm gonna have to put cuffs on you and read you your rights and the whole nine yards if you don't—"

"She's not guilty. I'm the one."

Moe waved the intruder back. "I'll let you know when it's time for a verdict, Tasha. First thing is to settle this disturbance, and it looks to me like this lady…"

"I'm doing fine, Tasha." And she was. She had the camera trained on her, the poofy-haired reporter hanging onto her every word, and the crowd hadn't lynched her yet. She gestured toward the front of the saloon, where most of the demonstrators were huddled together and holding up their signs. "These women are concerned about what this addictive vice is doing to their families, their children."

"We don't allow kids in here," Race pointed out. He figured he could handle this if he could just move the woman off the stool and get her out of the limelight. But she'd reclaimed her composure, and she wasn't going to quit now.

"There is a slot machine in every little outhouse in this town, Mr..."

"Latimer," Race informed her.

"Okay, I think we've got enough on the interview," the reporter told the cameraman. "Let's get out of the constable's way, but be ready to roll the camera again if he starts to arrest anybody." She laid a hand on Hannah's shoulder. "I liked that slot machines in the outhouses line. That was good."

Officer Bartok leaned toward Race and used the barrel of the confiscated weapon as a pointer, indicating the red Exit sign. "I figure the rest'll probably follow this one out the door."

"She wasn't trying to hold me up with that." Race offered a lopsided smile as he slid a glance Hannah's way. "Not this time, anyway."

She wasn't about to return any smiles at this point. "I know you were trying to embarrass me with the pistol, but you're mistaken if you think you're getting the last laugh, Mr. Latimer."

"Actually, I'd like to think there might be more laughs down the road. You're a very funny lady." He braced his elbow against the bar and kept right on smiling. The music of tumbling coins rang out from one of the slots on the far wall, followed by a winner's whoop. The protest hadn't diverted everybody. "You want me to feed Critter while you're in the hoosegow?"

"Critter?"

The thought took her tone down half a peg, and she turned to Moe, who was messing around with the side of his belt. Race was more interested in the look in the woman's eyes. She was thinking about the consequences now, and in a minute he could offer another drink, maybe a handshake, and let everybody get back to business with no harm done.

"You're not going to keep me in jail . . . very long, are you?"

"I told you, ma'am, I gotta do this."

At the sight of Moe's handcuffs, Race stiffened. The lady who belonged at the lake looked up at him, her blue eyes brimming with both fear and defiance. Damn her, she took pleasure in offering up her slight wrists in sacrifice. Race's hand shot out when he heard the first click. "Now, wait a minute, Moe . . ."

"Get a close-up of the cuffs."

"Standard procedure. No exceptions." Moe didn't look too comfortable with it, either, but he was one to go by the book. "We've really had to toughen up lately," he told Race before turning to the other demonstrators. "Now the rest of you can stay together and come along quietly, unless you're lettin' your friend here hang separately."

"We're together in this," Tasha called out.

"We need a bigger police force," Moe announced, partly to Race, partly to the television crew. "We only got two full-time officers."

But Race was watching *her*. Hannah, that was her name. *Give it up, Hannah. Tell him you'll back off, and he'll take the damn cuffs off.*

She was looking down at her wrists, and he was, too, thinking she could slide her hands right out, they were so small. *Come on, Hannah.*

But she wasn't saying anything, and she was going to jail.

Race grabbed the policeman by the shoulder. "Listen, Moe, as long as they're leaving, why don't we just forget the whole thing?"

"They're leaving because one of them is in handcuffs." He motioned to Hannah, who awkwardly levered herself down from the stool. Race would have offered a hand, but he wanted her to stay the hell up there, and he was only half listening to Moe's commentary. "Tell you what, this is something the Hospitality Association is gonna want us to nip right in the ol' bud."

"Yeah, but this little bud's kinda fragile-looking, don't you think?" Race said. He glanced at Hannah, but she was staring straight ahead, ignoring them both.

"You guys called me over here," Moe said. "If you back down, we won't be able to do much. Just so you know."

Race watched Moe usher Hannah, with all her innocence and false bravado, out the door. She'd gotten herself into this. She'd made her statement. She'd stood her ground. But, damn it, she was leaving his place in *handcuffs*.

"Looks like they're hangin' together," Billy said as they watched the camera crew, the demonstrators and the lawman make their exit. Already the slot machines were ringing in more bets. "Pretty small offense for a hanging."

"What do you mean, small offense?" Vicki demanded. "This kind of thing could ruin our reputation."

Good ol' Vicki was all business. "I don't know about yours, but mine's not worth worrying about," Race said. "I got a feelin' that's not true for, uh...for Hannah, there."

"Hannah?" Vicki echoed, stepping around to confront him nose to nose. "Have you been borrowing *sugar* from the neighbor?"

Because his nose was well above hers, he was able to ignore the challenge. "Wonder what her last name is?" He turned to the man behind the bar. "Did you catch it, Billy?"

"Hannah Quinn." Billy crossed his arms over his chest and tucked his hands into his armpits. "Never hurts to double-check the ID."

"Good man."

"They probably wouldn't mind letting her go if you didn't want to press charges."

"Hey, this is my place, too," Vicki reminded them. She looked from one to the other, disgusted that they'd both gone soft just because the trespasser had big, sweet baby blues.

"Friendliest saloon in Deadwood, Miss Vicki," Race said, turning on his considerable charm. "Our reputation just might profit from a generous and forgiving gesture." He pushed himself away from the bar. "Besides, my sister took me to see that movie three times, and I never liked it when little Alice fell down that rabbit hole."

"If she didn't fall in the hole, there wouldn't be a story." Vicki helped herself to a cigarette from Race's shirt pocket. Race struck a match for her. "And you can just tell—" she dragged on the filter until the cigarette was lit "—*that* one needs a story. What am I saying, story? She needs a life."

"She needs to go jump in the lake," Race said. He tossed the matches onto the bar and gave his partner a parting nod. "But she can't do it if she's in jail, now, can she?"

Hannah's stomach hurt. Her muscles had been wadded up so tight for so long that she ached with it, and if she didn't get herself into the the house quickly, she was going to be sick. She stood at her door like someone who'd had too much to drink, using both hands to make the key fit into the lock, while Critter whined at her elbow and wagged his whole body to prove how glad he was to see her.

"If you just had a hand, Critter, you'd be the best friend a girl could—" The key slid home, and Hannah finally stumbled into the front room. "There. Sorry I was trying to wish a hand on you, boy. Paws are great on a dog." She shook the one he offered. "I'm glad to see you, too, and I know you're hungry, but I've done it to myself again. Let my stomach get all tensed up."

The cramping made her feel nauseous. Critter went over to his dish and wagged his tail. He didn't understand nausea.

"Why do I do this? I knew I shouldn't have eaten that hot dog with those..."

She went looking for the hot water bottle and the heavy-duty aspirin. "It's all piling up on me at once," she said, talking to him from the bathroom. "Do dogs get cramps?" She found the hot water bottle, but the aspirin had gotten into the kitchen somehow. On her way to the cupboard, she glanced at the big blue dish and the dog sitting next to it expectantly. "You wouldn't know. You're a male. Males have no idea. Well, it's more than cramps, it's a combination of—"

Critter jerked his head up and pricked his ears, focusing full alert on the back door.

"What is it?"

Nothing. Critter lowered his nose to his dish to see if maybe something had appeared while he was looking the other way.

Hannah sighed and opened the cupboard door below the counter, where she kept the dog food. Oh, it hurt to bend over. "I can tell when you're not interested. Any little distraction," she said, deciding she was better off squatting than bending.

The dog came to attention again. A distant whistle drew him to the door.

"Oh, no, he's back," Hannah groaned. Critter's response was more receptive. He whined and scratched at the door furiously with both front paws.

"Traitor! Don't you know what he wants? He wants to gloat, that's what." She dumped a scoopful of dog food into the dish and returned the scoop to the large economy-size bag. "I don't suppose dogs indulge in gloating, so you wouldn't understand that, either. But you might say your friend out there let me off the hook tonight."

Critter sniffed at the food as Hannah pushed the cupboard door closed, but she could tell he was really more interested in what was outside.

"He'll *definitely* say he let me off the hook. The policeman told me—rather disgustedly, I might add—that Mr. Latimer decided not to press any charges, and then they let me go. So now—" The whistle sounded again, and Critter bounded to the back door. "I should call the police. *He* called the police. *I* should call the police." The dog didn't care what she did. He was going to get through that door, by hook or by claw. "Critter, don't do that. We're just going to ignore him."

Not a chance. The whistle sounded a third time, and the dog redoubled his efforts.

"Critter, stop it!" But he wouldn't. Thoroughly displeased, Hannah flicked the porch light on and threw open the door. "I've really had it with this." She was speaking to man and dog both as she slammed the door behind her and followed the dog, marching down the path to the lake. Critter took the plunge, and Hannah followed him, but only to the end of the dock. She stood there on the wooden planks, hugging her stomach and scowling at the two bobbing heads.

"Hey, looks like you did all right on bread and water."

"They didn't put me in jail." She hugged herself tighter. With her hands tucked under her elbows, she clutched at the fabric gathered over her hips. "But then, you know that. You dropped the complaint."

"I'm not much of a complainer." He was stroking the water, effortlessly keeping himself afloat a few feet out from the piling. "A person starts out as a complainer, then he ends up signing papers, writing letters and carrying signs. It's a big hassle."

"Not if you believe in something."

"Tell you what, lady, if you believe in putting us out of business, you're gonna have to deal with Vicki next time around. She's a lot tougher than I am." Bored with the conversation, Critter started churning around him like an eggbeater. "You wanna toss us a stick or something?"

"A stick?"

"Better yet, why don't you just peel down and jump in with us?"

"P-peel down!"

He laughed. "How do you like that echo? Bet they can hear you clear on the other side of the lake."

"I am not about to peel—"

"Come on in and cool off, Hannah," he coaxed. His voice seemed to be swirling around her now, as though someone were sloshing the two of them around in a jar. "It'll give you a new perspective, and you won't feel much like compla— Hey, what's wrong?"

"Nothing." Not much, anyway. She'd doubled over and had sunk into a little puddle of pain right there on the end of the dock. But she was working hard to make it look as if she'd just sat down for a rest. "I'm tired of all this commotion in the middle of the . . . night, is all."

"Rude dog," Race scolded jovially in Critter's direction. "Look what you've done to your—" Suddenly he gave a kick and glided close to the dock. "Something *is* wrong. Are you—"

"No, don't come out!"

"It's okay." He reached the deck, levered himself up effortlessly and climbed out of the water. "See, I'm decent. Bought these today." Water was still pouring off him as he snapped the waistband of his swimming trunks for her reassurance. "Are you sick?"

It took heroic effort, but she sat up straight and sucked in a long, deep breath. "I'm fine." She turned and found him right next to her, down on one knee, giving her a skeptical perusal. "No, really." And then came the dog, bounding along the dock and hell-bent to shake water all over her. "Critter?"

"You're not fine. You need help getting back to the house?" The humor had disappeared from Race's voice as he insinuated himself between Hannah and her dog's lapping tongue. "Cut it out, boy. The lady's had a rough night."

She wasn't sure whether the dog or the man had rocked her back on her heels, but suddenly she was in the arms of a man whose strength was as surprising as his sudden concern. Caught off guard, she was able to wrestle with only one force at a time, and the pain deep in her stomach was the more pressing. It was a feeble protest she made as she clutched his wet shoulder for balance.

"Mr. Latimer, I can walk."

"Race."

"No, *walk*. Just put me down, and I'll—"

"My name is Race, honey, and if you don't relax, you'll get the fireman's carry instead of the royal treatment." Her head dropped to his shoulder, and he took it as a sign of submission. "That's better."

She thought it only fair to enlighten him. "I might throw up on you."

"That won't be a first for me. Take it easy, now." He took the pine needle covered path in stride. Almost. "Ouch! I usually don't do this with bare feet."

"I can't imagine why not. You usually swim with bare everything."

"You noticed?" He chuckled as he mounted the back steps of her house. "I'm flattered."

He had to bend his knees to line his hand up with the doorknob. Even as she tightened her grip on his shoulders, she felt obliged to protest. "You can put me down now, Mr. Latimer. I think I can manage to—"

"You know, dogs can be taught to open doors. Pretty neat trick. I think we oughta see if Critter's up to it." The dog scurried in under Race's elbow as he managed to juggle both door and Hannah, deftly getting them all inside. "Bathroom or bedroom?"

"Please, just . . ." She waved her hand toward the living room.

"Sofa." He deposited her there, tucking a small pillow beneath her neck as she let her head drop back to the arm of the sofa. Still leaning over her, he studied her face. She wondered what stage of horrible-looking she'd reached. "Do you need to see a doctor?" he asked.

"No. It's just . . ." She scooted up a little and tried for levity. "This always happens to me when I get arrested."

"Which is, what? Two or three times a week?"

"Which is never." She closed her eyes, wishing he would stop looking at her. "I'm a novice at this and obviously not very good at it."

"A glass of brandy would settle you right down, Hannah."

"Or knock me out completely. It's going away now. I'll be fine. If you need a towel, there's one in the bathroom."

He followed the direction of her gesture and disappeared into the bathroom. She heard water running. He returned with a white bath towel draped over his neck and the hot water bottle in his hand. She thought it was to his credit that he'd chosen boxer-style swimming trunks rather than some little bikini thing. But these white trunks fit him well enough to make her want to look at more of the man than she ought to. When he knelt in front of the sofa and she smelled the damp heat of his skin, she had to swallow to keep her mouth from going bone dry. His shoulders were broad enough to block most of the light from the kitchen.

She looked up and found him staring, too. Without a word, he lifted her hands and tucked the red rubber pouch beneath them, pressing it firmly against her belly. And without looking down, she told herself that the warmth came directly from his hands and that there was healing in his dark, sympathetic eyes.

He stood slowly, still watching her as though he expected her to say something to stay his course. Her eyes followed his compelling ones, and she wondered what she might say. What would a more sophisticated woman say in response to such an unexpectedly tender gesture? When he turned away, she felt strangely bereft.

"What are you doing?" It was a silly question. He'd already taken two pine logs from the crate next to the big stone hearth.

"Building a friendly fire." He tossed in some kindling and struck a match as he spoke. "No brandy or whiskey in the house, huh?" He turned for the answer he expected, and she shook her head. "Where's the tea, then? I know you've got tea."

"The small canister on the counter. Why are you doing this?"

"Because I know what ails you," he said as he padded into the little kitchen, lifted the kettle and judged that there was enough water in it. He turned the gas burner on high.

"You were scared spitless when they clapped those handcuffs on you, but you toughed it out. Gotta hand it to you, the way you kept your chin up when mean ol' Moe marched you out the door. I shouldn't've felt too sorry for you since you were doing your damnedest to cause trouble for me, but you kinda had that trapped animal look in your eye." He lifted a flowered mug from the little tree that stood on the counter next to the canisters. "I've got a real weakness for trapped animals. Sometimes in a fire you'll see them running the wrong way, and you'll want to drop everything and try to head 'em off."

"In a fire?" She wasn't following him, even though she admired every move his body made. It surprised her, watching him pour water over the tea bag, that the process came so naturally to him. He didn't strike her as a tea man.

"Yeah. That's how scared you looked. Just like Bambi's mother. Honey?"

"I don't remember."

He laughed. "I mean, it's gotta have honey in it or it's no-good." He found the jar behind the first door he tried and used the wooden dipper to stir some in. "Try this."

"Thank you." She sipped the hot brew. It tasted sweet and felt good going down. "I *was* scared. But I really am opposed to all this gambling."

"I know. You sat right on top of one of my bar stools and told the whole world what a bad place I'm running."

"And I meant it." Her eyes followed him as he moved about the room, stoking the fire, petting Critter on his way back. "So I really wish you wouldn't be too solicitous."

"Does that mean neighborly? I've got a right to be neighborly. I'm staying at Vicki's place, next door."

"Oh." She didn't know her neighbor at all, but she wondered if he made tea for her, too. "*Staying* there?"

"I'm not around the Plugged Nickel much. Vicki keeps it running. I'm kind of an absentee partner."

"I see."

He sat on the floor right next to her, and she knew she ought to tell him not to worry about getting the furniture wet. But she didn't. He leaned his shoulder against the sofa cushion, and she thought about touching his smooth skin.

He tipped his head forward, ruffled his damp hair with both ends of the towel and came up looking as if he'd just gotten out of the shower. "The fire feels good, doesn't it?"

She cleared her throat. "Yes, it does."

"Demonstrating like that is kind of nervy stuff. You ought to stay out of it."

"I've got nerve," she insisted. "I've got plenty of nerve." *Not enough to lift her hand a few inches unless she could come up with an excuse.* "Not the kind you have, but enough to take a stand."

"You took a stand, which won't change a damn thing, and now your head's spinning and your gut aches." She was holding her tea in both hands, and the hot water bottle had slipped. He smiled and adjusted it over her stomach. "You don't want to be sitting in jail, Hannah."

"No. But someone has to speak up."

"You've got a pretty voice for it, too, but money speaks louder. The money's just too damn good. And it's good for the town. Look at all the business it's—"

"I think a petition would be next in order. You can't go to jail for that." She hugged the hot water bottle with one arm while she sipped her tea. Then she recalled, "You can go to jail for swimming in the nude. I checked."

"Did you, now?" he asked, chuckling. "And did you sign a complaint against me?"

"No."

He was grinning, and mischief danced in his eyes. "You didn't have to look, you know."

"I wasn't expecting—"

"Neither was I. So I got these—" he leaned back and snapped his elastic waistband again "—just for you."

"As long as you're my neighbor's guest and you're properly dressed, there's nothing I can do to stop you."

"You can join me." He winked at her. "Anytime."

"You must have ice water in your veins."

"Actually, I'm hot-blooded." He touched the back of her hand to prove his point, frowned a little, then took her hand completely in his, more to test than to hold. "My hands are always warm. Yours are cold, even with the hot stuff you've been touching. Still scared?"

"No," she said too quickly.

"Good." Smiling, he settled her hand back over the hot water bottle.

"I really hated the handcuffs." He nodded as though he knew from experience what she meant. "And the finger-

printing. It made me feel like a criminal, even though..."
She looked into his eyes to assure him, "I'm not one."

"You're treading on thin ice. They wanted me to sign a complaint."

"I do..." Oh, Lord, those eyes were teasing one minute and dangerously dark the next. "...appreciate the fact that you didn't."

"Can you say, 'Thank you, Race'?"

"Thank you—" it was hard to look into his eyes, but she could say it "—Race."

"No problem." As though he'd gotten what he wanted, he left her side and moved closer to the fire. "Did Moe give you your gun back?"

"I wish you'd forget about that. Pointing that thing at you was a stupid move, stupid and childish and—"

"Don't ever take up poker. You're not much of a bluffer." The raised hearth offered him a place to sit. "You feeling all right now?"

"Much better, thanks." She sipped her tea and tried to think of something less personal to talk about—at least, less personal for her. "Did you know that a man who has a wife and children to support lost his whole paycheck at your blackjack tables the other night?"

"A grown man with a completely functioning brain in his head?" He shook his head in amazement. "Then it's up to him to use it, right? I'm not twisting anyone's arm."

"But you're obviously a caring person."

"Yeah, well..." He gestured toward her with one hand as he stood up again, holding both ends of the towel, still slung around his neck, with his other hand. A man about to plead his case. "I'm not going to walk away from a woman who's doubled over in pain, if that's what you mean. But I'm not a fool, and I'm not going to walk away from a great business opportunity, either. A guy walks into the Plugged Nickel to play blackjack, he'll get himself a fair game. We don't ask him how much he can afford to lose. That's his business.''

"It's bad business."

"I'm making good money at it, and it's put Deadwood back on the map. Everybody's benefiting from it in some way. What business are you in?"

"I'm a social worker."

"Terrific. A social worker." He started to pace, but he turned with another open-handed gesture. "You're a good example. I'll bet business is booming for you, too."

"We're not *looking* for *business,* we're—"

"You're getting it sent your way. People being what they are, you'll never find yourself out of work, and neither will I."

"I don't want people to need my services, but when they do—"

"I don't want people to gamble away their paychecks, either. That's up to them. Live and let live, right?"

"I suppose that's one way to look at it."

"It's the only way." He jerked the towel off his neck and tossed it onto a chair. "I'm going to swim back where I came from now," he decided. "You'll be okay?"

"Yes." She thought about offering him something to eat or drink, just to get him to stay a few more minutes. But the wiser part of her nipped that thought in the bud. Instead she said simply, "Thank you."

"Stay out of those wicked saloons from now on if you want to stay out of trouble."

"And out of your way?"

"Can't promise I'll stay out of yours. There's an undertow or something keeps pulling me over this way." He grinned.

The dog picked up on Race's intentions and followed him to the door, wagging his tail. "See ya, Critter," he said; and the dog whined shamelessly just to have the man pet his head. "No, you stay with your mama. Be a good watchdog." He looked up, caught Hannah watching him and gave her another flirty wink. "Keep the bad guys away."

After he'd left, Critter stood by the back door, still whining.

"A lot of good you're going to do," Hannah grumbled.

Chapter 3

Hannah hung around the Center until everyone but Nettie had left. She was tired of the daylong rehash of the sit-in. Embarrassed by it, really. The story had been told from all perspectives. A geriatric gambler had talked Celia out of her seat, so she'd been jockeyed out of action early. Marta had stood on her chair and waved her ALL BETS ARE OFF sign, and, sure enough, she'd seen herself on the KWST night report. The sign, lips, neck and shoulders—that was Marta. Tasha had made a lot of noise. Hadn't everybody heard her yelling "Throw the bandits out"?

"But, Hannah, you really came through for the cause," she went on now, nodding at the others. "Didn't she? Wasn't she great?"

It was agreed more than once that Hannah was great. And the television coverage had reportedly sparked at least one heated discussion in the grocery store. Rumor had it that a customer at the gas station had turned her nose up at the slot machine there and professed to "agree whole-heartedly with that blond girl on TV."

Hannah felt like an imposter. She had been a reluctant sit-in recruit, yet she'd ended up splashing her face all over the ten o'clock news. She wasn't even sure how it had happened, except that she'd been provoked by a rubber band. All of a sudden her mouth had been running at the same time as the camera.

Not that she'd said anything wrong. It was just that she hadn't intended to be the center of any attention. The worst part of it all was the way the words "next time" kept coming up in the conversation. Next time we'll do this or say that. Well, next time it was Tasha's turn.

Nettie was unimpressed. She'd kept to herself all day. She'd offered neither criticism nor congratulations. In fact, she'd hardly spared a glance from her work. So Hannah had waited for time alone with her. Nettie's silence was heavy with something. Displeasure with her, Hannah was sure of it. Whatever she had done, Hannah wanted to be forgiven. She wanted Nettie to tell her that she hadn't done anything that terribly stupid.

When everyone else had left, Hannah brought Nettie a cup of coffee, for which she received a nod and a curt thanks. She pulled up a chair, selected a penknife and started stripping the bark from a willow switch, the way the older woman had taught her to.

"It won't really make any difference, will it, Nettie?" she said. "What we did won't change anything."

Carving the bill of the basket that would be shaped like a duck absorbed most of Nettie's attention. "Why do you ask me? It doesn't concern me. I told you that."

"I know." Hannah sighed and voiced her true feelings on the matter for the first time. "I made an absolute fool of myself."

"No more than the others. You have plenty of company."

"More than the others, yes. As it turned out, I was the one who looked...who acted..." She tossed her head, impatient with herself. She'd ended up arguing last night when she had intended to be completely collected, absolutely stoical and totally cool.

"That's why you went," Nettie said flatly. "To act. To make a show."

"To make a point." She thought she had done that much. She waited for Nettie to confirm at least that, but the woman went on perfecting the shape of the duck's head. Hannah cleared her throat. "I made a point, anyway." No response. "I did, didn't I?"

"If you made your point, then what bothers you?"

"What bothers me is that I didn't mean to put myself at the center of it all. I meant to be there for moral support for Tasha and the others." She watched Nettie select a strip of red willow from the table. She knew the woman was listening, but she needed more response. "I'm not an activist. Not front line. I'm more like..." *Look at me, Nettie. See that I'm more like...* "Support troops."

"But you were right when you said it won't change anything. It will cause trouble. Police trouble. Courtroom trouble and newspaper trouble." Nettie's hands stilled on the duck's head, and she looked up now, a new soft sheen in her eyes as she entreated, "Let it go. Maybe people will lose interest in the gambling, and it will go away."

"Maybe they'll wise up and drive it away."

"I wouldn't count on that. But maybe something new will come along in a different town, and the gamblers will all go there." Nettie's skeptical smile belied her own words. If such a thing happened, it would take time. "Troubles come and go. You know that. After a while, people won't want to live this way anymore. So they'll find another way."

They shared a quiet time, with Hannah stripping bark while Nettie shaped the duck's skinny neck. Nettie was not one to tell Hannah just what she wanted to hear, and it always took a while for Hannah to hear what Nettie had said. Nettie was a deep cache of experience, and Hannah needed to draw on that. She'd learned to draw wisdom from the woman in silence as much as in words. Sometimes just being in Nettie's presence helped Hannah to sort things out. Even now, as she thought about Nettie's aversion to "police troubles," she remembered Race's comment that she wouldn't "want to be sitting in jail."

Impulsively she broke the silence. "Remember the man I told you about? The one who swims at night behind my cabin?"

"I remember that you admired the way he looked—" Hannah glanced up to catch Nettie's knowing expression "—from behind."

"Admired? Did I say 'admired'?" Nettie shrugged, and Hannah knew that it didn't matter what words she'd used. "Well, he's the man who owns that casino. The one where we had our sit-in."

The older woman's eyes widened, and Hannah thought, finally I've told her something she didn't already know. Now Hannah had a story, and she leaned into the telling of it.

"His name is Race Latimer, and he's not the sole owner of the Plugged Nickel. He has a partner. Vicki Potter. My neighbor." This was the part that bothered Hannah, and maybe Nettie, too, for she'd glanced away. "He must be staying there with her," she said, and resigned herself to it with a shrug.

"You said you never saw the face of the man in the lake. You said it was too dark."

"Well, I've seen it now. He recognized me first, and he . . . well, he let me know he was the one." Absently she set the penknife aside on the table. "It's a handsome face, Nettie. He has dark eyes that can make you forget where you are or what you said last. When he teases, they sparkle, sort of like yours do." Nettie shook her head and pushed the notion away with an unbelieving gesture. But Hannah insisted, "That's how you give yourself away. A piece of yourself, anyway."

"You saw all this last night when you were arguing with this man in front of the people from the TV station?"

"I don't think they showed the argument." She hoped they hadn't. She hadn't watched the broadcast. "He could have pressed charges against me—against us—but he didn't, and last night, after I got home, he . . . I saw him again." Nettie's hands were still now, too, and she looked at Hannah with some anticipation. "He's not what you would expect a casino owner to be like."

"What would you expect?"

"I wouldn't expect him to let me off the hook the way he did." But it was more than that. "I didn't expect to like him."

"The man in the lake, or the man who owns the casino?"

"Either one."

"They both disturb you," Nettie guessed.

"Yes."

"Because you disapprove," came the reflective response. "Of what?"

"Not the man himself, but the things he does."

"He did something good. He kept you from sitting in jail."

Can you say, Thank you, Race?

"Even for an hour it would have been awful. I know that." And even as she said it, she felt foolish. How could she presume to know from mere mental images what Nettie knew from bitter experience?

Well, she'd worn the handcuffs. She'd had her fingertips pressed in ink. "I was ready to accept the consequences. And I don't approve of nude swimming, or taking money from someone in a poker game."

"Then don't do those things, Hannah."

"But they're wrong," she claimed stubbornly.

"And you want to be right. So be careful what you do, and you won't be 'wrong,' like this man." Nettie smiled indulgently. "The man who let you go free when he could have pressed charges."

Hannah bristled as she reclaimed the penknife and began shaving the peeled stick down into a rib for a basket.

"Now, tell me what you liked about the man *himself,*" Nettie said gently.

Without looking up from her task, Hannah reported dutifully, "He was concerned about me, I have to admit that. He knew I was scared. The handcuffs, the fingerprinting and all that . . ." She gave her head a quick shake to dismiss the memory, then smiled when another replaced it. "He made me a cup of tea. Of course, he said whiskey would have been better if I'd had any."

Nettie listened intently, and because her expression hadn't changed, Hannah found herself explaining both sides against the middle. "That was the saloon owner talking. You see? There are too many sides to this man. It's hard to figure out who he really is."

"He's my son."

"What?" She hadn't heard right. Had she said . . .

"Race Latimer is my son," Nettie repeated. "No one here knows this. Not even Race. He doesn't know who I am, and I don't want him to know."

Nettie was stunned. The child Nettie had given up, the one she seldom talked about, was Race Latimer?

"His father raised him. I gave him to Phillip Latimer when he was two years old, and I've stayed out of his life ever since."

"And now?"

"He doesn't need to know about me now. I came to Deadwood for reasons of my own. He's here for his. He doesn't know anything about Nettie Couteau."

"If he hasn't heard your name mentioned by now, he will sooner or later."

"His mother was Annette LaFrambois. An unmarried woman who had an affair with a married man. It is possible that he knows who I am, knows my married name, and chooses not to acknowledge me. Then..." Nettie glanced away and tugged at that always errant shorter piece of hair that escaped the clip at her nape. "Then I guess we have an understanding in a way. But I don't think he knows. I think he forgot Annette LaFrambois long ago." Nettie shook her head. "She wasn't worth remembering."

"Oh, Nettie." It was painful to watch her, painful to listen and to imagine, but neither Nettie's voice nor her expression betrayed that pain. When Hannah would have touched her hand, Nettie took up her weaving again, refusing to be pitied.

It wasn't pity Hannah wanted to offer, but hope for change. "Everything's different now. What happened to you was...was awful, and I'm sure if you told your son the whole story—"

"No." A hard look from Nettie was meant to set Hannah straight. "I gave him up. No one forced me to. I gave him up and went on my way. And that was only the beginning of my shame, as you well know. I see him on the street sometimes, and I remember the little boy who tangled his fingers in my hair and hung on so tight. I wanted to let him take that much—that piece of my hair. Something he could hold onto. But I took that from him, too."

Memory softened the look in Nettie's eyes, but the soft feeling was not for Hannah. It was for Race.

"He screamed when his father took him. He reached for me. He looked so small and so scared. 'Hold him tight,' I said, because his father was looking at me as if I'd just handed him a wild porcupine and he didn't know how to handle it. 'Hold onto him. He's pretty strong for such a little guy.'" She chuckled and said, "He almost got away. I see him on the street now, and I think about that time. That terrible look in his eyes."

Hannah remembered his eyes, too. Dark and compelling, but he had a capacity for caring. A man like that could forgive.

"You must have had good reason," Hannah said. "It couldn't have been easy to give him up that way."

"Yes, it was. I couldn't do what I wanted, whenever I wanted, not with a baby around. It was easy to pack his things—he didn't have much. It was easy to make his father take him. I knew it would be. One thing about Phillip, he knew his responsibilities. I knew he would raise his son and teach him to be a white man. A Latimer. He looked a lot like a Latimer, even then. Not blond, of course, but not as dark as me. He would have respect."

While Nettie spoke, Hannah watched the woman's hands carefully working the willow over and under. Working hands. Hands she, herself, admired. Respected.

She thought of brown leather, worn by the elements and by continual use. Nettie worked tirelessly at her craft, as though she were trying to make up for lost time.

"As for me," Nettie concluded, "I had nothing but trouble to give him. Nothing but bad to teach him. Those were my reasons for giving him up."

Hannah didn't know what to say, and Nettie knew full well that wasn't like her.

"Do you disapprove?" the older woman asked. "Do you disapprove of the things I did?"

"It's all in the past now, Nettie."

"But I can't change it. Everything is different, yes, but those things can never be changed."

"Maybe you did the right thing."

"If I did, it was for the wrong reason," Nettie assured her. "But he's doing good now. He's a fire fighter, you know. For the Forest Service."

"He did say something about firemen, but not that he was one himself. He said he was making a lot of money at the Plugged Nickel."

"He was a fire fighter before he got in on that place, and he still is. A smoke jumper out west most of the summer." Her eyes had brightened again. She studied Hannah. "You like that better?"

"Well, Nettie..." She waved the penknife in the air and tried to be exasperated, although Nettie's smiling eyes made it difficult to pull it off without smiling back. "Now this crazy man who's suddenly turning up everywhere turns out to be your son."

"But you liked him before you knew that, and I think you'll be seeing more of him." When Hannah started to protest, Nettie waved the attempt away with a snappy piece of willow. "There's a reason why he's turning up everywhere. There's a purpose."

"I can't imagine what it would be. He's staying with the woman who—"

"The woman's not important," Nettie said, and Hannah enjoyed the way Vicki was so easily dismissed. "I've kept my distance, but I know him better now, just from what you've told me. The kind of man he is." She smiled. "He turned the other cheek for you, didn't he?"

"Nettie, I didn't *strike* him, and I'm hardly much of a—" The expression in Nettie's eyes reminded her to be honest with herself. "Yes, I guess I did threaten him. In all fairness, I have to admit he showed no malice in return."

"Just the opposite, in fact," Nettie pressed. "He treated you good."

Hannah saw the pride in Nettie dark eyes. The men in Nettie's life had not treated her well. She had been ignored by her father, cast aside by her lover and abused by a succession of men until finally one had been required to pay.

"He did," Hannah admitted.

"You can't tell him about me without my permission, isn't that right? Even if you're not my counselor now."

"You know I wouldn't betray a confidence, professional or otherwise."

"Good." Nettie nodded, and she went back to work on her weaving, mouthing the word twice more. Then quietly she recited the convictions she stood by rigidly. "His mother was Annette LaFrambois. She deserted him long ago. The rest . . ." She didn't have to remind Hannah that the rest was privileged information. "He doesn't want to know the rest."

"You don't have to punish yourself."

"I don't punish myself. This way I see him sometimes." She made it sound as though it were truly sufficient. "I've kept track of him. I've always kept my ears open about the Latimers and what they were up to. It's a big name in South Dakota. I heard about Race being on the outs with his dad, about him getting in with the Forest Service. Even in the pen, you hear things through the moccasin telegraph. He doesn't know his Chippewa relatives, but they know him."

"Nettie, he isn't a child anymore. Why not just tell him?"

"Because he isn't a child anymore," Nettie echoed. "It's not like he'll ever need me, and I don't want to stir up old ghosts." Ghosts that echoed within the walls of the big empty room as the women talked. Nettie believed in ghosts. She dreaded their interference. "It can't hurt, can it? To let me have . . . just this much?"

"I think you deserve more." The old woman shook her head. "I do, Nettie."

"You're a good girl." And then came the touch. Nettie's leathery hand on Hannah's young, supple one. "It's good this way. This way I'm not making any trouble for him. You understand?"

Race wasn't sure why he wanted to see her again before he left for Montana. There wasn't a snowman's chance in hell of scoring with Hannah Quinn. He'd be lucky if he got as far as first base with her, which was a hell of a way to waste his last night in Deadwood. He should have been making friends with a good-time sort of woman instead of pounding on Hannah's heavy pine door.

He had to be getting old. Hearing that dog whip himself into a barking frenzy on the other side of the door seemed kind of nice. He hadn't planned on getting sentimental about faithful dogs and one-man women for another ten years, at least. But he had this funny, expectant tingle deep in his gut as he stood there waiting for the door to open.

It creaked on its hinges as she stepped around it and peered through the screen, wide-eyed and pretty as a picture in a kid's storybook. Just that flushed and fresh-scrubbed looking. "Oh," she said, surprised. "Mr. Latimer. Aren't you a little early?"

He checked his watch reflexively.

"You don't usually come floating by before midnight," she explained.

"Oh, yeah." He wasn't dressed for the lake, but she wasn't going to see much of that for herself unless she let him in. "Well, you complained about the hour. I thought if I came early, maybe you'd join me."

"In that icy water? You're the only swimmer I've seen out there so far this spring. My constitution is no match for yours."

"It wouldn't hurt to get your feet wet, kinda toughen up gradually." Her cute grimace made him laugh. "Maybe I could talk you into it over supper."

"I was just going to fix some—"

"I'm inviting you out. Sort of a bury-the-hatchet supper between temporary neighbors."

"You're my neighbor's ... houseguest." He wondered what the pregnant pause was for. "And her business partner. And..."

On the second pause it dawned on him. "And that's it. Vicki's living in town now."

"Oh."

"'Oh, that's different,' she says."

"I wasn't thinking—"

"Yes, you were. You were filing through the Commandments in your head, looking for one that says, 'Thou shalt not covet thy neighbor's old man.'"

Critter, yapping and running back and forth like a caged monkey, effectively drowned out Hannah's protest.

"Hey, Critter, wanna tell the lady to open the door so I can get my face properly licked—" He gave Hannah the eye, along with his special slow smile, the one guaranteed to charm her.

"—by whoever's glad to see me."

"I'm sorry. I didn't mean to keep you standing outside. It's just that this is such a—" she opened the door, and as soon as he stepped inside, the dog was all over him "—surprise. Critter, mind your manners."

"He is," Race said, laughing as Critter happily licked his cheek. They played around like two kangaroo boxers. Then Race took the dog's big head in his hands and shook it affectionately. "Thanks, buddy. You've got a thick T-bone coming for getting me past the front door."

"You're inviting Critter out to dinner, too?"

Critter plopped his butt on the floor and gave them each the big-eyed puppy treatment.

"A doggie bag'll do it, huh, boy? Otherwise you've gotta wear shoes and a shirt and all that." Critter woofed, and Race interpreted. "He'll settle for two doggie bags if I promise not to keep you out too late. Of course, we'll have to drive to Rapid to get anything decent."

"I could offer you a decent meal right here," Hannah said. And he was tempted. She looked as though she'd made herself comfortable for the evening in a soft blue blouse and easy-fitting white slacks. He could have made himself comfortable, too. But that wouldn't have been the best way to bury the hatchet.

"I'm sure you could. But I'm talking about decent doggie bags." He motioned for her to turn around. She gave him a quizzical look, but she complied. "Just checking you over. The shirt's fine, but you'll need shoes."

"Well, I guess supper would be fine, too," she allowed. "But swimming is definitely out, and you won't change my mind about the gambling issue, either. I'm still opposed to it."

"That's all right. I have nothing but respect for a woman who sticks to her guns." As she started to turn, a little too self-assured for his liking, he added, "Even if they only shoot rubber bands."

"Will I ever live that down?" she asked with a groan. He only smiled. She squared her shoulders and retreated to the bedroom for her shoes.

"Probably not," Race muttered to Critter as he absently petted the dog's head. "And you're not as determined as you think you are. What should we work on first, Critter? The moonlight swim or the gambling issue?"

Critter's tongue lolled as he commenced panting.

"My sentiments exactly. I don't give a damn what she thinks about gambling."

Hannah was unaccustomed to riding in a pickup truck, but she knew that it was the vehicle of choice for most South Dakota men. She could see why. She'd spent her life looking up at people most of the time, but seated in Race's pickup, she was riding high above the highway with the wind from the open windows making free with her hair. The sun was sliding toward the dark peaks, and the sky was fading to a pale, hazy blue with a peach underbelly.

He didn't talk much as he drove them to Rapid City. It was probably just as well. She was glad he didn't ask her to suggest a restaurant, because she wouldn't have been able to come up with one since she seldom went out to eat. But she couldn't help wondering what he was thinking and why he wanted to spend the evening with a woman who had waved a sign protesting his place of business in front of a television camera.

Whatever the reason, she was glad for it. She was glad he had gone to the trouble of putting on a sport coat with his jeans and wearing a spicy, masculine fragrance. She wondered whether those efforts had been just for her, as he would have her believe the purchase of swimming trunks had been. He was certainly getting closer to the kind of apparel she thought suitable. Or the degree to which a man ought to be dressed, which was completely.

And she was getting closer to admitting that this man would catch her eye and make her heart beat a little faster no matter what he wore. Indeed, he did favor his mother. She should have seen the resemblance immediately in the way they both smiled with their eyes. And in the widow's peak in his dark hair, much like Nettie's. His hands on the wheel—as Nettie's were when weaving her baskets— strong, sure, work-roughened and deeply tanned.

"What's it like to be a smoke jumper?" she asked.

He glanced across the pickup cab's interior, looking surprised, as though he'd forgotten she was there. "My memory must be going. I don't recall telling you I was a smoke jumper."

Hannah squirmed, remembering that it was Nettie who'd told her. Lord, she was going to have trouble keeping it straight who'd told her what, and she was going to have to learn to be a little cagey about this confidence she was bound by professional ethics as well as honor to keep. Eventually the problem would be moot, though. Sooner or later, mother and son would meet. Hannah was sure of it.

There's a reason why he's turning up everywhere. There's a purpose.

They were to come to know one another at last, aging mother and grown son. What else could God have intended by bringing them so close? And if Hannah were to be an instrument, so be it.

An instrument, she told herself. But not a Judas.

"Someone at the Center mentioned that, um, she'd heard that you…" She wasn't going to lie, but she did have to hedge around the whole truth, which wasn't easy. "I mean, we talked about the Plugged Nickel, and the fact that you weren't actually there that much."

He smiled. "You were discussing the players, right? Was this before or after you staged the big game?"

"Afterward. I was giving you due credit for letting me off the hook. And one of the women said that you also work for the Forest Service, which I find very interesting."

"You like that better, do you?" When she didn't deny it, he took a firmer grip on the steering wheel and attended to the road ahead. "I'm heading out for Montana tomorrow."

"Is there a fire?"

"Up in the Bitterroots, where they have to use jumpers." Race signaled for a right turn into the parking lot of Chub's Steakhouse, but a silver sports car shot across the intersection and zipped in ahead of them. Race shook his head and made his turn. "Guess this guy heard something about a fire, too. Either that, or he knows there's only one parking place left at Chub's. You like steak?"

She admired his cool. "I'm sure I can find something on the menu that I'll enjoy."

"They serve the best steak in town here, but if you're into eating only what's 'good' for you, we can go—"

"No, this is fine," she said, touching his arm to assure him. "I'm really very easy—" her touch drew a slow, heated gaze that made her stomach flutter "—to please. I mean, I like almost anything."

"Really?" He watched her hand make its retreat, and then he smiled. "I would have sworn you'd be pickier'n hell."

They were given a secluded table in the dark, rustic restaurant. The decor was characterized by black vinyl and rough pine, and the air was heavy with the aroma of steaks on the grill. The grill was situated in the center of the dining room. If Hannah hadn't been hungry for beef before she went in, she was by the time she sat down. A small lantern in the middle of the table held a white votive candle, and the napkins were blue bandannas.

Race allowed that Critter would be happy when they both ordered ribeye steaks. While they waited, he sipped his beer and she her iced tea. She started to say that Chub's Steakhouse seemed to be getting along well without slot machines, but she changed her mind. And when they were finished eating she almost said, yes, she would mind if he smoked, but she changed her mind about that, too. He was leaving tomorrow, and she didn't want him to go off thinking of her as "pickier'n hell." Picky sounded too much like peevish and fussy. She wasn't that.

"Is it a big fire?" she asked.

"I guess they sent in one crew yesterday, but they figure it'll take at least one more. It's early in the season for a big fire. Still, we've got some dry spots around the country this year. Including here."

"So they just drop you out of a plane in the middle of nowhere, and you put out the fire," she said. "It must be a dangerous job."

"Oh, I don't know. Once you make the jump, it's pretty much like fighting fire anywhere else. Dirty, tedious, backbreaking work." He leaned forward, resting his forearms against the edge of the table and lacing his fingers together. "But it's challenging, you know? Because fire is such a wily opponent."

"And powerful," she supplied, although she could have been persuaded that it was no more so than he. He was a powerfully built man. His hands fascinated her. Long fingers, richly tanned . . .

"So you outmaneuver it. And no two fires are ever the same." He leaned back abruptly, retrieving his cigarette from the ashtray. "Anyway, they've had me training fire fighting crews this spring, working out of the Custer District. Working with new recruits can be a dangerous job. Sometimes they don't listen worth a damn."

"Sometimes it seems like my clients aren't listening, either, and then all of a sudden something clicks, and they take hold of things." She watched his lips take hold of the cigarette. She could almost taste the smoke in his mouth, and she found herself repeating words, just to be talking. "Take hold of . . . their lives."

"I know what you mean." He exhaled.

Hannah hated smoke, and she wasn't sure why it was so fascinating to watch this man's every move, but it was.

"This bothers you, doesn't it?" he said as he crushed the remains of the cigarette in the ashtray. He eyed her knowingly. "You should've said something."

"It's not that bad. Really." He hadn't guessed the whole of it, thank the Lord. The fascination part.

"I don't want you to lie to me, Hannah. Ever. About anything." The look in his dark, deep-set eyes was intimidating, and she glanced away so that she could assure herself she hadn't lied to him about anything. Ever. Strictly speaking.

"Okay?" he insisted. "I meant it when I said that I respect a woman who sticks to her guns. I won't quit smoking for you, but I don't have to do it around you."

"It's not a big issue, really." Not as big as telling the truth, the whole truth and nothing but. Oh, Lord, she had to stop squirming over everything this man said and did.

"Tell me more about training fire fighters."

He set the ashtray aside. "They put these guys together on a crew, and for a while they're running into each other, tripping over their own bootlaces. Just when you think one of 'em's bound to kill somebody with his Pulaski, things start clicking into place, and you've got a team."

"What's a Pulaski?"

"It's a fire fighting tool, sort of half hoe, half ax."

"And are you training smoke jumpers?"

"Oh, no, not here. You have to go to one of the aerial depots for that. In the off-season, jumpers can be detailed where they're needed, which is why they decided I oughta start training fire crews. I'm actually just a fire fighter who jumps out of a plane to get to the fire. Of course, once you're on the ground..."

"It's a dirty, tedious, backbreaking job," she echoed, smiling. "You must be very good if they've made you an instructor."

"They've found worse ways to keep me busy off-season." He shrugged, then allowed himself a small measure of credit. "I've been at it a while, been a crew boss..." He smiled. "Yeah, I'm pretty good at it. And the South Dakota assignments are welcome, now that I've got business interests here." He made a toss-away gesture before he reached for his coffee. "Anyway, I guess the Forest Service wanted somebody like me to come in and work with Indian recruits."

"Because of your Indian heritage?"

The look in his eyes hardened. "What makes you think I have any Indian heritage?"

She'd done it again. Hannah's face felt warm, and she knew the telltale blush was creeping up her neck. Lord, she couldn't seem to keep her feet out of her mouth tonight.

She cleared her throat. "I guess, your coloring makes you look a little..."

"You're a whole lot redder than I am right now." A cool moment passed before he shrugged it off. "Black hair, brown eyes, some Indian blood. But no heritage."

"I really didn't mean to be rude."

"Chippewa," he said, as though she'd asked.

The fact that she already knew brought on another twinge of guilt, and she studied the last of the coffee in her cup while he went on telling her things she wished she hadn't heard before. "On my mother's side, I'm Chippewa. But I don't remember her. My father's white, and he's the one I lived with growing up. So I don't know much about being an Indian, if that's what you mean by 'heritage.' But the Forest Service recruits a lot of Indian fire fighters, and they figured they had this Chippewa with a lot of experience in the field and some off-season time on his hands." He hesitated, then quietly confessed, "I didn't much like it at first."

"You've never been close to anyone on your mother's side of the family?" The asking stirred up more uneasy feelings, but it seemed a logical question, given the course of the conversation.

"No," he said tersely.

Obviously, not a door to be tampered with.

"But you don't really need the job anyway, now that your casino is doing so well," she ventured, going back to safer waters.

"Yeah, but if I quit smoke jumping, I lose half my appeal. With you, probably ninety percent." He chuckled when she started to protest, so she gave up and just shook her head, grateful to be led away from the terrible temptation to pry for Nettie's sake.

"I like the job," he told her. "I don't even mind breaking in the new guys, now that I'm getting the hang of it. I've had a lot of different jobs in my time—building houses, punching cattle, dealing cards. I like working outside, especially when the weather's good. And when it's not so good—" he lifted one shoulder in a half shrug "—I like to have a beer and deal some cards. No harm in that. The Plugged Nickel is an investment, and dealing blackjack is entertaining once in a while. Just like gambling."

"Some people get addicted to gambling," she reminded him, dutifully remembering her *Thou shalt nots*.

"You name me one thing that somebody somewhere isn't addicted to." He jabbed a finger in the air as he set up to make a point. "The New Moon Center. That's where you work, right?"

"Yes."

"I noticed the column in the newspaper listing all the meetings they hold there. There's an 'anonymous' for everything, including eating. People have to eat."

"It's not eaters. It's *Over*eaters Anonymous."

"So, see? You and your friends could stage a protest right here." With a broad gesture he indicted the room full of tables, then jerked a thumb at the one closest to them. "Look how much food that guy has on his plate. He might get addicted."

By the looks of the pudgy-faced diner, he already was. But the added pounds hadn't affected his hearing. He stopped shoveling steak into his mouth long enough for a brief glare.

"Shh." Hannah glanced left, then right. "*We* might get thrown out."

Race smiled, his eyes alight. "We might get on TV. Besides, that's the guy who was driving the silver 'Vette, so we know how serious his problem is. Of course, if we make a pitch for outlawing food, we'll probably end up in the psych ward rather than the county jail."

"You're being ridiculous." He raised his eyebrows as if to say "Aren't *you?*" "But I wasn't," she contended. "And, anyway, there won't be any more meetings or any more Center if something isn't done about the lease rates. The church can't pay those incredible increases."

"Put in a slot machine or two."

"Right." On the tail end of a sigh, she had a second thought. "Have you ever been inside the New Moon Center?" He shook his head. "I'd like to give you a tour. I think if you saw what goes on there—"

"Hey, I have all the respect in the world for what you do. I just think you have to get real about some things, Hannah. For instance, people have to eat."

"But—"

"And," he said, cutting her off with a raised finger, "gambling has been one hell of an economic shot in the arm for Deadwood. The town was flat broke, and now it's flush with cash, almost overnight."

"The invitation stands," she said flatly.

"I'm leaving in the morning."

The reminder fell heavily into the space between them and left them silent, looking at one another, assessing, wondering what plans to offer and what promises might not be out of line. Then candlelight burned in his eyes and glimmered in his thick, dark hair.

"When will you be back?" she asked.

"That depends on the fire season. I usually try to get back when I have a break, but I never know when that will be." He gazed at her in the candlelight and spoke softly. "Will I see you?"

"I . . . don't know."

"You're not going to lose your lease this summer, are you?"

"We're not going to lose it at all if we can help it." Just one of the many reasons for saying, "No, it's too awkward. No, it's too confusing. No, it's impossible."

But *no* wouldn't come.

Instead, she surprised even herself by asking, "Would you mind if I wrote to you?"

"You mean . . . letters?"

He made it sound like a foreign word. "Yes, letters. Where do you stay?"

"I'm based at West Yellowstone, but I'll be staying at a fire camp until the fire's out, or until they move me someplace else."

"Does the mail reach you?" she pressed.

"I don't get much mail. The only person who ever writes to me is my sister, Lannie." His level stare seemed to challenge her to back off on her offer. "I'm not much for writing back."

"As demanding as your job must be, I'm sure Lannie understands." Hannah smiled. "I will, too."

"Look, it's fine if you want to write to me," he said almost grudgingly. "But I'm not looking for another sister. And when I get back this way, I'll be knocking on your door."

Chapter 4

After digging fire lines up in the high country for two weeks, coming back to a dormitory bunk was the worst part of Race's job. The first night he was always too tired to care. But by the time he'd had enough sleep so he didn't feel so much like a zombie, he was looking for another call. This time of year it probably wouldn't come right away. It wasn't quite the end of May, and the fire season usually didn't heat up until the middle of June.

When there were no calls, fire fighters either spent their days packing parachutes and checking cargo boxes, or they were detailed to other ranger districts to work on forestry projects. Dead-time detail that made you wish you were doing something else. Race wondered if someone else had finished out the training down in Custer, or if his crews had been pronounced fit for duty. After all the time he'd invested, he wanted to see for himself if he'd turned out a good hotshot crew. He had a little slack time coming, and decided he would put it to good use.

The aerial fire base was three miles outside the town of
West Yellowstone, which offered minimal diversion. He'd
been there earlier to pick up some cigarettes and a couple
of magazines, but he hadn't felt much like hanging around
the tourists and listening to fishing stories. He'd ended up
leaving without either. The cigarettes were just more
smoke, and the magazines...well, he did have other
reading material. Two letters, three pages each. Both
signed "Yours truly, Hannah."

The first one had been dropped, along with a load of
supplies, at the fire camp in the Bitterroot Mountains.
There he'd directed two hand crews of smoke jumpers in
controlling a fire started by lightning. The fire had been
christened the Goat's Ridge Fire. After they'd mopped up
and struck camp, he'd been assigned to a second incident,
and he'd carried the letter inside his shirt. He wasn't sure
why. Maybe for luck.

He'd practically memorized the first one by the time the
second letter arrived. There usually weren't too many guys
around—West Yellowstone housed only a small smoke
jumper force—but he made sure he was alone whenever he
read his letters. Somebody was bound to figure out that
he'd read them half a dozen times already.

Either that or they'd razz him about the fancy paper. It
was kind of a soft white, the color of piano keys, and del-
icate-looking next to his rough, brown hands. He wondered what kind of flower that was in the upper left-hand
corner of the first page. Its five petals turned back, blush-
ing with a hint of pink, as though the bold yellow stamen
in the center somehow embarrassed them. He covered it
with his thumb, memorizing the embossed shape. It had a
female feel to it.

He'd been thinking he ought to answer. In fact, the wads
of yellow paper snuggling up to his hip attested to the fact

that he'd done more than think about it as he sat there on
his bunk with his back braced against the wall. The blue-
lined pad from Stockert's office and the ball-point pen
from Deadwood's Saloon No. 10 lay nearby, waiting for
him to try again.

That paper was going to make it a tacky-looking letter.
And if Hannah could have seen the advertising on the pen
he was using, she'd probably cringe. Hell, he was lucky he
could even find a pen. He couldn't remember the last time
he'd written a damn letter. God help him, he couldn't come
up with a single sentence that didn't sound like something
out of a note passed by a gawky school kid.

Why didn't hers sound like that?

Dear Race,
    I think it's almost warm enough to swim in the lake.
It's late, and the night is unusually hot and still. It
seldom gets like this in the Hills at night. Critter's sitting right next to my feet, but he always seems to have
one ear cocked toward the lake. Like him, I almost
expect to look out the window and see you swimming
in the cool water. Last night I took him outside and
waded in up to my knees. The way we did the last
night you were here...

Not quite up to her knees, as he remembered. Midcalf
was as far as he'd gotten her to go that night after their
dinner date. He'd imagined dragging her down until she
was in over her head, and then it had suddenly occurred to
him that the notion of dragging her down in any way was
like taking a quarter turn on a wrench that was attached to
his gut. She deserved to be lifted up and held high, just for
the warm way she smiled. He doubted she had any idea
how sexy she'd looked when she'd stepped into the water

and that beautiful shiver had shimmied its way from her shoulders to her toes.

Even after he'd warned her about slippery rocks, she'd almost gone down on one. She'd laughed as she'd tipped and swayed, trying to catch her balance. Reaching for her had been a reflex. Until that moment he'd felt pretty ridiculous standing in the water with his pants rolled up like some geek. But when she'd grabbed his hand, foolish feelings had evaporated. In his mind he heard the laughter go still again. He smelled the water and the field flower scent of her. Her hair was the color of moonlight. The breeze toyed with the full, filmy skirt that kept flirting with the lapping water. He remembered the way her eyes had glistened when she lifted first her chin, then her lashes. If it hadn't been for Critter bounding into the water with that damned stick in his mouth . . .

He had no trouble picturing the way he would have kissed her. He just couldn't imagine how he would have stopped.

"Hey, Race, it's chow time."

At the sound of a boot on the back step, Race slipped Hannah's letters under his pillow and slid over, sitting on the crumpled evidence of his attempts at letter writing. It struck him that maybe the round wads were like eggs, and he nearly cracked up at the thought of hatching a letter while he sat there jawing with Al Stockert. He managed to suppress all but a smirk as Al let the screen door swing shut behind him.

"The beef's nice 'n rare, and the biscuits'll melt in your mouth." Race's grin stopped Al in his tracks. "What?" The big man checked his denim shirtfront. "Have I got crumbs on my chin, gravy on my tie, what?"

"I'd like to see you in a tie," Race said as he laced his fingers together behind his neck and tipped his head back against the wall. "You ever wear one, Al?"

"Not if I can help it. Why?"

"Couple of weeks ago I was going out to a restaurant, and I thought maybe I oughta wear one. Looked through all my stuff. Couldn't find anything but the string ties we've got the bartenders and bouncers wearing at the Plugged Nickel. I found a jacket, but I guess I don't own a real tie."

"I think I got a couple somewhere. Next time you're feelin' fancy…" Al put his foot on the seat of the wooden chair next to Race's bunk and laid his forearm over his knee. "Who were you out to impress?"

"My Aunt Harriet," Race said derisively. Al was always asking him about his love life. Probably because Al had been married since the last Ice Age. "I've got a three-day weekend coming, and I'd like to spend it in South Dakota."

"Gus is taking a tanker down that way in the morning. You can hitch a ride with him." Race nodded, and Al expounded. "It's pretty dry down there this year. The Bighorns are running a high fire index, too, along with the Bitterroots. The crews you've been training are bound to be working soon."

"I wasn't finished, you know. The Basic 32 is a joke. We were up to eighty hours of training, but we could have used more."

"You need a hundred and ten hours to turn out a good hand crew. But they'll catch up. The Indian crews are some of the best ones we've got." Al took his foot off the chair and sat down. "How's business in Deadwood?"

"Best investment I ever made." Race laughed. "Hell, it's the only investment I ever made. Maybe some of my dad's business sense wore off on me after all. Probably shock the hell out of him if he knew how much money that place rakes in.''

''You gonna quit jumping?''

''Why would I wanna quit jumping?'' He quirked an eyebrow in Al's direction. ''Now, bustin' my buns digging fire lines and getting my eyebrows singed, that I might wanna quit someday. But the rest . . .'' He rolled the back of his head from side to side against the hard wall. ''I don't know what it is about a wildland fire. It eats up everything in its path and dares you to try and stop it. It's like some guy twice your size saying, 'Wanna step outside, boy?' And you know if you don't, he's gonna trash everything.''

It sounded pretty sentimental, but he knew Stockert understood. His body had long since surpassed the two hundred pound weight limit for smoke jumpers. He was in charge of aerial operations at West Yellowstone, but he still liked to get soot under his nails whenever he had the chance.

''The wildlands need fire when they get overgrown,'' Al said. ''It's part of the cycle.''

''Yeah, but we've got damn little wildland left. If we don't manage it, it'll all be gone,'' Race recited for the man who'd been his instructor. Then he smiled. ''Does that sound pretty good?''

''I'm impressed,'' Al claimed. ''Was she?'' With a frown, Race feigned ignorance. ''The woman you're writing to. Bet she didn't hardly miss that tie when you fed her that line.''

Chuckling, Race admitted, ''Can't very well tell her the real reason I'm keeping this job is that I'm a thrill-seeker, pure and simple.''

"'And, honey, being with you is the biggest thrill I've had all week, so what do you say we...'"

"Nah, not this lady. She's not even my type." Lowering his arms and folding them across his chest, he amended. "I'm not *her* type. I don't know why she even..." *Wrote to me.* She'd said she would, but he hadn't expected her to. After he'd left, she should have come to her senses.

"Well, I'll let you get back to your letter writing." Al heaved himself out of the chair, pointedly glancing at the yellow pad on the floor as he straightened his back. "Just tell her you want to see her again. That's all you have to say."

Race looked up in mock despair.

"You make a living jumping into fires, boy. Just tell her." He reached down and swatted Race's denim-clad knee. "You better come and get something to eat before it's all gone. Looks to me like you'll need your strength when you get back to South Dakota."

Hannah was more than surprised when Race showed up at the New Moon Center at lunchtime. Dressed in jeans, black T-Shirt and a battered straw cowboy hat, he was the last person she would have expected to come rapping at her office door. He looked tired. His face was drawn, and there were dark circles under his intensely dark eyes. Not his usual cocky self, which made his visit seem all the more surprising.

"Didn't you get my letter?" he asked.

"No." News of a letter was, in fact, astounding.

"Guess I beat the mail, then." He leaned his shoulder against the door frame. "How about a Nickel's worth of lunch?"

"You mean, have lunch in a saloon with all those slot machines ringing in my ears?" Actually, he looked as though he needed peace and quiet more than she did. It probably wasn't the best time to try to make a terrific impression on him, but he was there, and he might as well see, she decided. "How about a New Moon lunch? I'd love to show you around."

"I don't think I'm up for seeing a bunch of women in some kind of counseling sessions," he said wearily. "Especially women who'd just as soon scratch my eyes out as look at me."

"Oh, not within the walls of the New Moon Center. Everyone's safe here." She checked her schedule quickly, then slid the book into the top drawer of her desk. "It's nothing personal, Race. It's just principles. That's all."

"Yeah, but after two weeks of battling smoke and flames, I don't have the energy to deal with principled women." He adjusted his crumpled brim, almost as though he were tipping his hat to her. "Which are the meanest kind."

"Oh, really?" He wasn't smiling. She wasn't going to let herself get prissy, but sometimes she couldn't tell whether he was teasing her or just plain cutting her down. "Well, you won't get to see any sessions, I'm sorry to say. That would probably open your eyes a little, but, of course, they're private. Let me show you the shop and the craft room."

"And the tuna salad and carrot sticks?" He was following her down the narrow hall, dragging his feet. "Let's compromise and go to the drive-in for a burger and fries. Then we can talk about..." They'd reached the door to the playroom, where little voices were clamoring for lunch. "Kids?"

"Okay," Hannah said as she opened the door and gestured toward the table in the middle of the room. "Let's talk about kids." He'd said the word gently, and she suspected a soft spot he probably didn't know he had. "We have a small day-care program, which we started for our clients. Lately, with all the No Children Allowed signs springing up all over town, there's been a demand for drop-in-care. But as you can see . . ."

"Jeez. That's a lot of kids."

"Which is why we need more space, not less. If we lose our lease . . ." The woman in charge looked up from the trayful of half pint cartons of milk she was dispensing, glanced at Race, then at Hannah. The expression on her face warned of a wolf loose in the lamb's fold.

"Marta, this is . . ." Race was ignoring the introduction, attending instead to a little dark-haired boy who'd escaped, carrot in hand, from his chair at the lunch table to check the man out. Race hunkered down to meet the boy at eye level.

"Well, you remember Race Latimer from the Plugged Nickel," Hannah said in a cheerful attempt to make the requisite introduction.

"I remember," Marta said, coolly.

"They got you eating carrot sticks, huh?" The boy grinned and offered Race a taste. "No, thanks." Undaunted, the boy stuck the end of the carrot within half an inch of Race's mouth. "Okay, one bite. Thanks. I know what you're up to, partner, and I can't say I blame you. But you've gotta eat some of it, too."

"Race, this is Marta Turnbull."

"Hi," Race offered, sparing a quick nod while he shook off the carrot stick the little boy was still angling to get him to polish off. Race laughed. "What's this guy's name?"

"That's Josh."

"Hi, Josh. No, you eat it." Race guided the hand with the carrot back to the little boy's own mouth, then ruffled the mop of brown hair as he stood up again. "I don't know a hell of a lot about kids, but this is a cute little guy. Does his mom work here?"

"His mother's with our program, yes. Thanks, Marta," Hannah said with a parting wave as she closed the door to the playroom. "It would be nice if we could expand a little," she told Race. "I'd like to open the day-care program up to more people, but we just don't have the space, and we can't afford to lease any more. Nobody can unless—"

"Unless you put a few slots in the lobby," he said as he followed her down the hall again. "What could it hurt? The money would be going for a good cause, right?"

She turned on him, astounded. "Do you really think we should have people cussing at slot machines right down the hall from this playroom?"

"It wouldn't be anything they haven't heard before," he insisted, but her glare evoked his retraction. "Okay, maybe not right down the hall."

She nodded, satisfied with her small victory as she moved on to the next door.

But the next door led to the craft room, and Hannah hesitated to push it open. Some of the women would have gone home for lunch, but a few usually stayed, and Nettie would be among them. Hannah hadn't exactly planned this, but she'd conjured the scene many times in her idealistic mind. The two were bound to meet eventually. It wasn't as if she were taking him there to actually *introduce* Race to his long lost mother. She was just showing him around. She couldn't very well *not* show him the craft room, could she? And if Nettie *chose* to reveal herself to him, and if there were tears and apologies and forgiveness, wouldn't that be...

"So, what's this? The cafeteria?"

"Um, we don't have—a cafeteria. We have a small kitchen. This is—" She opened the door, took a deep breath and ushered him into the room that had become the center's hub. "This is the craft room, where we make many of the gifts and..."

Nettie looked up from her basketwork and brushed the ever-straying short lock of gray hair away from her face. She glanced at Hannah, then at Race. He noticed her immediately, and Hannah wondered whether it was instinct. A bond that had never quite broken, perhaps. There was nothing in Nettie's expression that might give her away. There was no sign of recognition in Race's eyes. Yet mother and son were staring directly at one another for the first time since she'd shoved him, screaming in protest, into his father's arms. There was still time for them, Hannah told herself. Still lots of time.

"...the beautiful crafts that we sell in our shop." Hannah cleared her throat, trying to banish the pesky frog that was threatening to betray her. Nettie retreated first by turning to select a slender red willow branch to work into her basket.

"This is also where we hold some of our classes," Hannah said quietly, noting that Tasha was sitting at a table with Celia and two other women. Their luncheon conversation had ceased, and all four were staring as though two naked people had just walked in the door. "And... and where we sometimes have social functions..."

"And plan your protest strategies," Race put in under his breath.

"Some people have lunch here." She ignored his comment and pointed to a pass-through window. "The kitchen is through there. Ladies, this is Race Latimer, who, as you probably know, owns the, uh, the Plugged Nickel.''

''Part owner,'' Race corrected as he shoved his hands into the back pockets of his jeans and shifted his weight from one foot to the other. ''You all look familiar, but I don't believe I've had the pleasure.''

Tasha snickered.

Celia pushed her chair away from the table and started stuffing sandwich wrappings into a brown lunch bag. ''You've had the pleasure of parting my husband from his paycheck,'' she muttered loudly enough for all to hear.

''Race is really interested—'' Hannah didn't know whether to lead him over to the table or stay close to the door ''—in seeing first hand . . .''

''Dragged me into the lionesses' den, didn't you?'' he accused under his breath. ''If I stay for lunch, I'm the main course.''

'' . . . what New Moon is all about. Now, he didn't press any charges against us when we staged our demonstration, and I think we need to keep the channels of communication open so that—''

''Thanks for not putting us in jail, *Mr.* Latimer.'' Tasha made no attempt to temper her sarcasm as she interrupted Hannah and followed Celia's lead in clearing her place at the table. ''Most of us have kids to take care of while our husbands, if they're still around, are likely to be hangin' around your place rather than ours.'' She gestured toward the rafters. ''Which is why *we're* here.''

''Tasha, be fair. Not everyone in the program—''

''Okay, I'm sorry,'' Tasha said, but the apology was for Hannah. ''When people come to look the Center over, we're supposed to be hospitable, so welcome to New Moon, Mr. Latimer.'' She crumpled the top of her lunch bag as if she were wringing out a dishrag. ''And, by the way, we'd like a little support from the so-called business community—which at this point is a pack of booze vendors and cardsharps—*if* you wouldn't mind."

"Nice to meet you, too, Tasha," Race said. "I'd offer to buy you all lunch, but I see—" the group filed into the kitchen and out the back door "—you weren't very hungry." He pulled the brim of his hat down to his eyebrows. "Guess I should've called first."

Hannah was stunned. She turned to Race, who shrugged it all off, clearly too tired to care. "I'm sorry," she offered. "Sometimes it's hard to separate the issue from the individual, and I guess you represent—"

"Hell, I don't even *know* those women. I don't know that blond lady's husband. I don't lure innocent little kids into betting their savings on a shell game, and I don't deal from the bottom of the deck," he said bitterly. "I went in on a deal to buy a little bar in a little town. And then the little town got a new law passed, and we all lucked into a windfall. For that they wanna crucify me?"

"No, I'm sure they wouldn't want to—" Lord, she was sorry she'd initiated this. Awareness, maybe some kind of compromise—that was the best the Center could hope for right now. She'd thought the co-op members would be pleased to see one of the casino owners show some interest in what was going on at New Moon.

"I'm really sorry. They're not usually that...vocal."

"Vocal?" He chuckled. "Nice try."

Nettie was still there, saying nothing, probably wishing she could wring Hannah's neck. "Race, I'd like you to meet Nettie." Hannah quickly lopped off the last name and decided she wouldn't offer it unless he asked.

"Only if I didn't buy her son his first drink and ruin his life," he said only half-jokingly. But when Nettie's expression changed for the first time, he responded to her apparent surprise. "I didn't, did I?"

Nettie shook her head.

Hannah's throat went dry as Race ambled over to the corner where his mother sat with her half-finished basket. The two women exchanged glances, one pleading, one apologetic.

And then a promise. *I won't give you away.*

And another. *If you do, I won't forgive you.*

"Good," Race was saying. "Then it's a pleasure to meet you, Nettie."

She offered him her hand, and if she voiced a greeting, Hannah couldn't hear it. She knew that Nettie was doing her best to remain expressionless. She wasn't succeeding. The light in the older woman's eyes was unmistakably a mother's pride. Hannah half hoped Race would see it, recognize it and accept her on the spot.

But he didn't.

"What's this you're working on?" he asked. "Some kind of basket?"

"Yes," she said as she fingered the woven rows of the part that was finished. "It's just a basket."

"That's willow, isn't it?" Race asked and Hannah held her breath as she watched him examine the assortment of branches on the table in front of Nettie. There was red bark and gray, along with natural material that had been stripped. "You, um . . . you from around here?"

"I live near here," Nettie said.

"Is this basket weaving . . . is it, like, Sioux?"

"The Sioux aren't basket makers." Nettie spoke quietly into the unfinished basket she held in her lap. "The Chippewa make these baskets."

"Chippewa." He said the word carefully, measuring it and assessing its ramifications. Then he rapped his knuckles on the table once as if he were waking himself up from a reverie. He exchanged looks with Hannah, then made an unexpected offer. "So what about you, Nettie? Wanna go out with us for a quick burger?"

"I have too much work to do." She looked up at him, her eyes alight with a wistful smile. "But thanks for asking."

"Maybe next time," he said, and he pointed to the basket with its willow ribs sticking up like fingers ready to catch a pop fly. "I'd like to see the finished product."

Hannah was so pleased with his interest, she was bursting to show him a whole roomful of his mother's baskets. "You haven't seen the shop yet. We have some of Nettie's work, some wonderful—"

"Hannah, I'm tired." He offered Nettie a nod, took Hannah by the elbow and steered her toward the door. "I don't want to meet the lady who's running the shop, see, because all these women think I'm the bogeyman. So introductions really don't make much sense." He pushed the bar on the door and gestured for her to precede him. "Now, I don't know exactly why I did this, but as soon as I got to town, I came over here."

She stepped into the hallway and turned to look up at him as he closed the door behind them. They could hear the children laughing and baby talking in the playroom. He stepped close to her, and she felt that he wanted to touch her, but he refrained. He simply looked at her. Her mouth, her hair, her eyes.

"Actually, I *do* know why. Because you wrote me letters." One corner of his mouth turned up in a smile. "So I came to see you. But not here." He glanced toward the end of the hallway. "You coming?"

"Where are we going?"

"To the bogeyman's pickup, but since it's high noon, you're probably safe."

She paused to check her watch, but he was already on the move. "I have a group scheduled for one-thirty."

"I'll get you back in time." He turned and extended his hand to her. "Come on."

They ordered lunch at a drive-in and took it to one of the many picnic spots along the winding road north of Deadwood. Race wasn't as hungry as he'd thought, and the shot of caffeine that came with the icy jumbo slurper he'd ordered didn't do much to perk him up. But it was good to stretch out under the towering lodgepole pines on the old army blanket he carried in the pickup, prop his head on his arm and look up at Hannah. He liked the sweet, simple way she wore her long, blond hair and the unpainted tone of her skin. He liked the way she nibbled her fries from end to end, licked her finger and her thumb, then smiled at him as though she'd polished off a gourmet's delight.

"Aren't you going to eat yours?" she asked, glancing at his untouched box of shoestring fries. "They're done just right."

"I can see that." He smiled lazily. "Help yourself. I'd rather watch you."

"Are you being picky?" she teased as she snatched a four-inch fry from the red and yellow box.

He started to laugh, but then she offered him the potato the way little Jason had fed him his carrot. The move surprised him. He used her method of attack, proceeding slowly as he neared the end. He caught her fingertip between his lips, then caught the look in her eyes as he sucked the salt from her skin. "Uh-uh," he said when the finger was withdrawn. "I want the rest." He flashed her a playful look as he caught her thumb, held it between his teeth and licked the fleshy pad.

"You are being picky," she said huskily.

"Damn right. Told you I'd be knocking on your door." He glanced at the box. "Beautiful day in the garden, isn't it? Why don't you offer me another bite?"

She brushed her hands together, then adjusted her cotton skirt over her lap as she shifted her seat slightly. "I was hoping after you ate that you'd tell me all about the fire," she said as she pushed the box of fries closer to him. "Where it was and what you had to do to put it out."

"I had to take a really, really deep breath—" he demonstrated, sighing dramatically "—and blow very hard. For two weeks."

"You must be worn out." She couldn't resist smiling.

"Damn right." He rolled over onto his back and tucked his hands behind his head. "A lot of thanks I get from the average American citizen over at the New Moon Center."

"They don't know what you *really* do for a living."

They didn't? "I thought you said somebody in your program told you what I do."

"I mean—" She hesitated, and he figured she was probably trying to remember which one out of that crabby crew had offered this particular tidbit. "Obviously they know who you are without really knowing—" she shrugged "—who you are."

"Well, you sure picked the wrong way to introduce me. You could have said, 'This is Race Latimer, who's been fighting forest fires for the last two weeks.'"

"You're right. That's what I should have said." By way of apology, she fed him another French fry. "But, of course, they've seen you at the Plugged Nickel. That night, anyway. And they probably all know that you work for the Forest Service, too. It's just not the first thing that comes to mind."

He covered his eyes with his forearm, and sighed long and deep.

Her voice came to him in the dark now, like a lullaby. "You're very tired."

"*Very* tired." If she fed him some more, he'd eat. If she didn't, he'd drift off right there under the pines. "I should have gone up to the cabin and just crashed for a while."

"You probably had to stop in and pick up the key."

"I've got a key."

He didn't have the energy to wonder what she thought about that.

After a moment she asked, "Did you really answer my letters?"

"Said I did." Short, sweet and to the point, just like Al had suggested. *I'm coming to see you, Hannah.* He uncovered one eye and squinted up at her. "You write nice letters. I hope mine got lost in the mail."

"Why?"

"Because I couldn't think of anything good to write, except that I was coming back for a while."

"That was good."

"And I wanted to see you. Is that good?"

"It surprises me a little."

"Me, too." He braced up on his elbow again, figuring that if he kept his eyes closed much longer he'd be out, and she'd have a hell of a time waking him up. "That Indian lady's Chippewa, huh? What's her last name?"

"I'm really not..." She started fussing around with the food, carefully wrapping the remains of his hamburger as though she thought somebody might want it later. She seemed to be avoiding his eyes as she spoke. "Last names are a private matter, um, usually. At the center, you understand."

He decided not to remind her that she'd mentioned other last names. Maybe some were staff, and some were clients. But he wasn't out to put her on the spot, and he wasn't interested in sticking his nose into other people's business, anyway. "My mother was Chippewa. I guess I told you."

"Yes."

"I'm enrolled as a member of the Turtle Mountain Chippewa in North Dakota." Which was his personal business, but for some reason, he was telling her about it. "I didn't know I was enrolled until I was grown. I guess my dad didn't know, either. I was kind of surprised she'd bothered to do that." Kind of surprised to hear himself talking about it, too, but meeting the Indian woman had tugged at a part of him that always seemed to be hungry for something.

He helped himself to a French fry. "Anyway, I don't know anybody from up that way."

"You've never tried to find your mother?"

"No." Ordinarily that would have been the end of it, but his brain was running on autopilot, and so was his mouth. "She knew where I was, and she never came by. I don't know what I'd say to her if I saw her. Hell, I don't even know if she's alive."

"You might have other relatives somewhere."

"I've got enough relatives that I hardly ever see." And not enough time for the people he'd like to be getting to know better. "Why don't you take the afternoon off, and we could just lie here and watch the clouds roll by?"

"I can't, Race." But he could tell she wanted to. "Besides, I don't think you could stay awake for the show. I'm going to drive you up to the cabin."

"You don't have time," he said as he levered himself up to a sitting position.

"Yes, I do."

"Then what happens to my pickup?"

"I'll drive it home, and we'll get my car tomorrow." She laid her hand on his shoulder. "Come on, you ought to be in bed."

"Can't argue with that, but I'm not gonna make you miss your appointment." He touched her cheek and smiled. "Tell you what, though. That's the nicest offer I've had all day."

Chapter 5

It probably wasn't a good idea to disturb him, but Hannah was going to do it anyway. Race's pickup had been parked at Vicki Potter's cabin ever since Hannah had gotten home from work. Not that she could see it from her yard or even from her own access road. She'd actually walked over there twice, then changed her mind and walked back. This time she had manufactured—baked, actually—a viable reason to knock on the door. She'd made a little extra lasagna for supper. Well, how else could she make lasagna except to fill the pan? She'd tucked the casserole into one of the quilted cloth casserole carriers they sold at the craft shop, and she'd walked through the woods to the neighboring doorstep.

In the time that it took him to answer the door she almost chickened out. She was standing there with one foot on the step and the other on the gravel walkway, teetering between options, when the porch light came on and the door opened. She couldn't see much with the light in her eyes, but she recognized his broad-shouldered silhouette and his deep, mellow voice.

"Well, well. Miss Quinn." The screen door came open about six inches. "You're a little late, aren't you?"

Hannah plumbed the depths of her craw for a pocket of nerve and a bold reply. "Early, actually. I generally come after you with my little pistol sometime after midnight."

"Either I'm still dreaming, or this sounds a whole lot better than I remember it." The door opened wide. "Come on in."

He eyed her cloth basket as he stepped back, holding the door open for her. "I see you brought your basket of goodies, Little Miss Hannah. Good thing all the wolves got chased off long ago." He chuckled villainously as he turned on the swag lamp over the kitchenette table, but the humor was lost on Hannah. She was too busy questioning the appropriateness of what she was doing.

"I brought you some leftovers." She set her offering on the table and took note that the room was sparsely furnished and smelled of the surrounding pine woods. "I don't know why I made so much." *Stop talking like an airhead, Hannah. The stuff didn't just grow in the pan.* "I guess I had a taste for lasagna tonight. Do you like lasagna?"

"I'll know in a minute." He yawned as he padded toward the kitchen sink, raking his fingers through his hair. He wore nothing but a pair of jeans, and he looked as virile as he had the night she'd seen him wearing only moonlight.

Virile. She told herself to say good-night and take her leave.

Race turned the faucet on and cupped his hands under the running water. "Did you bring any coffee?" he asked before he immersed his face.

"You don't have to eat it right now." Watching him work on waking himself up, she suddenly felt terribly foolish, terribly transparent. "I'm sorry. I should have realized . . ."

He shoved his whole head under the faucet, so she doubted that he could have heard what it was she should have realized. Or that he cared. He slapped the lever down on the faucet and came up shaking his head, spreading droplets from pillar to post.

"It'll keep for days," Hannah said. "In the refrigerator, of course."

He pushed his wet hair back from his face and raked through it again with his fingers as he turned and caught her edging toward the door. "Where do you think you're going?"

"Home." After saying the word she offered a small, apologetic smile.

"You got me out of bed so you could drop this off and go home?" He pulled a chair out and indicated that she should sit. "I'm almost awake. Pretty soon, I'll start being almost nice. I'll get some plates." Halfway to the cupboard, he turned, glancing at the meticulously packaged supper. "Are you a good cook?"

"At least fair. That's just for you," she said with a hesitant gesture toward the casserole. She felt a panicky urge to take it back and add more meat or another layer of cheese. "I've already eaten."

"It smells good. Wish I had a beer to go with it, but the cupboards are bare."

"I was thinking you probably wouldn't have any groceries, since you've been gone a while. And that meant you wouldn't have anything for supper, so I just thought, since I'd made so much . . ."

"I came up here after lunch, and the last thing I remember was sitting down to take my boots off. I guess I was pretty—" He ignored her protestation and brought two plates down from the shelf while she uncovered the contents of the pan.

"Tired," she affirmed. He was sorting noisily through the utensil drawer. "You didn't need food. You needed rest, and I shouldn't have—"

"This looks great." Forks and knives clattered against the blue tin plates as he set them on the table and leaned over the casserole, inhaling deeply and expanding his bare chest in the way of a man anticipating culinary heaven. "Oh, yeah, this'll get me goin'. Mmm, pasta, garlic, cheese..." He took up a table knife and flashed her a grin. "See? I'm awake now. I'm being nice."

"Let me serve that up." He'd gotten to her with the fuss he was making over simply the smell. He relinquished the knife, and she chattered on as she served up the pasta, deftly juggling it between knife and fork. "It might all fall apart, and then it won't be stacked right, which would ruin the taste. There, see how that..." It reminded her of a brick sitting in the middle of an empty slab. She sighed. "I should have made you a salad. I had a little salad with it, myself, but I didn't make..."

"You mean you're just gonna watch me eat?" he asked as he seated himself.

"You watched me this afternoon."

"Yeah, but I was useful," he reminded her as she slid the plate in front of him. He looked up at her, his eyes smiling with boyish delight. "Are you going to lick my fingers?"

"I'll get you a napkin." She scooted behind him and tried the drawer next to the one that had produced utensils.

"I doubt if we have any in stock." His fork scraped the plate. Hannah slid the drawer closed slowly. The word "we" had rolled off Race's tongue too easily between bites. "I'll be up for the night, now," he said. "Can you handle that?"

"I can't stay up all night." She pulled out the chair across the table from him and temporarily perched on its front edge.

"Tomorrow's Saturday."

"The Center's open. We have craft classes going on, meetings . . ."

"You don't work on Saturday, do you?" She shook her head. He filled his fork, brought the pasta near his mouth and smiled past it. His eyes glittered. "So what's your bedtime, Little Miss Hannah?"

"Whenever I get tired."

"Once you rouse the wolf, you can't afford to get tired, honey."

"I thought you said there weren't any more wolves in these parts."

"Well, you never know, Little Miss Hannah. I hear they come down from Montana once in a while. Forest fires drive 'em out sometimes."

"There aren't any wolves in Montana," she said. She was sure she'd read that somewhere.

"Maybe not since this morning." He ate the bite he'd been delaying, then another. "You're much better than fair. This is the best goodie basket I've gotten into in a long time."

"How about some water?"

"Not to drink." He leered theatrically and delivered a singsongy, "The better for us to swim in, my dear."

"I told you, Race, you're not getting me—"

"Careful, Hannah." He punched the air with his fork. "It's risky enough to rouse the wolf. It's fatal to dare him."

As if on cue, they heard a plaintive howling not far beyond the cabin walls. Hannah's eyes widened, just for an instant. Then they looked at one another and laughed together.

"Good ol' Critter sure has great timing," Race said. "Is he on the prowl for female Critters?"

"He's no longer interested in female Critters." Hannah scooted back in the chair and pressed her shoulder blades against the padded backrest. She was wearing shorts, and her thighs stuck to the vinyl seat immediately. "Except me. He's very protective. He's letting me know it's time to come home."

"Nah, that's not what that means. He's letting *me* know it's time to play in the water." He finished the last of what was on his plate, then reached out to reseat the aluminum foil on the casserole dish, tucking the corners down firmly. "I'm saving the rest of this for breakfast."

"Lasagna for breakfast?"

"I got nothin' else in the house, honey. I'll bring you a clean pan tomorrow," he promised as he cleared the table in one fell swoop. The plates—one dirty and one clean—clattered into the sink. The pan was shoved into the refrigerator.

He disappeared into the bedroom and came back wearing his boots and pulling his black T-shirt on over his head. "Let's go out and say hello to Critter."

Always the anxious puppy when Race was around, Critter bounded back and forth just ahead of them as they picked their way along the dark path toward the lake. Race broke a two-foot stick off a deadfall and continued on. He knew the way. Neither one had much to say now, and

Hannah wondered what he was thinking. His steps were lighter than hers, and she wondered even more at what she was doing.

It wasn't like her to knock on a man's door in the middle of the night, to follow him through the woods this way when she knew full well that he had no more care for propriety than her dog did. Just like Critter, Race could—no doubt *would*—plunge into the lake without giving a second thought to the time of day or the temperature or what he wore... or did not wear.

Second thoughts. A lot of good they were doing her. She didn't seem to be turning around. There was another thought driving her—a curiosity, really, about the dark woods and the lake at night and the man who wanted to take her there.

If your friend jumped into the lake, would you jump in after him?

Well, maybe. From a deeper place in her brain came a strong primal coaxing.

See the way he slides his strong, lithe body along the path, his broad shoulders taking charge, leading the way for you. Go and see where he takes you. He's beautiful and good. Go and be with him for a while.

Critter loped to the end of the dock, his claws clicking against the wood. The structure was in need of a few new planks. Race found a spot to sit down and take off his boots and his socks. He shrugged off his shirt and tossed it over his tall, ornately stitched boot tops, making a little hammock between them. He braced his hands on the planks at either side of his hips and flexed his shoulders and expanded his considerable chest as though preening for some kind of challenge.

Beautiful was a superficial given. Good was, well, probably a lot deeper down. He looked up at her, gave her a teasing smile and stuck his thumbs in the waistband of his jeans as he tapped his fingers on the five brass buttons that held them closed.

"You're going to make me get my pants wet again, aren't you?"

"This was all your idea," she said tightly.

"But I know you won't go along with me if I do it my way." He stood up quickly, taking with him the stick he'd brought along. "So I'm making allowances for your modesty." Critter took his cue from the upraised stick and barked furiously. "That's right, boy. We're gonna look out for the lady tonight. Go for it!"

The stick and the dog flew almost at once, and Race cannonballed in after them. Hannah shrank back from the resulting geyser. Race shot back up with a toss of his head, bellowing, "Ahh-hh! I'm alive and kickin' now!" His grin seemed to bob in refracted moonlight on the waves he'd made. "Come on, Miss Hannah. Best thing is to jump in and take the whole shock all at once."

"I don't want to jump in and take—"

"Yeah, you do."

He was right, darn his beautiful hide. There wasn't an ounce of conviction in the feeble way she shook her head.

"Take you shoes off first, though," he instructed. "Look, you're standing right on the edge there, and you want me to reach up and pull you in."

"I do n—"

"Yeah, you do. You've gotta do it yourself, girl. Take the plunge, or stand there and—"

She put the brakes on her brain and heard no more of his cheeky counsel. Her knees flexed of their own accord, and she sprang off the deck. It was like leaping into an ice-fishing hole. She popped back up, sputtering and yelping like a whipped pup. And Race, bobbing close by, was laughing.

"All rii-iight! Look at her, Critter. She's one of us, now. Wet and wild."

"F-free-ezing!"

"You'll be okay in a minute." He moved in closer, and she grabbed for him, her legs churning. "Jeez, shoes and all." He chortled again. "Who says Miss Hannah can't take a dare once in a while?"

"M-mostly M-Miss Hannah." She didn't want to touch bottom, so she let him be her buoy. He took to the job automatically. "Sometimes the rocks c-can be hard on your feet. Yeow, it's cold!"

With both hands moored to his shoulders, she bobbed and shivered within the harbor he made for her. He pushed the hair back from her face. "Tell you what, the trick is to keep moving. Keep the blood circulating. So you're going to get rid of those shoes."

Below the water he found the inflated leg of her shorts, then her thigh, which led the way to her fluttering foot. She kept her grip on his shoulders and let him take first one canvas slip-on, then the other. "You don't want anything to slow you down now," he said as he tossed her shoes. She heard a thunk-thunk on the dock's rickety planks.

He slid away, his smile beckoning. "Now we're gonna push out to where we can swim." Hannah hated losing her anchor. She didn't like swimming all that much. She preferred canoeing on the lake and climbing the rocky paths around it. But Race was already propelling himself through the water with a leisurely but powerful backstroke, and she seemed to be paddling after him. There was a big air bubble in her blouse. She probably looked like a bobbing jellyfish, while Race sliced through the water like a sleek dolphin. He'd likely laugh at her again any minute, but she kept right on side-stroking along in his wake.

Critter was yapping his head off for another chance to fetch, and Race obliged him. Then Race disappeared beneath the water and Hannah felt him slip past her belly like an undulating water creature, too quick to be caught in anyone's net. He surfaced on the other side, blowing water like a sassy whale.

"Wanna dive off my shoulders?" He sounded only slightly short of breath. "No lifeguards around to blow the whistle on us."

"I'm just getting used to the water," she protested. "Sort of."

"See how you kinda just naturally drift over toward the neighbor's dock?"

Her back porch light shone through the trees. "Yes, I see."

"Don't know if it's fate or just undertow."

She fluttered her feet, still following him. "I think it's warmer over here."

"You may be right. I must have been lured by the warmth all those nights." He was drifting now, and she was closing in on him. "There's a friendly feeling over here. Kind of a promise in the air."

She truly wasn't as cold as she had been at first. Dog-paddling did seem to warm her up. "Isn't it dangerous to swim alone at night?"

"You're not alone."

"I mean for you. All those other nights."

"Probably." He circled around her, as though playing a game. "You'd better come with me from now on. Keep me safe."

"I feel like an idiot, swimming around in my clothes."

"See? You're headed toward the inescapable conclusion." Critter slid back into the picture like a beaver bringing in the next bit of building material. Race took the stick and hurled it ashore. "Bare is better."

"Oh, I don't think so." She watched Critter make a beeline for the stick, which had been chucked so far the dog would probably never find it. But he'd try, the dear old crazy. "Idiocy is better than indecency."

"You've still got too many hang-ups, Miss Hannah." The water lapped below his shoulders. He took her upper arms lightly in his hands and drew her close. The water made it all so easy. "You should see yourself. You look like a mermaid I saw in a movie once. Her hair was just like yours." He touched the mat of it that covered her shoulder. "Like yellow seaweed." He glanced pointedly at the cove between her breasts. She looked down. She could see the lacy cups of her bra. "'Course, she wasn't wearing a shirt."

"'Course, I'm not a mermaid." If she tried to adjust her shirt, she'd have to take her hands off his chest. She told herself he probably couldn't see much.

"I'm glad." His lips glistened with lake water, and his eyes glimmered as his leg drifted between hers, his knee brushing against the inside of her thigh. "In the long run it would be a terrible waste if you were."

"Race—"

She'd intended to say his name in protest, but the night was so close around them that the whispered word sounded like an entreaty. He answered in kind, making her name sound like soft music, as soft as the touch of his lips on hers. The brush of a bird's wing. She closed her eyes and lifted her chin, for if something so soft would come seeking, how could she turn away? His kiss came as a breath-stealing surprise, but not because it demanded. Rather it posed a tender offer. His lips were moist and sweet, something to be savored. She moved her lips against them, and the flavor improved.

"A freshwater kiss," he said, his breath still mingling with hers. He lifted his hand from the water and touched her lower lip with a wet thumb. She started to catch the drop of water with her tongue, but his lips got there first. He sipped, then kissed again, the tip of his tongue fluttering against the seam of her lips. "It tastes good, doesn't it?"

She wasn't sure she could use her lips for speaking now, but she managed the smallest, "Yes."

"Do you realize you're hanging onto me for dear life?"

She opened her eyes, and the night was there, and the shadowed face and the shoulders that made her hands feel so small. "Not exactly for dear life."

"Dear what, then?"

"I don't know. Dear . . . dear . . ." The bird's wing fluttered in her stomach. "Race, kiss me again."

This time his kiss demanded more, and she slid her arms around his neck and kissed back hungrily. He tasted of oregano and lake water, and there was wonder and warmth in his mouth. He drew her close and let her drift against him. The five brass buttons on his jeans became playing pieces for her belly. Say the magic word, win five titillating tokens. But words would have been a mistake with her breasts bobbing before his chest like two supplicants paying homage. For their trouble they were teased and made more needy. Her nipples hardened defiantly, but when Race ended the kiss, she wanted to defy that, too.

"Oh, dear Lord."

"I thought it was dear Race," he said, then pressed his lips to her temple.

"I think so, too." An icy hot current shot through her, and she shivered. "I really do."

"Should we go inside and dry each other off now?"

"No." She needed to take her clothes off, and she imagined him helping her. She steeled herself against the tempting prospect. "No, we shouldn't."

"Hannah," he coaxed, taking her face in his hands and forcing her to look into his eyes. "Hannah, you want to say yes. Look at the way you're still holding me."

"Because I'm cold." A fact that made her cling to him all the more, and yes *was* the magic word. "Because your kiss..." And the strength of your arms and the sound of your voice. "...Because I can't say yes, but I don't want to let go."

"You don't have to say anything or do anything. Just hold me, Hannah, and I'll make you warmer than you've ever been." He was moving slowly toward the dock, and they were holding one another.

"You make me more impetuous than I've ever been. Look at me." Even as she said it, she gained her release. She had to get hold of herself. They were standing waist-deep in icy-cold lake water, and she was shivering.

"I'm looking at you." He ran the back of his hand slowly down the front of the blouse that clung to her like another layer of skin. She sucked in a quick breath as she watched his hand disappear beneath the curve of her breast. "I want to see more of you."

"Oh, Race, you—" Her nipples throbbed. She either had to put them into his hands or back away. She did the latter. "I have to go in now. I'm acting too crazy. I have to go in."

"You're not acting." He caught her by the shoulders, and she looked into his eyes, seeing a glimmer of the very need she felt, and maybe even something of the fear. "It's

not in you to pretend. Not you, Hannah. Not the way
you—''

"I have to go in."

He permitted her to twist out of his grip, but he held her
a moment longer with that desperate look in his eyes. It
was harder to pull away from eyes than from hands.

He watched her clamber up the bank and scamper over
the path like a doe in flight. But she was a tenderfoot, and
he winced when she jumped back from an unseen bit of
treachery on the path, hopped on one foot a few times,
then continued with a little less zeal, trying not to hobble.
The pines swallowed her up, and he had half a notion to
follow her. He knew the advantage was his, and if he
pressed her, she would at least let him come inside.

Come inside. Be inside. Inside Hannah's house.

The better to seduce you, my dear.

Inside pretty Hannah, who'd written, *Dear* Race.

Not tonight, he told himself. A shiver claimed him, and
he pushed off the lake's silty bottom, stretching his long,
aching body into a crawl.

Not tonight.

Early the next morning Race showered, dressed and
went down to the dock. The newly risen sun painted tan-
gerine stripes in the quiet water. A blue-winged teal
skimmed the shimmering canvas, muttering small peeps as
he searched for his breakfast. Race muttered to himself
too, as he dodged a hole in the dock's planking. If he were
going to stay at the cabin, he ought to fix a few things. He
wouldn't mind owning a place like this.

He wouldn't mind owning *this* place. Next door to the
owner of the small, white canvas shoes—one upright, one
tipped over on its side, both still sodden—that lay at the

end of the dock. He smiled as he reached down to retrieve them. It was his turn to make a gesture.

She was dressed for work when she answered the door. Her hair was done up on the sides, fastened with her favorite beaded barrette, long and loose in back. Freshly washed. When she let him in, he stepped close enough to inhale the scent of citrus shampoo. She was a plain dresser—white cotton blouse, light blue skirt, little pearl earrings. Generally it took a little more style to catch his eye. Strangely enough, he found himself mentally extolling the virtues of simplicity. He decided it was too damned early in the morning to try to justify any of this. He offered up the clean casserole dish containing the folded cloth carrier that served as a pillow for her shoes.

"If the slippers fit, you get a date with a real live hero. Guy who fights forest fires." He lifted one shoulder in a shrug. "Sorry. We're fresh out of princes this morning."

"Um—" She seemed to be casting about for a response. Her eyes darted from his face to the shoes to the door that still stood open. "I'm sorry about last night."

"I'm not." He wanted to touch her now, but he knew better. "It was a start."

"A start?"

"You're reluctant, but you're not unwilling." She glanced away guiltily, and he felt bad for her. He didn't know why. He just knew he had to ease her mind to bring peace to himself, so he amended, "To do something a little crazy once in a while. It'll be fun to see how far I can get you to go." He smiled wickedly, returning all innocence to her court.

"Do you realize," she began as she let him return her possessions, "that we are on opposite sides of almost any fence you can name?"

He nodded. "Kind of adds a little spice to the recipe, doesn't it?"

"I was just about to have some plain old cornflakes in some skim milk. Care to join me?"

"Think I'll pass that offer up and wait for a better one." He stole a quick kiss. "Like the lasagna. You don't have to try the shoes on. I know they fit."

After he left Hannah's, Race drove down to the Custer fire team training camp and participated in a lesson in fire shelter deployment. His Indian crews were glad to see him, and he was surprised at how glad he was to see them. They were developing the esprit de corps that was vital for a good fire fighting team, and he found himself claiming a piece of that as he told stories about fire fighters, himself included, who had been entrapped by fire and survived in the aluminum foil pup tents known as shake and bake bags.

He recalled the time he'd managed to stop thinking of himself as a trussed-up turkey and had envisioned wide-open spaces for several hours. The trick was to avoid panic while keeping your nose to the ground, sweating like a plow horse and periodically calling out to four other guys bundled up in their bags. The story was a good attention-getter, but the entrapment he eventually simulated with bonfires separated the visionaries from the claustrophobics. Some of those boys would need more practice.

He was on his way to the Plugged Nickel late that afternoon when he spotted the Indian woman leaving the grocery store. He parked his pickup on a side street as he racked his brain to remember her name. Natalie or Nellie—something like that. He liked her, maybe because she hadn't given him that go-to-hell glare he'd gotten from the rest of the lunch crowd at the New Moon Center. Or maybe it had something to do with her being Chippewa, something he hadn't thought much about in a long time. Not until just lately, when he'd been asked to train the Indian crews, and then only when Hannah had asked him about his background.

Something about this Indian woman—the way she kept to herself, maybe, or the way her shoulders sagged just a little—something made him recall some of the old questions. A young boy's musings, mostly. Part of him was Chippewa. The dark part. The part of him his father had not loved.

He shut the pickup door and ignored the red flag on the parking meter as he watched the woman pass beneath the awning of a narrow storefront. Nettie, that was it. He called to her as he jaywalked across the narrow street that separated the rows of four-story buildings. She stopped, shifted her brown paper sack from one hand to the other, and he could swear she stiffened a little as she turned.

He smiled. She didn't. She looked a little dazed, and he wondered whether she recognized him as he picked up his pace toward the curb. She took a swipe at a bit of graying hair that had strayed from its clip. The rest of it was pulled straight back in a severe style that emphasized the careworn lines around her dark eyes and her drooping mouth. She'd said she was from Turtle Mountain. If he mentioned his mother's name, would this woman know her?

"Race Latimer," he announced as he approached. "Remember?"

"I remember." She spoke quietly, as though she didn't want to attract any attention.

He walked right up to her, anyway, and spoke jovially. "You headed over to the New Moon Center?"

She nodded.

"Me, too." He hadn't been, but he was now. He reached for the sack. "Here, let me carry that for you."

"It's not heavy," she claimed as she relinquished it to him. "Just some coffee and things."

He peeked over the sack's sawtooth rim. "The can alone's five pounds. See, I'm looking to do a couple of good deeds to polish up this bad reputation I've got over at your New Moon Center." He grinned as they fell into step together. "Think it'll do any good?"

"Why does it matter?" She tucked her black handbag beneath her ample breast and carried it close, as though she feared a purse-snatching. "You aren't the only person in town who owns a casino."

"Yeah, but I'm the only casino owner who's been targeted for nonviolent bulldozing by Miss Hannah Quinn and company." The woman stared straight ahead as they walked, but he thought he detected a hint of a smile. He figured Nettie had taken Hannah under some kind of motherly wing, and he was going to do a little fishing, just for the fun of it. "The only one who's willing to brush the tire tracks off his back and take her out to dinner." Yep, there it was. A little sparkle in the woman's eye. At least she didn't disapprove. "As far as I know, I'm the only one. She's not seeing anyone else, is she?"

"The Center keeps her very busy."

"It's always good to keep busy. I'm pretty busy myself." Nettie acknowledged his busyness with a curt nod. So, okay, she had his number. Might as well lay the cards on the sidewalk. "You can probably guess, she's not the kind of woman I usually go out with."

"She's a good woman."

"That's what I mean. We're probably wasting each other's time." No objection from Nettie on that score, which irritated him enough to let the old woman in on a news flash. "She brought me supper last night."

It wasn't the idea that she had waited on him that pleased him. He'd grown up in a motherless household, and he wasn't one to wait around for services of any kind. It was the pleasure he'd felt in finding her standing at the door, food in hand—food *prepared* by her hand—despite her own obvious misgivings about entering his territory. Crazy as it sounded, it almost seemed like a brave thing for her to do. Like claiming a stool in his bar. "Does she have family somewhere?" he wondered.

"Her parents were missionaries. She's lived in many places, all over the world."

"Missionaries, huh?" He laughed and shook his head at the idea of pursuing a preacher's daughter.

"You should ask her these questions," she admonished him as they reached the New Moon Center's two glass doors.

"No, the whole thing is crazy. I don't know why I'm asking *anybody.*" He shifted the grocery bag into the crook of his left arm and opened the door for her. Something about the gesture seemed to amaze her, and he lifted one shoulder, smiling sheepishly. "And I sure as hell don't know why I'm going through this door again."

"You have fine manners," Nettie said. "Don't see that too often these days."

"A fine lady taught me." The information seemed to surprise her, and he wondered if he had some kind of motherless look about him. Maybe old women had a sixth sense about such things. "My sister, Lannie. I was mostly a hellion when I was growing up, but Lannie made sure I knew better, even if I didn't—"

Nettie glanced behind him, and he felt Hannah's presence before he turned to find that she had actually managed to sneak up on him. "Well, well, Miss Hannah."

"Race," she said, and she glanced at Nettie, probably for some female signal, before she gave him a tentative smile. "I wasn't expecting to see you . . . here."

"We're destined to surprise each other."

Hannah was firing wordless questions at the older woman. Something like, "What have you guys been talking about?" Or "What have you told him about me?" Women had a way of getting the whole scoop without ever saying a damn thing.

"Actually, I just happened by when Nettie was coming out of the grocery store with this heavy sack, so I offered to give her a hand with it." He winked at Nettie as he made a production of lowering the "heavy" sack into her arms. "'Fraid this is as far as I can go, ma'am. The kitchen is surrounded by a webful of black widows, and I'm not anxious to get eaten alive."

"The Chippewa say that Grandmother Spider played a role in creating our world. She is a weaver, you know."

"Nope," he said, keeping his distance from the whole notion of grandmothers and spiders being related. "My Chippewa mother skipped out on me before I was old enough to acquire any appreciation for her kind of spiders."

"Nettie tells wonderful stories about—"

"There's no coffee made," Nettie clipped as she turned away from them abruptly and started down the hall. "I have to get the coffee made."

Race suddenly felt a little uneasy. "Did that sound bad? What I said about her kind of spiders?"

"No." Her hand on his arm was reassuring. It also made his heart do funny things, especially when he caught the sympathetic look in her eye.

"I didn't mean to insult her beliefs. It was—" he tried to shrug off everything but Hannah's hand "—kind of a joke."

"I don't think she was insulted." It felt strangely cold when Hannah's hand slid away. "Nettie's made it her sacred duty to keep the coffeepot full, and there are two groups meeting here this evening."

He had no interest in the groups, but the look he'd just seen in the Indian woman's eyes haunted him. He stared down the vacant hallway, still watching after her even though she'd already disappeared from his sight. "She's from Turtle Mountain," he mused. "I thought about asking her if she knew..." Abruptly he shoved his hands into his pockets and shook off the whole idea. "What's the point? I don't know anybody up there."

"Do you want to?"

He shook his head. "I'm always willing to meet people, but who wants to rattle old bones?" He checked his watch. It was long past time to get off this subject. "When do you get done here? Maybe we could grab something to eat."

"I have to facilitate one of the groups at five."

"Facilitate, huh?" He smiled, thinking it was a good word for what he wanted to do, too. "What time will you be hungry?"

"About five-thirty, but I won't be finished here until eight."

"I can hold out till then." He reached for the push bar on the door. "Meanwhile, I'll be 'facilitating,' a card game over at the—"

She suddenly clapped her hand over his mouth and whispered, "Hush!" They exchanged astonished looks, but his was tinged with delight as he watched her catch herself making a bold move. Slowly the spark of mischief dawned in her eyes. He smiled against her fingers.

"My spiders have ears," she warned.

Chapter 6

For the better part of an hour Race had watched Hannah nibble at the salad he'd considered a meager meal. It was all she wanted, she'd insisted. He'd tried to tempt her with sweets, and she'd accepted two bites of pecan pie from his fork, then no more. She'd been absorbed in troublesome thoughts—troublesome to him because he found himself craving her attention. Even her occasional brief and wistful smile had evoked his embarrassingly overzealous attempts to capture her fancy. Had he been thirteen he would have resorted to handsprings.

He'd suggested they take the long way home. As he negotiated another tricky switchback on the way to high ground, he admitted to himself that her agreement was more a case of her having offered no objections. But surely even Hannah knew what "the long way home" meant. She knew what was coming, and she wasn't just along for the ride.

He surprised himself a little when he found himself taking her to a place he'd vowed never to take anyone else. He'd thought to keep it free of associations with anything but solitude. At the top of a winding narrow road was his favorite pine-sheltered place on the rim of a bowl of mountains, filled to the quarter mark with crystal water. It was a place that drew him when he wanted to hear nothing but the wind in the evergreens and the resonant call of the cat owl, when he wanted to stretch out on his back and lose himself in the night sky.

His secret place, and he'd brought her there. It was just like doing handsprings.

He gave her the flashlight and blanket to carry while he held her hand, moved branches aside for her, and pulled her back from the short, steep drop-off he'd once discovered by skittering over too far and landing on hands and knees just in time.

"Why do we need this blanket?" she asked. She was whispering. It pleased him that she understood this to be a whispering kind of a place.

"It's the only way to take in the sights," he told her.

Breaking out of the trees was like stepping onto a platform—a free-flying, victorious feeling—and the small plot of grass, a nest in the rocky face of the mountain, beckoned the explorer to sit, rest and behold the starlit lake.

"It's beautiful here," she said as she helped him spread the blanket on the grass. "I take it we're not going swimming."

Down on one knee, he pivoted and peered down the mountain. "Not unless you're into cliff diving. Personally, I prefer to do my jumping with a parachute."

"I tend to be quite earthbound." She settled on the blanket, tucking her legs to one side and her skirt around them. "And this is a wonderful patch of earth to be bound to for a while, isn't it? You don't have to be a bird to get close to the sky if you know about this place."

"Getting close is a nice idea." He stretched out beside her. She smiled at him even as she lapped the front of her cardigan tight as a drum and wrapped her arms around her middle to keep everything in place.

He was undaunted. "As I see it, we have two choices. Talk or neck."

On principle she had to come up with a third. "Or we could just be together and look at the stars."

"That's for afterward." He put his hand on her skirt-wrapped knee. "After my choices, see, we'll know each other better, and we'll be content to just be together and look at the stars."

"Do you really want to talk?"

"I really want you to. You've been too quiet." He moved his thumb slowly, caressing her knee. She seemed not to notice. "I guess you have to listen to a lot of belly-aching at these group sessions, huh?"

"I wouldn't call it bellyaching."

"Well, whining around, then, everybody trying to outdo each other, misery-wise."

She gently *tsked* at him. "You ought to become a little more misery-wise if that's all the compassion you can muster."

"Most people are as miserable as they let themselves be," he told her as he edged over on elbow and hip. He wondered what kind of a pillow her lap would make. "If a man's gambling away his paycheck, his wife should give him the boot. Simple as that."

"There's nothing simple about splitting up a family. What about the children?"

"If there are kids, she's got all the more reason. What good is he doing them? Kick him out and don't let him come back until he shapes up.'' It was a philosophy Race held firmly, and he levered himself up to her eye level just to tell her so. ''Guy has a kid, the least he can do is support it. And if I had a degree, I could give that same advice and charge a fee.''

She tipped her head to the side as though considering a new side of him. So he thought people should take care of their kids. Big deal.

''You can give it without a degree the next time one of my clients' husband brings his paycheck to your blackjack table.''

''Give me a list.''

''I wish I could.'' Bracing her arm on the ground, she forgot herself and her sweater as she leaned into the discussion. ''They're not all men, you know. Women get hooked, too. Single and married women, mothers of young children. Does the same advice apply?''

''Kick the woman out?'' He gave it some thought. His father would have told such a woman not to let the door swat her in the butt on the way out. Some of the old man's notions had a lot of merit. ''I guess if it came to that. If she's pumping the grocery money into the slots, if she won't take care of her kids...''

''Sometimes they can't Race. Sometimes the problem becomes bigger than the person, man or woman, and they can't take care of *themselves,* which means the children—''

''Get the shaft.'' His tone lacked pity. He hated pity. ''Believe me, I know the story, even though I still can't figure it. It's a free country, and people make the damnedest choices.''

Hannah was bound and determined to squeeze some kind of sympathy out of him. ''Haven't you ever made a choice you've regretted?''

"I've made a few bad ones." He chuckled and shook his head. "Wasted time, mostly. It took me a while to figure out that I was never going to be my father's favorite son. I may be thickheaded, but eventually I get the message."

"And who *is* your father's favorite son?"

"That part doesn't matter." But she waited for an answer, and before he knew it, he was giving her one. "Trey, the fair-haired boy. Literally. His mother was the old man's wife, and mine was—" With an impatient gesture, he dismissed his phantom parent. "Who knows what mine was? The girlfriend, I guess. But Trey's my brother. I got no complaints there. He had the good sense to leave home long before I did." He smiled, remembering the day he'd quit working for his father. Trey had been there to shake his hand and wish him well. "You'd like Trey."

"I'd like your sister, too. Maybe even your dad."

Sitting beside him in a pool of moonlight, she looked like the kind of angel who could make the meanest miser part with a coin or two, just for the chance to touch her spun-gold hair. He reached over, laid his hand on her head and followed the silky fall to her shoulder.

"My dad would want to know what a nice girl like you was doing up here with a bum like me."

"I'd tell him we were just talking, and I'd tell him you're not a bum."

"No, I'm not. I've made some damn good choices since I stormed out of Latimer Construction on a powerful head of steam."

"Like buying into the Plugged Nickel?"

"Like bringing you up here." She let him toy with her hair as he spoke. He moved a handful of it to the front of her shoulder, then tucked it behind her ear, then stroked her temple. "After that blue funk attitude you were giving me during supper, the idea was to get *you* to talk."

"I am talking," she said, smiling. He could tell she liked being stroked.

"Then maybe we oughta set some ground rules. Don't you set ground rules for your group sessions?"

"What kind of ground rules?"

"I'll make one and you make one," he proposed. "You go first."

"Well, sometimes after group I'm lost in my thoughts, which is why I haven't been very talkative." She was studying the pearlized snaps on his shirtfront. With a forefinger, she pressed one. "But I can't talk about that, you see. So that's my ground rule. No asking me what's bothering me after I just had group."

"I probably don't want to know. It probably has something to do with the Plugged Nickel."

"That probably figures in," she admitted. She moved her finger down to the next button.

"You can't blame the business, Hannah. Bars don't create alcoholics."

"Gambling is different. In most places it isn't legal, or it's very limited, and there's a reason for that."

"Many reasons," he said, and she glanced up, waiting to compare hers with his. "I'd hate to see it open up any more in this area. Las Vegas, Reno, Atlantic City and Deadwood. That's enough. Otherwise the goose stops laying golden eggs."

"Poor little Deadwood's been completely absorbed by it."

"Poor little Deadwood," he echoed with a chuckle. "That town's tough as nails. Always has been. People love it because it's too mean to die. My business is legal, Hannah. I'm not the maker of your clients' problems."

"I know."

"Okay, here's my ground rule. Your clients are off-limits. My business is off-limits. Deal?"

"So what'll we talk about?"

He offered a slow smile. "You and me." Her chin was tipped up, waiting for his thumb to use it as a starting point for stroking her neck. Long, soft, lovely neck. He leaned closer, whispering, "And then maybe we can move on to option number two."

He gave her the kiss her supple lips were ready for, the leisurely, tender one that wouldn't scare her. Then he gave her a couple of inches of breathing space so she could savor the flavor of him and maybe decide to draw him back for another nibble.

"I think option one bears more..." He wasn't going to let her think too much. He pressed his lips to her cool forehead and breathed the scent of night air in her hair. "What exactly would you like to know—" she swallowed delicately "—about me?"

"Things you can't tell me, like..." He took her in his arms, the better to learn for himself. "What it's like to rub my cheek against your head and smell your hair." It was like snuggling with satin. "What this part of your neck tastes like." Salty-sweet, like fresh spring water. "Whether you kiss with your eyes closed."

"Aren't you supposed to?" she croaked.

"I don't think there are any rules." Gently he laid her on the blanket, cradling her in his arms to protect her, support her. "No ground rules, but if you keep your eyes open, you get to see the stars, and I get to taste..." Her sweet mouth inside.

Her lips parted for him, and he felt favored as his tongue touched the edge of her teeth on its way to warm, secret recesses. He felt her hands at his waist, holding him to her, and he felt his own heat rising. He lifted his head and smiled, feeling foolish for asking, "How about that?"

"I closed my eyes," she whispered. Her breath was quick. "I still saw stars."

"You mean I knocked you out?" His uneven tone wasn't as teasing as he'd intended.

"I think so."

"With a feather, hmm?" He brushed his lips along her cheekbone. "Just like this. With a feather."

"That can't be. I'm not a . . ." Sliding her arms around him, she welcomed his kiss, and he felt all the stiffness in her melt away. Hardly the same for him. When he came away, the rest of her claim slipped out slowly, like molasses. " . . . Pushover."

"Don't you think I know that? I know it, Hannah." Languid now, she looked less reluctant, more vulnerable. "You're so good. You taste like . . ." He wanted to shelter her, from what he couldn't say, but he felt a fierce urge to cover her and keep her safe as he peppered her face with small kisses. "Goodness," he whispered. "This is what goodness tastes like."

"Race, please don't." He drew back and looked for "don't" in her eyes. It wasn't there. He pressed closer to her, pelvis to pelvis, and she closed her eyes. "Oh, Race."

He knew the heat was rising in her, too. His hand sought her breast, and he felt the thudding of her heart in his palm. "I just want to touch you, Hannah. Just—"

With the release of a single button he was able to slip beneath her blouse and acquaint himself with satin and lace. And warm skin. And the shape of female flesh that fit so sweetly in a man's hand.

"Oh, dear Lord."

He hoped to kiss away all prayers and protestations. Her arms were still about his waist, and when his tongue touched the roof of her mouth, she whimpered in a way that made him feel drunk with the power he'd been storing for her since the first moment they'd met. Power to please her. Power to unleash sensations he knew she didn't know existed. It would please him simply to lead the way.

"I won't hurt you," he promised as he kissed the place where her collarbones met. "I won't push you over if you don't want to be—"

"You can't," she insisted, her voice husky. Her hands slid away from his back.

"I can't," he agreed, and he kissed her temple softly. "Put your arms around me, Hannah."

He kissed her lips again, and she did. He slipped his fingertips past lace, past satin and found her velvety nipple. With a teasing thumb, he turned it into a pearl and felt her go short of breath. He gave her his.

He rotated his hips once slowly, twice, and he felt her lift to meet him. He knew he would touch her first, make her need him more. He knew she battled with herself even now, for he felt the tension ebb and flow through her every muscle, and he could almost hear her brain chanting, "Want to. Better not. Need to. Better not."

"It's all right," he promised as he felt for the fastener he'd learned to find between a woman's breasts. "You'll be safe, honey. I have . . . I mean, I always carry protection for—"

"Safe?" She looked up at him, her eyes overly bright. "Safety isn't everything. Race, I'm not ready. I can't just . . ." Her words were rushed and breathy, as if she had to push to get them out. "Love is important, too."

Having been handed the big kicker, he backed off. He could offer some powerful stuff, but not that. There were plenty of ways of not being ready. She had hers. He had his.

"I'm sorry," she said. All he heard in her voice was relief. She put her hand to her chest, covering the unfastening that was his single transgression, and she stared at the starry patch of sky directly above her. "This is a wonderful place, and your kisses are much too wonderful."

"You're sorry about that?" He decided to comfort himself with a cigarette.

"No." She turned her head at the sound of the match. "I'm just out of sync with the times, I guess."

"You're a sweet lady." He held the match to the end of the cigarette, puffing until he had ignition. "And we're out of sync with each other. What I wanted to do—" a long stream of smoke dissipated, like his intentions, into the night "—was make love with you."

"I want love." She fumbled with the button on her blouse, and it gave him some measure of satisfaction to realize that her hands weren't steady. But, then, neither were his. "That's not quite the same as lovemaking, is it?"

"I think they're related," he allowed. "Sometimes."

"And I think they belong together." She sat up, studied him for a moment, then touched his cheek. "*Always*. Race, lately I think about you so much. I know I must seem very silly to you. Maybe old-fashioned, maybe just childish."

He didn't like being patronized. Not by a woman he wanted the way he wanted this one, anyway. He took another long drag on the cigarette. He almost told her he agreed on all counts, but instead he balanced his forearm on his raised knee, directed his smoke away from her and offered no comment.

"You're a risk-taker, and I'm not," she said.

"So, if I said I loved you, you'd be ready?"

"I haven't said *I* loved *you*." He glanced at her, wondering why he felt wounded. With grating patience she continued. "I won't say it unless it's true. And neither will you."

"How can you be sure?" He waited for an answer—something flattering, maybe. Either she didn't have one, or she knew something he didn't. He sighed. "We can have fairly safe sex, Hannah, but there's no such thing as safe love."

"Is that, finally, the risk that scares you?"

"No, it doesn't scare me." Neither did fire, but he was always careful not to start one. "No more than dragons and werewolves scare me." He spotted a flat rock beyond the edge of the blanket, and he stretched himself in its direction.

"You don't believe in love at all?"

"I don't know if I believe it's all it's cracked up to be." He pulverized the cigarette butt against the rock and wondered what she, in all her cherished innocence, could possibly know about the subject. "Have you found it to be?"

"I haven't found it yet."

Good. "Then you go ahead and hold out for it, and let me know." He was aiming for flippancy, but the idea that she would have to find it without him suddenly worked at his insides like a crab's pincers. Be damned if he would believe he was scared. Better to be straight with her. To smile and say, "You're right. I'm not going to say it unless it's true. I've got one or two principles holding up an already fairly sketchy conscience."

"I doubt that."

"You doubt the principles?"

"I doubt the sketchy."

She'd straightened herself out, gotten her clothes back in order, but the rigidity hadn't returned. He got the impression she'd discovered something—maybe that it wasn't as bad as she thought, or that she could handle him. He wanted to tell her he could handle himself, but he realized she'd just said that, only she'd packaged it in idealistic ribbons that had him chafing. He took a certain amount of pride in his sketchy conscience. And in the fact that he could be honest about its condition.

"Is it afterward yet?" she wondered.

It took him a moment, but then he remembered, and chuckling, he shook his head. "This doesn't feel like any afterglow to me. Some parts of me are hard to fool."

"You said afterward we could just look at the stars."

"Caught in my own romantic snare." He shook his head again and sighed with mock self-pity as he slipped his arm around her shoulders. "I do get to hold you for this part, don't I?"

"Of course. You have a very nice shoulder." She rested her head against him, and they lay down together. "Perfect support for star-gazing. You must work at it."

"That's one of the job requirements." He was boasting now, but she'd invited him to. "Daily workouts except when you're fighting fire, which is a hell of a workout in itself. Smoke jumpers can't weigh over two hundred pounds."

"No matter how tall?"

"Can't be over six-five."

"Maybe I could qualify."

"You're too small." He rested his chin on her head. He liked the way she made him feel when she snuggled against him, as though maybe she could depend on him for something. "You'd probably clear the minimum height—five feet—but you don't weigh any hundred and twenty pounds." She raised her head to question his boldness, and he smiled. "Just an observation."

"You're supposed to be observing the stars."

"I sleep with them a lot, but I'm afraid I don't know their names."

"Story of your life?"

"Oo-ooh." He clutched his belly dramatically. "Lady, that was a low blow."

"I know some of them. Shall I introduce them?"

In truth he knew some of the names, too. They shared knowledge and swapped star stories. She told him an African folk tale about the star trail, and he told her fire fighters' tales about the fire that left soot on the face of the moon and the summer the stars forgot to shine. Neither of them mentioned the idea of telling time by the stars. Time was not a concern.

Race spent the following day at the Custer fire management station. He drove back to Deadwood, bypassing the turnoff to the lake cabins—*cabin,* Vicki's cabin, not Hannah's. Time to mind his business, he told himself, and he headed for the Plugged Nickel. He took over for the dealer at his favorite blackjack table. The casual air with which he usually dealt the game was absent, though, and he waved away all short break offers. He needed the game.

At two in the morning Vicki managed to lure him away from the table with a cheeseburger and fries. He hadn't realized how hungry he was until he smelled the grease. The crowd hadn't dwindled much, but it wasn't hard to commandeer one of the three small supper tables. The late-night patrons were either serious drinkers or serious gamblers. Those who fell into both categories were by this time in serious trouble.

Vicki joined Race at the table, but she wasn't eating. She had a beer and a box of what was becoming a lucrative sideline. Coming up with ideas for new Plugged Nickel souvenirs was one of Vicki's favorite aspects of the business.

"I ordered some of these with our name on them." She brandished a lacy red garter under Race's nose and gave the elastic a workout. "What do you think?"

"*Our* name?"

"'Souvenir of the Plugged Nickel, Deadwood, S.D.,'" she quoted.

He squinted through the smoky haze. "All that fits on that little thing?"

"Of course." She snapped the garter against her own hand and dropped it back into the box. "Small print. The sweatshirts are selling great, and I'm already out of the black panties. I doubled the order on size five."

"Is that your size?"

"You know my size, cowboy." She smiled saucily and fluffed the blond hairdo that billowed beneath the brim of her black cowboy hat. "And you were right about putting the little plugged nickel on the left cheek instead of..." Vicki winked. "You know, where *I* wanted to put it."

"You've gotta learn to be a little bit more subtle, Vicki. A little more—" he had long, silky, natural blond hair on his mind "—ladylike sometimes."

"*Ladylike!*" Vicki bristled, and it occurred to Race that if anybody in the place had been drifting off, she'd woken him up in a hurry. "What the hell kind of fun is that? Somebody's looking to buy a souvenir of Deadwood, he wants it to be just as bawdy as the legend. That's exactly what you said." She stuck her lips out in a pout. "Once upon a time."

"Well, yeah, bawdy..." He leaned over and peered into the box, which contained an assortment of items that fit the description. The six-shooter on the men's briefs had been his idea, too. "But with the right touch of restraint."

He recalled pointing out to her that a Colt .45 was carried on the hip.

"We got lots of restraint in our ladies' lingerie, Race. We got the nickel sittin' over to the left like a cute little tattoo, just like you said." There was that brassy smile again. "I liked it so much, I had one done."

"One what?"

"A tattoo. A plugged nickel." She stretched her back and postured, with her hand resting high on her backside as she leaned across the table toward him. "Care to have a look?"

"I'm still eating." He picked up his cheeseburger.

"Afterward."

"Afterward?" He remembered using the word with Hannah. Damn, he didn't want to think about Hannah now. He wanted to be tempted to take Vicki up on her offer, and thinking about Hannah didn't help. "We decided not to mix business with pleasure, and it's made a better partnership." Which was the one and only reason he wasn't tempted, he told himself. "And a pretty good friendship."

Vicki looked disappointed. She helped herself to the dill pickle spear she knew he never ate. "So what's she like?"

"Who?"

"Miss Goody Two Shoes. You're seeing her now, aren't you?"

"Right now I'm seeing you and a plate of French fries."

"And thinking about Hannah Quinn."

"We've been out a couple of times," he admitted, then modified, "casually." The look in his partner's eyes said she didn't buy the modifier. He tipped his chair on its back legs as he pushed his plate away. "Come on, Vicki. You said it yourself, she's not my type."

"No, but you're her type." He started to laugh, but she signaled for silence, and he actually wanted to hear her out. She wagged the pickle instructively. "Every Goody Two Shoes secretly yearns for a guy like you—one with a wild streak as deep as the Broken Boot Mine. You are the bad boy of her dreams, Race Latimer, ripe for reform. In fact, she's sure if she goes mining way down deep in that big barrel chest of yours, she'll find this incredible lub-dubbing nugget of pure gold."

"Get out of here, Vicki."

She stuck the pickle in her mouth and made a circle with her hands, fingers palpitating. For effect she added wild, silly eyes, and the pickle ended up looking like a tropical fish on its way to being swallowed. He couldn't hold back on the laughter any longer. "You're really reaching now. Hannah Quinn won't even ..." He glanced away, shaking his head.

"Won't even what?" Vicki asked rhetorically after biting off a piece of the pickle. She looked at him speculatively, chewing slowly. She knew him well, and she'd gotten him to say more than he'd intended to already.

"Bet you a nickel she will," Vicki pressed.

He glared, but her knowing look softened him. She nodded, satisfied he'd capitulated to her superior powers of prognostication where another woman was concerned. There was also no point in arguing about a thought he hadn't even completed. Enjoying the upper hand, Vicki kept right on chewing and nodding. "Eventually she will, and then you'll be right back to mixing business with pleasure."

"How do you figure that?"

"She's sitting on prime Deadwood real estate." She finished off the pickle, leaving her hand free to wave away any technicalities. "Well, the church is, anyway. And if they sublease that property, she's out of a job. When the lease is up, she's out, but then again, the sooner the better.

"Nothing personal, Race. Purely business. I want to diversify. Get a second location that's big enough for a nice restaurant, pretty crystal chandeliers, velvet drapes." He could see the vision in her eyes. It was a good idea. His business sense agreed with hers. "I want a casino with a little Monte Carlo style. Real tasteful."

Trouble was, his sketchy conscience was filling out more all the time. "They want to diversify at the New Moon Center, too," he told her. "They want to expand their day-care program."

"What for? People with kids are moving out of this town."

"Which is maybe what they should do," he said, trying to imagine them all packing up and leaving at once. Might be the best thing for them, gettin' outta Dodge. Or Deadwood, same damn thing. He'd drink to that.

"Definitely." Vicki tapped her finger in the middle of the water circle Race's beer bottle had left behind. "After they shut the whorehouses down a few years back, the people with the kids and the station wagons took over, poking around in the relics of rowdiness. Upstanding citizens getting a big thrill out of viewing places where things used to happen. But now the tables have turned again, and Deadwood's back in business."

"Parental discretion advised," he added.

"No kidding. I say we bring in a pied piper to march the little rug rats down the road." Her eyes danced to the tune of her idea. "All the damn protestors are sure to follow right behind them."

"Leave the town to us ramblers, gamblers, and thieves."
Race figured he could talk himself into this with another
beer.

"The kind of people who built it in the first place,"
Vicki credited. "The New Moon Center can't afford to sit
on that property, Race. Churches depend on charity, and
people get real short on charity when they see they can
make a buck. Which reminds me, there was another salesman in here today peddling metal detectors."

Race grimaced. He had his limits.

"Well, we might wanna think about it. A guy got a gun
past the bouncers in the No. 10 Saloon last night. Nothing happened. He just waved it around. Turned out it
wasn't loaded. But we've had some sore losers in here
lately."

"Maybe we should put up a sign that says Quit While
You're Ahead. Give 'em something to think about."

"All we want them to think about is the next bet," Vicki
insisted as she swiped a cold fry from Race's plate. "You'd
better stay away from that sweet-faced little church
worker." Race rolled his eyes. "I'm serious. You're getting soft in the head."

"Let's get the metal detector. I don't want any gun-
slingers in here." He surveyed the saloon decor. There were
holsters hanging on the wall, but no guns. "The *illusion* is
fine. That's all we want."

"You're chasing illusions, all right," Vicki said quietly.

They stared at one another. She was no dummy. But he
was no chump.

"The only thing I ever take the trouble to chase is fire,"
he assured her. "Nothing else runs as wild."

"Except the Race Latimer we all know and love."

Chapter 7

"Why do we always end up talking about men?"

It was a good question. Hannah raised her eyebrows and shrugged, a speculative gesture meant to indicate that the group was responsible for choosing its direction and that Tasha probably knew the answer herself. It also was one of those smug looks Hannah had learned from her mother, and she hated it. But she used it in self-defense when she knew that more of a response would only prompt more questions. Right now, she had no intelligent answers to offer.

She'd coasted through the morning group, and it hadn't gone well. She'd been wishing she were somewhere else, doing something different. Getting some experience, maybe. She wasn't the right person for this job. She didn't know anything about relationships, and she knew she had no right pretending she did.

She'd had friendships. She'd dated safe men whom she'd kissed in a friendly way. Nice men, whom she'd met in class, or who were friends, or brothers of friends. Predictable men, who had continued to call until she'd turned them down enough times that they finally got the message.

"I guess we get what we deserve," Tasha said, pulling Hannah's mind back to the group. "We let them drive us crazy. They don't have to be a problem for us, but we act like we've got nothing better to worry about than what they're gonna pull next. Right?"

Hannah managed to smile. "I think you've hit the nail on the head."

"Yeah." Tasha sat back and surveyed the faces in the group. The women who had been where she was now. "So I wonder if Mick's ever gonna bring my car back."

"You let your ex-husband take your car?" Hannah could have kicked herself immediately for sounding surprised.

"Well, yeah, I think I mentioned that half an hour ago. His pickup isn't running."

"I didn't realize he still had it," Hannah said, remembering that the reference to a pickup had made her think of Race's sleek blue one, which she'd seen sitting in front of the Plugged Nickel when she'd come to work that morning. Which had led her to wonder whether he'd spent the night with Vicki, which was none of her business, really, but still. . .

All those whiches were reasons for her to be in group herself, asking people like Tasha for advice.

Well, maybe not Tasha. Not if she was trusting the notorious Mick with her car.

"You know, you're right," Tasha said. "The more dangerous they are, the more attractive they seem to be. But I'm wising up fast. I got the petition drawn up. I'll give you one to circulate around." She lifted the flap on her huge, brown vinyl handbag, then paused, mentally back-tracking. "I guess I left them in the car. I'll get you one tomorrow. I hope."

"Petitioning to shut down the casinos?"

"Not shut them down," Tasha said as she shoved the bag between her chair and Celia's. The limited space in Hannah's office required a tight circle. "Just go back to the way it was before."

"How far back?" It was a question Hannah could hear Race asking. Back to the bordello days? That wasn't much of a stretch. How about back to the heyday of gold miners? Right next door in the town of Lead the Homestake Mine was still chunking out gold, and there were still a few prospectors around. It wasn't hard to argue that Deadwood hadn't changed much in a hundred years.

"Back to sanity," Tasha said. She glanced at the clock on the wall. "And I've gotta hoof it over to the school to pick up my kid."

It was time to quit. Hannah opened the door to turn her group out to deal with the streets of the town "too mean to die."

Nettie was waiting in the hallway. "I have a message for you, Hannah." But she would not share it until the last of the women had filed out the door.

"Soon as I track down my car, I'll bring over those petitions," Tasha promised as she let herself out the front entrance. "You want one, Nettie?"

"I'll leave all that to you guys."

"I need help with this. I can't be doing all the writing, all the running around, all the—" The front door clicked shut behind her, cutting Tasha's list short.

Hannah turned to Nettie, who reported, "You had a visitor a little while ago."

"Race?" The older woman nodded. "Oh." Hannah's doubts flew out the window, and disappointment drifted in to replace them. He'd actually stopped in again, and she'd missed seeing him, missed speaking to him, missed even the opportunity of saying hello. "While I was in group? Did he say—"

"He was on his way back to Wyoming, and from there to a fire in Idaho, he said. He left this for you." Nettie handed her a plain white envelope.

She couldn't wait to tear into it, but the contents were not what she expected. "It's a check." Wonder of wonders. She slid it out, read it, blinked and counted the zeros. "Nettie, it's a check for five thousand dollars."

Nettie smiled as though this were no great surprise to her. "He said it was his gift for the New Moon. I told him he sounded like an Indian, the way he said it. He just laughed."

The pleasure Nettie took simply in relaying her son's message didn't escape Hannah's notice, but that for now was secondary. "He already left?"

"He couldn't wait around, he said."

Hannah checked the envelope again. "There's no note or anything." She felt bereft, even a little cheated. "Idaho?"

"He said the mountains in northern Idaho, where they can only reach the fire by air."

"Oh, my." Hannah tossed the empty envelope on her desk, which stood near the office door. "I know he loves his work, but it sounds so dangerous, jumping out of a plane and into a forest fire."

"But isn't he one of those men you talk about sometimes?" Nettie challenged. "The kind you say are attractive to women because everything about them seems dangerous?"

"I think I said that again this morning," Hannah admitted as she studied Race's bold, blocky handwriting on the check. "That's textbook, though. There's more to it in an emotional sense." Unconsciously she put her hand on her chest and tapped as she explained. "They're dangerous to us personally, emotionally. They take our very breath away, and when we lose that we seem to lose all sense of..." Nettie knew, and her smile made Hannah laugh self-consciously. "All sense, right? I'm sure he's very good at what he does and that he takes every possible precaution and that it's perfectly safe and—" She bit her lower lip. "I'm sorry I missed seeing him before he left."

"He said to tell you his address is still the same."

Dear Race,

Your generous donation to the Center will be put to good use in our day-care program. I'm guessing that's the part of New Moon you like the best. I remember how sweet you were with Josh, letting him feed you his carrot. Clearly you have a gift for communicating with children. When the fire season is over and you have more time, maybe you'd be willing to visit with our preschool group. They'd love to hear your stories about fighting forest fires.

I think about what it must be like for you to face a raging fire in the high mountains. I know it's a "dirty, tedious, backbreaking job," and I know you're experienced and highly skilled, but fire is fire. It scares me. Once when I was living with my parents at a mission in Africa, I saw a whole village go up in flames. It sounded like a tornado, and it was hard to separate the screams of the animals from the human screams. I think about you, and I remember the heat and the spreading flames, and I pray for your safety.

I've been thinking about the beautiful spot above
the lake where we went star-gazing. I think about going back, but I don't think I could find it by myself,
and I don't think I'd want to be there without you. It's
your place. I was your guest.

When you come back, I hope you will be my guest.
I don't know any wonderful secret places like yours,
but I can make a passable meal and serve it to you at
my table this time, instead of yours.

I know you're busy, but it would be good to hear
from you. Just tell me that you're safe.

Hannah

Race tried to keep the paper clean, but the little flower
in the corner was spoiled by one of several of his sooty
fingerprints. He was taking a water break. He'd sat down
on a fallen lodgepole pine that was only half charred, and
he'd downed as much tepid water from his plastic canteen
as he could stomach. Then he'd taken the letter out of his
pocket again because he'd forgotten how she'd signed it.

Just "Hannah." Not "Yours truly." Not that it meant
anything. People didn't really mean "yours truly" when
they put it in a letter. But she'd written it before, he remembered, and he wondered why she'd left it out this time.

He also wondered why he was thinking like such a fool.
Isolation, he told himself. The letter was as close as he
could get to a woman right now, and he was hanging onto
every damn word. But the words had come from Hannah, and as long as she seemed to be stuck in his head, he
felt pretty good knowing he was on her mind, too.

She was giving him a hell of a lot of credit he didn't deserve. He smiled. He liked that. "A gift for communicating with children." He didn't know a damn thing about

children, but if she wanted to believe he had a way with them, he figured it was a point in his favor.

She also had a pretty glorified image of him "facing a raging fire." It was pretty calm now. The dragon had roared through these woods, all right, but they'd beaten him back. Only the smoke remained, drifting on the shafts of sunlight that pierced the thick stand of pines. The air smelled of sap and soot, and the mountain was quiet. Too quiet. The wildlife had fled, but not for long. There was plenty of vegetation left, and a little rain would make it all green again soon.

Race had been cold trailing most of the day, feeling the dead fire's blackened edge with his hand and digging out the occasional live spots. Hardly glamorous work. He was tired and dirty, and his back was sore. It hadn't been much of a day for heat and spreading flames, but he knew when he crawled into his sleeping bag and reread his letter by flashlight, the night would be. In the dark he would imagine Hannah, and he would feel the heat.

He lit a cigarette—his first in two days—and studied the wispy black script on the second page. He knew damn well what spreading flames she remembered. He wanted her to tell him how it felt. If there had been a phone within reach, he would have called her.

Remember when I kissed you, Hannah? Remember when I touched your breast? Tell me about the flames, Hannah. Tell me how they warmed you deep inside your belly the night I touched you.

"Hot enough for you, Latimer?"

Race stiffened as though the friendly voice had coated him with starch. He didn't know why he felt like a kid who'd been caught doing something he shouldn't, but he resented the feeling as much as the intrusion. He took a long, slow pull on his cigarette without turning to acknowledge his fellow fire fighter, and he slipped the letter into his breast pocket, handling it less carefully than before.

"What's the problem, Baker?"

The reply was quick and amiable. "No problem. Just asked if it was hot enough for you."

Race looked up and offered a crooked smile. "Not quite. Can you turn it up a little?"

"I just barely got it turned down a notch, buddy." Baker took a step back as Race stood, abandoning his seat on the fallen log. "We move out first thing tomorrow, right? Assuming it's out," Baker added. He took off his hard hat and streaked the grime across his forehead with his sleeve. "Damn, it'll be great to take a real shower and sleep raw between real sheets."

Baker reached for the cigarette Race offered as a gesture of pardon for the intrusion. No words were necessary as long as the offer was accepted. Baker gave a nod of thanks and located his own match. "I'm thinkin' heaven must be made of clean, white sheets."

"Sounds like paradise to me."

With a subtle chin jerk and the thrust of his lower lip, Baker indicated the paper peeking out of Race's shirt pocket. "Letter from home?"

"Uh—from a friend." More than a friend. Hannah was where he wanted to be at the moment, but he wasn't sure if that meant anything like "home."

"Wish somebody'd write me a letter." The smaller man shoved his flame-resistant gloves halfway into his pants' pocket, leaving the fingers protruding in a bunch. "Write and tell me about the world that isn't either on fire or all burned up."

"Hey, we did ourselves proud on this one. Look at this." With a sweeping gesture, Race noted the number of trees still standing. "Mother Nature's gonna heal these scars in no time."

"We did pretty good, didn't we?"

Even though Baker was not based at his depot, Race had worked with the man before. Still, he knew little about him except that he was an Indian, which was self-evident, and that he knew his job. Normally, Race didn't ask too many questions, but the shared victory, topped off by sharing a smoke, invited at least some small talk.

"You got a home, Baker? I mean, besides a bunk in a jump base dormitory."

Eyes fixed on Race's letter, Baker puffed on his cigarette in silence. Finally he looked up at the treetops. "My ol' lady left me for a shoe salesman."

"The hell," Race said, sympathizing. He ignored his usual inclination to drop the subject. "How long ago was this?"

"Two years." Baker stared at the ground and continued to smoke. Race was ready to accept the brief silence as the end of the conversation when Baker added softly, "And three months. Give or take however long it had been goin' on before I caught her with him."

"What did you do?"

"I walked." He stuck his thumb in the pocket that held his gloves. "All my stuff fit into two boxes and one plastic trashbag. She sold the house we had in Billings, and I paid the realtor's commission." Then he smiled. "Only paid five dollars for the divorce, though. I went through Tribal Court."

"So, what, you've got no home now because you've got no wife?"

"I usually pick up a short-term lease during the off-season. Nothin' you'd wanna call home. Makes a difference when you've got somebody there, you know?"

"Or somebody close by," Race said.

"Somebody looking for you to be there with her. It's for damn sure we've got nobody close by up here." He surveyed the treetops, as if there might be a chance of somebody coming in from on high. But then he shook his head. "Not a woman within fifty miles."

"Don't be too sure. There are women on one of the crews I trained this spring."

"They weren't jumpers."

"They might be. One of them—" Race smiled as he remembered the woman and the way she'd taken charge of her team. "Wilma Bird from Rosebud. She could dig a trench faster than any man on the line." He figured she was crew boss material. So was Baker. "Where are you from originally?"

"Hardin."

"Crow?"

"On my dad's side," Baker reported. He studied Race for a moment, as though sizing him up for something. "I figured you for a Chippewa."

Race nodded briefly, confirming an association he usually dismissed with a wordless warning against broaching the subject again. "My mother was from the Turtle Mountain Reservation. I've been to Crow Agency. Driven through, anyway." He shrugged. "Never been to Turtle Mountain, far as I can remember."

"I have. It's nice up there. Nicest part of North Dakota, if you ask me. You never visit your relations up there?"

"I wouldn't know who they were, and they wouldn't know me." Didn't bother him. Never had. *So why did it keep coming up lately?* Maybe this time it was just the fact that Baker had lost his wife, but he still had people at Crow Agency.

Hell, Race had people. He had Lannie and Trey, and maybe if he'd look in on them once in a while, Trey's kids would even grow up knowing who Trey's brother was. Might be nice, being an uncle to his brother's kids, buying them candy and comic books and giving them piggyback rides the way Trey had done for him.

"What do you say we mop this thing up, Baker? I'm ready to do something a little more dramatic, like maybe—" Race grinned, thinking about Hannah, hoping she would keep right on thinking of him "—dropping out of the sky onto another burning mountain."

The next assignment took Race back to Montana, but it could have been Idaho again, or California. There were too many dry spots, and Forest Service personnel were getting spread pretty thin. He'd had little rest between fires, but that was okay. He wanted to earn himself a chunk of time off.

Hannah's letters kept coming. He had no trouble finding time to read them over and over, but he had a hell of a time writing back. He managed one note to her five.

Dear Hannah,

It's great to get your letters up here in God's country. They help to remind me that this really is God's country and not the Devil's own inferno. This fire's been pretty shifty, just like ol' Lucifer himself, whose ways a woman like you could only know about secondhand. But take it from one who's done some dancing with him—he's a foxy one. And so is this damn fire.

We're working long hours, and it's good when they bring in supplies and there's a letter for me. It rounds the day out real nice. Not that I expect you to write every day. Who could come up with something to write every day? You can sure tell I can't. But on the days when your letters come, the food even tastes better. And we get pretty tasty food here because the Forest Service knows it's good for morale to feed us well.

Your letters are good for my morale.

See, every time I start a letter, I have to trash it because it starts sounding stupid. You'll probably think I'm getting sentimental, like maybe the air is too thin up here or something. Oxygen can be hard to come by in a fire, anyway, so maybe that's my problem.

I wish you could see this place. The sky is filled with smoke, but there's a green valley spread out below where I'm sitting now. Pretty little stream running through it. I should be hearing birds, but I know they took off for safer places to perch. I hear fire burning hard at my back, and I don't want it to eat up this little valley. That's why I'm here. I don't know for how long, but we'll stick it out. If we can't save this valley, we'll save the next one over.

I've got to go shift some people around and get back on the line myself. Everybody's dog tired. I have to make these guys take rests or they'll keep going till they drop. Smoke jumpers are a stubborn breed. I guess I fit that description in more ways than most.

I don't know how soon you'll get this letter, but I want you to know I'm okay. I want you to keep writing. Truth is, I miss you, Hannah.

Race

The next day they broke camp and slung the gear out by helicopter longline. When he got back to the jump base, he tried to call Hannah. It was after nine, at night. Twice he let the phone ring a dozen times or more while he stood there in the small booth, mentally summoning the sound of her voice to his ear. It didn't work. He finally gave up and tried his sister, Lannie. He could count on Lannie to be glad to hear from him.

"How's everybody?" he asked eagerly. "How's Trey?"

"Oh, Race, Frankie's going to have another baby. Isn't that wonderful?"

Frankie was Trey's wife, and she'd already given him a son. "Yeah, that's great." Race heard the clucking sound Lannie always made when she scolded him, and he realized she detected a lack of sincerity. Downright sarcasm, in fact. Where had that come from? "I mean it. I think it's great." He wasn't jealous. Hell, he could have had twenty kids by now, and their twenty mothers would have considered themselves lucky, right?

Right. Try telling that to Lannie, and she'd find a sweet way to tell him to cut the bull. Okay, so Trey was a lucky man. Next time Race saw him, he'd tell him so.

"How about you and my favorite brother-in-law?" he asked.

"Not yet. We're ... we're trying, but ..."

Race laughed. "I just meant how are you guys doing? What do you mean, *trying?* Don't tell me anything that'll destroy my innocence, Lannie."

"What innocence?" It was good to hear Lannie laugh so readily. "We're doing fine. George has a wonderful new physical therapist. You'd hardly believe he was ever injured. He's able to work full time now."

"Yeah?" Race lit a cigarette. It was still hard for him to think of George Tracker as Lannie's husband, but he surely liked hearing the happy lilt in his sister's voice. "Doing what? Construction?"

"Finish carpentry. He does beautiful work." She paused. "I know you haven't asked, Race, but Dad's doing okay, too."

He hadn't asked because he expected no less from that tough old bird. "That's good. I was getting around to him. Anybody going down to the Hills this summer? I get down there as often as I can, even though I can't plan very far ahead. Maybe we could arrange—"

"Maybe you could arrange to come home for a weekend, Race. You haven't been home in eons."

"The business in Deadwood takes most of my spare time." The usual excuse wasn't enough this time. "That and... I met this woman."

"A woman?"

"Yeah." He chuckled. He could almost see the little hearts dancing in Lannie's eyes. "Damnedest thing. She's the last person in the world you'd expect..." Last *he'd* expect. Lannie had always had this notion that a "nice girl" was going to come along someday. He'd translated that to mean boring—exactly the kind of man he had *hoped* would come along for his long-suffering and under-appreciated sister. Then she'd fallen for a notorious, hell-raising Indian, and Race had just about lost his cool. Well, to be honest, he'd acted like a jerk, trying to tell Lannie how to live her life.

He wondered whether Hannah had any brothers. If he were Hannah's brother, he'd be calling himself outside for a fight just for thinking about her.

"She's a social worker. Works for a church program."

"What's wrong with that?" Lannie sounded delighted.

"She hates gambling. Doesn't drink, doesn't—" he dropped his cigarette on the concrete floor of the telephone booth and ground it out beneath his workboot "—smoke, doesn't..." Just thinking how impossible it was made him shake his head. "There's a whole bunch of good stuff that's not on her agenda."

Lannie wasn't discouraged. "What does she look like? I'll bet she's lovely."

"I wouldn't bet against you. She's got hair the color of the August moon, and her eyes—" He could just see Lannie smiling on the other end of the line. If he had to say something stupid, Lannie was the one person he could say it to. "She's got pretty eyes. They're blue, like yours. And she writes to me. You know how I met her? She staged a sit-in at the Plugged Nickel. Otherwise, she wouldn't be caught dead in a place like that." He sighed. "Which means I've got no damn business..."

"Being in love with her," Lannie concluded quietly after several seconds had passed. "Yes, you do. You have every right."

Race laughed uneasily. "I wouldn't go *that* far. This is still your brother, Race." It gave him a feeling of relief to affirm the relationship, that they were family and that she understood who he was. "Are you happy, Lannie? I mean, George is treating you right, isn't he?"

"He's wonderful."

"Yeah, well, he's not good enough for you, but I never met anybody who was." He remembered when hired thugs had beaten George nearly to death, leaving him with disabilities from which he was still struggling to recover. Sounded like he was doing it, though. Lannie's devotion was a beautiful thing. It had taken Race a while to accept the idea that the better part of it belonged to George now. "I'm glad the two of you... I'm glad it turned out for you."

"Thank you."

"Listen, don't you be trying anything too hard, okay? After you get to be a certain age..."

"I know," she said with a sigh. "I'm over the hill. If I don't get pregnant pretty soon, I guess I should give up on the idea."

"Hey, I'm kidding. You're not old. You always take me too seriously. I hope you get what you want." He pictured her ever-too-thin body and chuckled. "Fat as that lady you used to sing to me about. The one who swallowed a horse."

"She's dead, of course," came the deadpan reply.

"Yeah, but she did it all wrong. You get pregnant, Lannie. You tell ol' George I said I didn't think he could do it, and he'll get the job done for sure."

"He does beautiful work," Lannie repeated. Then she giggled like a teenager.

The sound made Race's heart ache, and he couldn't tease her anymore. "You raised me when you were too young to be saddled with a responsibility like that. Now that you've got a husband, I hope you have a kid of your own. You deserve the whole nine yards, Lannie."

"You do, too. You deserve a home and family."

"Just the thing to cramp my style," he said, desperate to lighten up. "Listen, I'd better—"

"What's her name?"

He was quiet for a moment. He wanted them to meet, face to face. His sweet sister and... "Hannah. Her name is Hannah."

"Pretty name."

"You'd like her. She's like you. She's a good person."

"Bring her home to meet us, Race. You've never done that before—brought a girlfriend home to meet us. And it's been so long since we've seen you."

"I know. I keep saying next month, next winter, next spring." He'd been back twice in six years. The cold look in his father's eyes had dampened the spirit of the visit the first time. The second time he'd avoided the old man completely. "It's hard to go back now, it's been so long."

"Bring Hannah."

"You're a hopeless romantic."

"I'm a hope*ful* romantic, and I've never met anyone with hair the color of the August moon."

"I don't believe I said that." But he knew Lannie would never make fun of him for it.

There was a tap on the glass behind him. He turned. One of the pilots was giving him the cut-it-short sign. "Keep your shirt on, Draper." He turned away, guarding his right to a private goodbye. "I've gotta let someone else use the phone. Take care of yourself, Lannie. You're the best."

"So are you."

Like hell he was. There wasn't much goodness in him when he got the news about the fire in the Custer District and all he could think about was finding a way to get himself assigned there. He wasn't thinking about rescuing the beautiful Black Hills, historic Deadwood, or even the Plugged Nickel. His first thought was, that's close to Hannah. He knew he'd have to do some fancy talking. Smoke jumpers were needed in a lot of places, but they didn't do any jumping in the Hills. There was plenty of access down there. He figured he'd have to come up with some angle.

And he did. The Indian crews he'd trained needed an experienced crew boss. He claimed to be the only man for the job.

Chapter 8

Critter seemed determined to destroy the back door. As soon as it opened, he came bounding inside like a corn-fed Shetland pony, and Hannah went down on her knees for a playful greeting. He'd been roaming the woods later than usual, and she was glad to have him back so she could lock up for the night. So glad, in fact, that she sang to him. "Yes sir, that's my doggie. No sir, not my froggie."

The back door was still open, which shouldn't have bothered her, but she felt self-conscious all of a sudden. Then she heard a deep chuckle, and she knew why.

She pivoted, rising slowly on the awareness that someone waited in the dark, someone Critter was willing to bring into the house even though his mistress was dressed in her flannel nightgown and ready for bed. She knew who it was—could *feel* who it was, even though the chuckle was generically male. Her heart hammered at her ribs when she saw his silhouette in the doorway.

"Race?" He just stood there, and since she hadn't turned the porch light on, all she could see was his shape. A quick flood of excitement washed self-consciousness across the floor. "The door's open. Shall I get you a towel?"

"I'm dry, like everything else in this tinderbox country."

He stepped inside, and she resisted the urge to go to him like a lover expecting to be embraced. But she wanted to be. She took two steps, her bare feet sticking to her freshly waxed kitchen linoleum. He wore jeans and a blue chambray shirt. She saw no sign of soot on his clothes, but he looked tired, as though he'd been working late. He didn't smile. He just stood there by the door, looking at her. Waiting for something. She moved closer, and she could tell he'd just showered. His hair was still damp, and he smelled of soap and water.

"It's so good to see you," she said. She dearly meant it. "Did they send you to fight the fire?"

"I sent myself. Been down there for two days." His first smile was for the big yellow Lab, who padded across the floor and licked his hand. "'Atta boy, Critter. You're my buddy. *Her* doggie, my buddy. Go lie down, now."

Hannah was amazed when the dog obeyed. "How did you get him to do that?"

"Just give him a masterful tone and a little respect." He flashed the pup an okay sign. "That's another one I owe you, big fella."

"How bad is it?" *Go put a robe on, Hannah.* "Everybody's been driving down to take a look, but I've been staying out of the way."

"Good girl."

"You can see it in the sky, though." *Never mind. Just pretend you're wearing one.* "It's like that awful city smog. It's coming this way, isn't it?"

"We've got two fires now—well, three incidents, technically. With the kind of winds we've been getting during the day, we're having a hell of a time staying ahead of them. Unless the winds give us a break, I'd say we'll be looking at some pretty widespread burning." He reached for her suddenly, hands on her shoulders, and drew her a step closer. "You smell sweet."

"You do, too." Beneath the voluminous nightgown her body tingled from nape to heels when he rubbed her shoulder blades with the feather-light touch of his fingertips. Her mouth went dry, and she had to swallow before she could ask, "Why didn't you call me when you got here?"

"Haven't had time." He was watching her closely, and something in what he saw brought on a crooked smile. "Couldn't get to a phone. Afraid you'd run if you knew I was coming. Take your pick."

"Run from what?"

"From me. From all the things about me that you can't accept."

"Oh, Race, please don't think I'm some kind of judgmental Puritan. I'm not." She wanted to prove it by putting her arms around his waist, but the blasted things wouldn't move. "Just because I don't approve of—" a quick toss of her head was meant to dismiss the obstacle she hated to name "—certain kinds of entertainment doesn't mean I don't accept you. And I'm not mentioning the forms of entertainment because I assume the ground rules are still in place."

He tipped his head in assent, and she slipped out of his grasp and hurried to offer more that might please him. "I can make you some coffee," she said, fluttering unproductively near the electric percolator. "Instant would be quicker, but I can...or how about something to eat?" She turned to find him watching her quietly. "Are you hungry?"

There was hunger in the eyes that riveted her as he shook his head. But it wasn't for food.

"Come and sit down, then." She lifted her hand toward the couch and started to lead the way. She knew she wasn't fooling anyone by playing the gracious hostess in her white flannel nightgown, but the chatter came automatically. "We won't build a fire in the fireplace. I'm sure you'd hardly find that relaxing. But I could turn on some music. Of course, there's no television, but you probably don't..."

It all came to a halt when he put his hands on her shoulders again. She closed her eyes and savored his nearness, scant inches from her back. "I'm trying to be cute and coy and casual," she admitted. "It's not working."

"It's not necessary. This isn't a casual visit."

"I know."

"Do you want me to leave?"

She shook her head so quickly it was awkward. His subtle kneading of her shoulders relaxed her, but his own breathing, warm against the side of her face, came ever harder, more uneven as he ministered to her.

"I'm not the best thing that ever happened to you, Hannah. You know it, and I know it."

"I don't feel that way."

"But you know it's true. I'm not your kind."

She turned quickly. "No. I don't feel that way, either, but it's funny...I've thought...so many times, I've thought, I'm not *his* kind, not the kind of woman he finds attractive. Not the sparkly, fun-loving kind I often wish, sometimes even imagine myself being. Last week I was looking at dresses in a store in Rapid City, and I wanted— don't laugh—I wanted to try on a black one with sequins.''

"Did you?"

It surprised her that he would even ask. "I *almost* did. Maybe next time." She offered a shy smile. "Of course, I won't come out of the dressing room."

"I don't want you to dress any differently or act like someone else. You've got me turning myself inside out as it is." His touch—three fingertips against her cheek—was as shy as her smile. "Don't change because of me."

"Every time you touch me, it changes me. I can feel it." She closed her eyes, hoping for more. "It feels good."

"I want it to be good." Then his voice went flat, as though he were obligated to poke holes in a myth. "But there's no way it can be. Not in the long run. Not for you, anyway."

"Why not?"

"Because touching and kissing isn't enough." A muscle twitched in his jaw as he drove his fingers into her hair and held her face close to his. "Because I want to bury myself inside you and stay there for a long, long time."

"Through the night?" Her soft voice was a counterpoint to his, but she kept it steady. She couldn't let him scare her now.

"You see?" The hands that cupped her head stiffened, then relaxed as though the man of action couldn't decide what action to take. "I'm not your kind, Hannah."

"I don't know what that means." She lifted her hands to his waist and saw the light flicker in his eyes when she settled them there. She spoke even more softly. "I do know that what you just said sent wonderful shivers through my whole body."

"You need to be careful, honey. That's exactly what it was meant to do." Half smiling, he let his hands come down to touch the stand-up ruffle at her neck and follow the one flanking the buttons that started beneath her chin. "This is just like you, this nightgown. It's the kind I've imagined you wearing."

"I'm probably the only woman you'd fantasize about in a flannel granny gown."

"You're the only woman I fantasize about at all lately. I've been imagining a lot of things since I left, but they all seem to start and end with you." Tracing the yoke of the gown with his fingers, he seemed to be memorizing lines even as his thumbs strayed to discover the swell of her breasts beneath the flannel. "Were you wearing this when you wrote to me about the way the breeze off the lake blows through your bedroom window at night?" He tipped his head to one side and blew on her neck.

"Last night the breeze through my window—" she lifted one shoulder and shivered as she recalled "—brought the smell of fire."

His eyes smoldered. "Can you smell fire on me?"

"A little."

"It's in all my clothes. Even the ones that haven't been out of my duffel bag."

"I like it better than cologne. It's part of your work. The dangerous part, the part that..." As though drawn by the smell of fire, she leaned closer, touched her face to his shirt and inhaled deeply as his arms at long last came around her. "Oh, Race, I'm glad you're safe."

"I'm glad you care that I'm safe."

"Of course I do."

"I've thought about you lying in the dark on top of your bedsheets, and I wondered why you didn't take this off." He moved his hands over the flannel on her back, massaging her, making her melt against him. "You said you were hot. I wanted you to let the cool night air bathe your body."

"I always wear my—" She swallowed. The breath in her seemed to come from an oscillating fan. "Some kind of nightgown to bed. I'm used to—" She remembered daring to write about being hot in bed, couching the comment in a weather report that had nothing to do with the real message, the one he'd obviously read loud and clear.

She tipped her head back and looked up at him. "I thought about you, too. So much. Have you been fighting the fire for two solid days? You look so tired. Did you just get home?"

"I don't know." The question stood in his eyes for a long moment before he gave voice to it. "Am I home yet, Hannah? Oh, God, how I've wanted—"

She parted her lips with no ready answer, and he spared her—spared them both—by covering them with his own. She welcomed him, greeted him demurely with a tongue less adept than his, but equally willing. It was a kiss made sweeter by delay, but the waiting had made them both blatantly greedy. He tipped his head for a new angle, a deeper draft of her. She met him eagerly, and they kissed each other breathless, then gazed at each other in amazement, for in all the anticipation, neither had imagined hearts pounding quite like this.

"You thought about me, too?" he asked. "What kind of thoughts?"

"Missing you. Wishing..."

"Wishing what?"

"Wishing you weren't a dream. Wishing you'd come stealing in the night and not be a fantasy."

"Come stealing into your room when you're asleep? I thought about that, but you never told me your bedtime." He smoothed her hair back and admired each part of her face in turn, as though studying facets of a jewel. "I couldn't wait any longer. I needed to see you."

"You didn't have to wait."

"You understand, don't you, Hannah?" He searched her eyes, and she saw the need in them. "You've roused the wolf. He steals your dreams, and tonight he is no fantasy."

"I understand." He held her so tightly that she couldn't touch his face the way she wanted to. She looked directly into his eyes. "I'm glad you're here. I want you to stay."

"After tonight you might wish you had the dream back. It's a lot safer."

"I'm glad you've come," she said, because she knew he needed to hear it again. "But after you find out how...how terribly dumb I am, you might wish you'd stayed away."

"Dumb?" He smiled, touching his forehead to hers, and she made a fleeting wish that what he knew about lovemaking would transfer from his head to hers. Then she took it back when, heads still touching, he shook his. "Sweet Hannah, I didn't come here to give you a test."

"Good, because it wouldn't be fair." Eyes closed, she whispered her secret. "I'll need you to teach me first. Teach me what I'll need to know to pass."

"It's not like that." He stepped back a little, looked into her eyes and held her shoulders tightly. Had she said something wrong? "I promise you, it'll never be like that. Trust me."

Again he shook his head, and this time he backed away completely. "What am I saying? You'd be crazy to trust a man like me."

"Why? Are you going to hurt me?"

"I don't know. I don't want to, but I'm a man, and you're so..." Whatever she was, he waved it away. The impatience of his gesture stung her, and she stepped back herself, wrapping her arms around her middle, feeling suddenly chilled.

He looked at her again, and his face softened. He reached out, touched her chin and spoke as though he owed her some kind of amends. "I've wanted you since the night I first saw this sweet face. I wanted to protect you from anything that might hurt you, but here I am."

She let her arms down slowly and moved closer. He was here, and she was glad. Couldn't he see that? Nervous, yes, but not afraid, not of Race.

He cupped her face in his hands. "I wish I could say the right things, whatever they are. A better man would make better promises."

"The minute he broke them, he would become the worse man. The lesser man." It was her turn to touch his face, the hard angles of his jaw, the smoothly shaven cheek, the sensual lips. "I won't settle for the lesser man."

"Who do you want, then?" He took her in his arms, because he knew the answer. But he needed to hear her say it. "Tell me who you want, Hannah."

"I want you."

His kiss promised that she would have what she wanted. Good promise or bad, it was the only one he could grant. She slid her arms around his neck and invited him to deepen his kiss. She wanted the full measure of him. Once committed to the task, he must not hold back, no matter how much teaching he had to do. Once committed, she wanted to learn.

"Show me where you sleep," he entreated, a heated whisper in her ear. "Take me to your bed and let me feel the breeze through your window." She shivered, as though she felt it, and he looked into her eyes. "Do you want me to take you? Is that the way your dream goes?"

"Yes," she admitted, although she hadn't intended to tell him. "That's the way my dream goes."

"Are you sure I'm the one?"

"Could you let it be someone else?"

"No," he said quietly. "Could you?"

"No. It has to be you."

He lifted her in his arms and carried her to the bedroom. The window was open, and pines, which blocked all but a glimpse of the lake, were rustling in the breeze. It was not a large room, and although it had the rough-hewn feel of a cabin, she had softened it with ruffled curtains and pillows, a Boston rocker with a cushion tied to the seat, and a night-light for reassurance. She wondered whether it seemed too fussy to him, or too plain, or too cramped. She looked up, thinking maybe she'd ask.

He hadn't noticed. He located the essential piece of furniture, laid her across it and himself by her side. Smiling, he stroked her hair and kissed her forehead as though he'd bought himself a present and taken it to his own room, and now he was telling himself, yes, this is just what I had in mind.

"I want to be good to you, Hannah. If I please you, it's okay to tell me. I want you to." His stroking was exquisite, but it felt best when his fingertips passed over her nipple. She moaned, and he joined her, making it a duet. "That's it, isn't it?" he whispered. "It pleases me, too. It pleases me so much, I want to kiss you there."

But instead he kissed her lips while he undid the nine buttons on her nightgown. Nine buttons. He gave her a kiss for each one, and she almost forgot that with each button he came closer to finding her naked beneath the heavyweight flannel. He kissed his way down her neck as he moved the nightgown aside. She tingled with anticipation even as she burned from exposure when he lifted his head and looked at her. No man had seen her this way way before. Flat on her back she imagined she had nothing for him to look at but two funny-looking eggs that had been shoved to either side of the pan. Sure enough, he smiled again.

"Remember that song, 'Be My Baby'?" He teased her nipples with his thumb and made her insides turn into a soft-swirl ice-cream cone. "Can I be your baby, Hannah? Will you let me..." He lowered his head and suckled her left breast until she was past worry, past thought, past even wondering why a man would want to do such a thing. "It tastes good," he told her. "It tastes like honey."

It felt good, but she couldn't believe he tasted anything. "It's supposed to taste like milk."

"Breast milk is sweet." He nuzzled her right breast, and she sucked in a deep, anticipatory breath. "Or so I've heard. I know yours will be."

"Oh, Race, do that again." His mouth made her ache, and his tongue made her tingle. "And again, and again, oh..."

But when he started to remove her nightgown, her muscles tightened. He slowed the pace, giving one breast a parting kiss before he levered himself above her on his forearm.

"Take my shirt off for me, Hannah." He took her hand and pressed it against the soft cotton cloth. "Just unbutton it for me." She took a deep breath and did as he asked, unfastening the buttons all the way to his waist with nearly the same brand of boldness he'd shown, except that she lacked the finesse to kiss him at the same time.

"Now lay your hands on me," he instructed.

She did, tentatively at first, but his smooth, hard chest was irresistible to her feminine touch. He groaned and rolled to his back, taking her with him. Seizing on her newfound brass, she kissed the part of him nearest her mouth and slid her hand over his hard abdomen. The puckering of his flat nipple against her lips surprised her. With a quick motion he unbuckled his belt and covered her hand with his, moving it almost imperceptibly until her little finger slipped beneath his waistband. She felt the small hollow of his navel.

"We're going to take our clothes off and come to know each other very, very well." His voice was gravelly, but his hands were sure and steady.

"But I'd feel better if—"

"When you sleep with me, you lose the nightgown." He gathered it from the bottom. She closed her eyes when it reached her hips. He hesitated, then lifted it over her head quickly, as if he were removing an adhesive bandage from her skin. "I promise, you won't miss it. I want to see you, Hannah."

"But I'm not—" She turned her cheek against the quilt that covered her bed.

"Yes, you are." She felt his gaze and heard the approval in his voice. She sought his eyes, and she found it there, too. "Oh, yes, you are."

"But, Race, you've still got..."

"I won't for long." He took his shirt off, tossed it away and settled down to stroke her. "Right now, I want time to touch you." He polished her nipple with the tip of his tongue, and his stroking hand moved over her belly, over her protective thatch of hair, slipping between her thighs. Reflexively they became a vise.

"Shh, Hannah, just listen to your body." He kissed her eyelids and said, "Close your eyes and listen. I'll make your body sing." More kisses relaxed her. More stroking coaxed her thighs apart. More caressing made her ache sweetly, made her go soft and moist between her legs even as a vibrant urgency throbbed within her and she yielded to his pleasuring hand. The sheer sensuality unnerved her, but she could no more turn away than stop herself from pleading to him in a way that some part of her warned she'd later regret.

"It's all right, Hannah. I know what you need." His voice chased all misgivings away, while his thumb tickled one small button and activated explosive sensations in her body. She quivered, at once stimulated by him and repelled by the response rising within her. "That's right," he urged. "That's beautiful, honey. You're beautiful."

Gallantly he pulled her shuddering body into his arms and absorbed her involuntary gasp in a deep, driving kiss. His belt buckle bit into her flesh, but she barely felt it, pressing herself against him, trying to hide in him, trying to get closer. His jeans rubbed against her thighs, and between them came a hard bulge, striking a spark more deeply within her than anyone could possibly reach. It became a slow burn, and she pressed against him even harder. She wanted the spark fanned or doused. In a moment she would be begging shamelessly for one or the other. Instinctively she tried to push Race's pants out of the way and free him to come to her.

He kissed her between whispered words of encouragement while he shucked his jeans, feeling wonderfully favored by her ineffectual attempts to help him. There could be no doubt that she wanted him, even needed him. For the moment he could believe it was right and that he was the right one. When he was as naked as she, he guided her hand between his legs, still easing her with his kisses, teasing her with his tongue.

"Will you take me inside you now, Hannah? Will you let me carve a place for myself, and will you forgive me if—" He took her hand away, thinking he would explode if he didn't do it now, sheathed himself first to protect her, then to be one with her. "Forgive me if I hurt you this time."

"You won't—" But there was a quick, sharp pain, and she felt a terrible need to pull him inside and push him away, all at once.

"Oh, Hannah, I'm sorry." He could see he'd hurt her, and he didn't know whether to go forward or back, even as his seams were about to bust wide open.

But Hannah tipped the scale. She tightened her arms around him and bravely lifted herself to receive more of him. "I'm fine," she whispered, her voice thinner than he would have wished. "I need you, and there's nothing to forgive, except for my awkwardness. Please show me." And then the words that inflamed him beyond all reason. "Please love me, Race."

Make love to her, yes. That he could do. That he *must* do. He exhorted her to relax as he raised her knees to ease his way. Then he relieved her of his weight and tagged the rhythm of his stroking to her quickening breaths, until the crescendo of her release triggered his own shuddering climax.

Hannah awoke to the warm touch of his lips against her shoulder. She knew his scent first—lemon-scented shampoo and smoke and musk—and then the awareness of his hand in her hair, followed by his weight against her and the overall aura of contentment that all this brought her.

"I have to go," he said softly, close to her ear.

Her eyes flew open. In the gray light she saw that he was dressed, and she remembered that she was not. She adjusted the covers under her arm and wondered whether Race had covered her. She remembered feeling perfectly languid and perfectly content to lie close to him, gloriously naked. "But it's not even—" She glanced toward the window. "It's hardly daylight."

"I know it's early. I have to get back to work." He drew back, his arms braced on either side of her. "I didn't want you to wake up and think I'd skipped out on you like some no-good lobo."

She knew better than to ask him not to go at all. "When will I see you again?"

"I've been watching you sleep and asking myself the same question." He laid a possessive hand on her thigh, rubbing gently as he straightened. "We're working twelve-hour shifts. I shouldn't be here now, but I haven't had much of a break in the last two weeks, and I—" He gave a quick shrug, apologizing to no one. "I just came, that's all."

"You still need rest."

"*You* still need rest." His gentle thumb traced the shadowed hollow beneath her left eye. "I kept you up past your bedtime last night, didn't I? If you go back to sleep now, you can get in a couple more hours before you have to face your—" He paused, searching her face for an answer before he asked, "You okay?"

"I'm fine," she said too quickly.

He watched her for a moment, and she wished she'd had the grace to hide an emotion as useless and embarrassing as disappointment. "My sweet Hannah," he said, as though naming her for the first time. "It was wrong for me to stay, and now it's wrong for me to go."

She touched his cheek and smiled a little too brightly. "If you had left last night, I would have followed you right out the door. My letters followed you, didn't they? There are probably some that haven't even caught up with you yet."

He caught her hand and brought it to his lips. The gesture, so unexpected from such a man, pushed Hannah's heart into her throat.

"I'm not an impulsive woman, Race. And I'm not sorry. Are you?"

"That's like asking a starving man if he's sorry he found food."

"Food." And the chance to delay his leave-taking, even briefly. "Let me get you something to take with you. It'll only take a min—"

"I'd rather spend the minute holding you," he said as he slipped his hands beneath her shoulders and gathered her into his arms. She went willingly, hugged him eagerly. "The sky's getting pink," he said. "There's a nice breeze coming off the lake now. Can you feel it on your back?" She nodded, rubbing her cheek against his shirt. "See how that nightgown gets in the way? The cool night air bathed us last night, didn't it? *Afterward.*"

"After we bathed each other in sweat," she remembered, smiling into his white buttons.

"And kisses."

"And kisses," she acknowledged softly. "Is the fire spreading very fast?"

"It will be if we keep this up."

"I mean down south."

"I mean that, too." He chuckled. "Oh, you mean the *forest* fire. We thought we had it contained, but then some loggers got another one going, and the first one slopped over and merged with the second one, and now there's another one. Yeah, it's moving pretty good." He kissed the top of her head. "At least you know I won't be too far away for a while."

"Does that mean I'll see you again?"

"You think there's a fire or a storm or any other disaster big enough to keep me away?" He drew back so that he could look into her eyes when he teased her. "Maybe if the New Moon ladies staged a protest in your bedroom, but otherwise—"

"What if I told you I loved you? Would that be disaster enough?"

His smile faded. She'd caught him off guard. "That wouldn't keep me away, either, Hannah. You wouldn't say it unless you meant it."

"That's right. So here's something to take to the fire with you." She put her arms around him and spoke softly, close to his ear. "I love you, Race."

Chapter 9

It was shaping up to be the worst fire season the Black Hills had suffered. Those who recalled the Deadwood fires of '59 said that no fire could beat that one for pure drama and destruction, a claim that generally triggered nostalgic recountings beginning with, "I remember where I was when I first smelled the smoke." People loved to remember how the whores with hearts of gold, women the town had scorned, had served up meal after meal to the fire fighters. Indeed, those who remembered the fire of '59 were sure Deadwood would never know its like again.

But the rangers who knew the parkland best were shaking their heads and walking away from talk of the days when a fire was a fire and a whore was an angel. They knew that fire in the past was a hell of a lot nicer than fire in the present, and that presently the Hills, with all its billboards and tourist traps, could very well become an inferno. Conditions were so dry that tree roots were conducting flame below ground, underneath fire lines. The

wind was pushing the flames above ground at rates the
weather, fire management and Forest Services had under-
estimated.

Fire fighting forces had been divided among three incidents: the original Argyle Fire, still burning in the south-
ern part of the district, and the White Tail Fire, which had
merged with the twin blazes christened Hellfire and Brim-
stone. The latest outbreak, to which Race and his crew had
been assigned, was the Fishtail Fire, a large-crew fire that
was becoming a direct threat to Deadwood and the surrounding area.

What his Indian squads lacked in experience, they made
up for in spirit. Race had put together the best "strike and
move" team he'd ever seen. Wilma Bird headed up the line
of twenty fire fighters, who worked quickly and effi-
ciently together, like a precision drill team, to gouge a fire
line out of the ground. His Dog Soldier squad had mas-
tered the art of leapfrogging, with each individual assigned to a specific task on the line. Whether it was
clearing, cutting or digging, the specialist moved in
quickly, made his mark and moved out of the next team-
mate's way. Good team players had a way of making the
coach—in Race's case, the crew boss—look good.

But it was frustrating when the team worked well and the
fire still had the upper hand. Race wasn't one to give up his
line easily and head for the trucks, but it was happening a
lot with this fire. It was important to keep one foot in the
black and your face to the fire. Race adhered to the lesson
old Wild Bill forgot only once: never let the aggressor get
behind you. He repeated the maxim with every retreat, but
he'd found himself a crew that didn't enjoy running any
more than he did. As crew boss he was responsible for first
aid and was constantly being told, "Hell, that ain't nothin'
but a scratch."

After four days in a spike camp, Race was glad when the troop trucks came to take his crew back to the main camp, where they could shower and rest. He rode in the back with them, sharing the bumpy ride, bone-weariness and the heading-home talk. Rumor had it that the Forest Service was running low on professional teams and that the military might be called in.

As the trucks pulled into the main camp, Wilma Bird was indignant. "Sure, we'll get this thing contained, and then the marines'll come in and claim to have saved the Black Hills."

"Hey, the army's the one with all the experience savin' the Black Hills from the Indians." Roger Shooter was the crew's historian. He braided his hair with strips of red wool, and he liked to tease Race about being on the opposite side of an old rivalry. "'Course, you Chippewa wouldn't know about that."

But Race was learning his role. "Yeah, well, I hear you Sioux expect to get the last laugh when and if you ever get your Black Hills payment from the government."

"When I'm too old to spend any of it."

"What do you mean, Shooter, you're already too old, but it ain't stopped you yet." Wilma shared Roger's heritage, but not his vision. She jumped down from the truck and poked him in the arm on her way past. "We're not taking any money. We want the land. I got a spot picked out for my cabin." She looked up at Race, who was fishing in his pocket for a cigarette. "Right near where you're staying, boss. Down the road from Sin City."

"Hey, that whole area's going up in flames," Charlie Chasing Hawk said as he hopped out of the back of the truck and joined the group.

Race forgot about the cigarette. "Where'd you hear that?"

"Moccasin telegraph." Charlie's grin faded when he realized it wasn't being met in kind. He jerked his chin and puckered his lips toward the truck driver, who was still sitting behind the wheel. "Actually, Brown heard it from his cousin who runs a dozer. Dispatcher reported they were evacuating that whole area."

"Not Deadwood."

"No, not Deadwood. Not so far." Charlie hitched up his saggy jeans and jerked a thumb to the north. "But all them cabins and stuff on the lake, they want people to hightail it outta there."

"So we've got a twenty-four-hour break comin'," Roger said. "You leave anything important out there, boss?"

It wasn't a something. It was a someone. She'd be in Deadwood at the New Moon Center. She'd be taking care of evacuees, feeding little kids and comforting other people who were about to lose everything they had. She wouldn't be hanging around a smoke-filled cabin.

Hannah told herself exactly what she'd told the state troopers at the roadblock. All she had to do was call to her dog, get him in the car and head back to Deadwood. The police were more interested in keeping tourists out of the area than they were in preventing residents from saving their possessions, but the wind was moving an escaped fire in the direction of the lake.

"Right now, the only thing between that fire and your cabin is dry trees, lady, so get your pooch and get out fast."

She found the approach to the cabins. Smoke gathered in the treetops and hung there like a big umbrella, but she didn't see any fire on her side of the road. She wondered where the fire trucks were. There should have been trucks and ladders and hoses out there working to save the cabins.

After she'd turned, she realized how thick the smoke really was. She left her little yellow car in the middle of the gravel road and made a mad dash for the cabin. "Critter!" she called, and then she covered her nose and mouth with her hand. Her eyes burned. She scampered around the perimeter of the cabin like a cornered cottontail, intermittently hollering and then covering her face before calling out again. She kept thinking she heard barking, but it was only the distant sound of a motor or the swish of the trees.

The silence was eerie. No voices, no animal noises. Hannah's heart was pounding too hard. It hurt to breathe. Call and listen, call and listen. No answer but the wind, which seemed to be gathering force. Hannah hurried into the house.

The rooms were filled with a blue haze, and even though everything was just as she'd left it, the house felt empty and forlorn. And doomed. The clock on the wall read seven-nineteen. The kitchen was clean, the sofa pillows in place, the fireplace yawning black and empty. In that moment Hannah knew it was all waiting to burn.

"Oh, Lord," she whispered. "Oh, Critter, where are you? Oh, Lord, I have to do something, quick tell me what to do, what to do."

Her eyes were tearing. She tried to take only shallow breaths as she ran around in circles gathering a few pictures of her parents, Critter's leash and his dish and a small jewelry box. She stuffed them all in a canvas sack. Then she had another thought. Socks. She wasn't wearing any. Yes, Mother, clean underwear, too. Oh, and her nightgown and the basket Nettie had given her to keep her recipe cards in.

Don't go so fast. You're getting out of breath.

There wasn't any breath. Only smoke.

Move faster. You've got to get out of here.

It was coming. She could hear the monster coming, but not the dog.

"Critter! Come on, Critter, plee-eease come."

The roar of the fire was drowning her out. Drowning her out? It sounded like a freight train headed straight for her! She dashed out the front door. Oh, God, the trees flanking her driveway were burning, and the brush around them and the—

She jumped back, shrieking, when a tall sturdy pine whooshed like a flame thrower, bursting into fire and pointing its menace at the sky. She couldn't see her car, but she knew it was closer to the tree than it was to the house. She'd burn up if she tried to drive through that fiery curtain.

"Criii-terrr!" The scream ended in a paroxysm of coughing as smoke billowed into her face.

Water. She had to get to the lake. She sprinted through the front door and out the back, clutching the few possessions she'd chosen to salvage. Her shoes barely touched the needle-strewn path as she pumped her legs like the anchor runner on a relay team.

And then she heard a clear, strong voice call her name.

"I'm here!" she squeaked. The shouting and the smoke had destroyed her voice. She peered through the trees, but she couldn't see anyone, although she was sure the voice she'd heard belonged to Race.

Her canoe lay beached at the water's edge. She dropped her bundle next to it, picked up a stick and pounded on the hull, hoping to draw his attention.

"Hey, don't destroy our transportation!"

She'd never seen a smuttier, grizzlier, more beautiful face in her life. Beneath the yellow hard hat, behind the fire fighter's goggles, there was no mistaking him. If she'd had a voice, she would have sung, "Hallelujah!"

As it was, she could barely welcome his approach in a whisper. "Thank God . . . Race . . . can't find Critter."

He didn't seem to hear her. "We're gonna have to use the boat, honey. Get hold of yourself, now, we haven't got time for—" He spared her a glance as he flipped the boat over. "Paddles, good. If that car doesn't blow, it means you're out of gas, and I'm gonna give you hell for that, too. Now get in."

"Help me find—"

"What is this stuff? Here." He tossed her bag into the canoe, took off his field pack and slung it in next, reaching for her. She'd been crying, but by this time she was nearly out of control, panicking because she couldn't make herself understood.

Ba-boom!

Hannah screamed. Race grabbed her and tossed her into the canoe with slightly more effort than he'd expended on the two bundles. He handed her the paddles and pushed off, wading in past his ankles before he hopped into the craft.

There was only one seat in this thing! It was obviously an old tub, and he wondered distractedly what surplus store had palmed it off on her. "You've gotta help me paddle," he ordered as he slid one of the oars from her grasp and pushed her toward the seat in the bow. He took the other paddle and knelt several feet behind her.

"Please listen to me." She gripped the oar with both hands as she turned, beseeching him with a pathetically tear-streaked face.

"Hannah, do you feel that heat? It's about to get a hell of a lot hotter. Now turn yourself around and paddle." He waited until she complied before he looked back toward the house. Through the smoke and the trees, he could see encroaching flames. "And don't look back. There's nothing back there you want to see."

"But I'm glad to see you."

Raspy as it was, that much he heard. "I'm...glad to see you, too." With a quick swipe, he pushed his goggles and his hat off between paddle strokes. He dropped them on top of his field pack.

"Critter's back there, Race, I couldn't—"

Her voice came in snatches, and he understood her tortured message, but knew they had no time. "Just paddle the boat, honey. Don't think. Just paddle the boat."

He knew she was fighting exhaustion, and he admired the square cut of her shoulders. She tried hard to control the tremor that betrayed her fear. She looked much the way she had sitting on the bar stool in the Plugged Nickel, and when they reached the middle of the lake, she turned on him with the same determination she'd shown that night.

"We can't go any farther."

"Hannah, we'll get across the lake and we'll—"

"No!" She shook her head defiantly. "We'll keep calling him. He'll swim out to us." She waited for him to agree, but Race couldn't bring himself to offer false hope.

His unrelenting stare didn't discourage her. "You know he's a wonderful—" Her voice gave out again, and she pressed her hand to her throat. He could feel the pain inflicted by her near-dry swallow. "—swimmer. He'll come to you, Race. You call him."

Race turned toward the burning shore. "Critter! Come on, boy! Come on, Critter!"

"He's just like a child. Sometimes if he's getting into something, he hides and he won't come." She managed to look hopeful. "Try again." He wished the look on his face could be more like hers. She believed. Not in him, necessarily, but in miracles that might come through unexpected channels. "Please, Race."

It was then that he realized he would never be able to refuse her anything. If she asked him to walk back into the fire and she had that look in her eyes, he'd do it for her. She deserved miracles, and he wanted them to come to her through him. Some of them, anyway. Whatever miracles could be squeezed through the conduit of a proud and unsentimental soul.

He had to turn his back on her to give the whistle. It hurt too much to see her like this, knowing there really wasn't a damn thing he could do to get her dog back if he'd gotten himself trapped in the fire. Watching her cabin burn wasn't much easier. It looked like a black skeleton, and he could just make out the bedroom window, filled with red flames.

"Critter! Come on out here, boy!"

God, it hurt to see all those trees burning and to listen for an answering yap he knew he wasn't going to hear.

"I don't care about the cabin," she said softly behind him. Then he heard a brave little sob. "I don't care about my clothes or my car. Race, please call him again. He's out there."

"Critter! Come on, big—" Resenting his helplessness, he bit back every curse he knew. He struggled to keep the worry from making spaghetti of his vocal cords. "Come on, big guy!"

He felt her hands on his back, and he was afraid to turn around. His eyes burned, filling with tears—from the smoke, mostly—but he didn't want her to see. She was bound to get the wrong impression. His throat burned, too—from all the screaming he'd done, surely—and he felt as if he was about to shatter his molars from clamping down on them so hard. That damn crazy dog wasn't coming.

"Get your tail out here, you stupid fleabag!"

"Race," she whispered. The sound of his name nearly broke him. He felt her forehead pressed against his back.

"The cop said you'd gone back to the cabin." He'd wanted to berate the man for letting her go back, but a cop wasn't a fireman. If he'd never experienced this kind of fire, the man couldn't have known how unpredictable its behavior could be. So Race had said nothing.

But the closer he'd gotten, the worse it had looked. "Your driveway was burning, Hannah. I got close enough to see the car, but couldn't get to the house. I had to cut down toward the lake. I kept thinking that's where you'd go. That's where you'd have to be." The paddle that lay next to him found its way into his hands, and he gripped it. But it was no weapon against fear. "I've never been scared of fire. *Never*. Not till today." He closed his eyes, recalling the face he'd seen in the flames.

"I'm afraid of fire."

"I know." He willed himself to remember that close calls didn't count. She was fine. She was there with him, and she was safe. He took a deep, cleansing breath and turned to face her. "You told me about the one you saw in Africa."

"Animals get so confused, sometimes they'll go back into a burning barn."

"Sometimes people do, too."

"It moved so quickly. I thought I had more time. I thought I could make a run for it, but all of a sudden it was like a wall around me." Her eyes widened, as though she saw some distant truth. "Critter is such a good runner. He must have gotten away from it." She put her hand over his on the paddle. "We have to wait for him. He'll come back, and he won't know where I am."

"Hannah..."

"I'm not leaving him out there. I'm not leaving, period. I'm—" Her demands were lost in the sound of a shattering explosion on shore. With a ragged scream she jumped, perilously rocking the canoe. Race hooked his arm behind her neck and pressed her head to his chest. "He'll come, Race," she sobbed. "If we call him, he'll come."

He surveyed the lakeshore. Her car must have blown. Or maybe it was his pickup, although he'd left that out in the middle of the road. The fire was crowning out, shooting to the treetops and advancing across the canopy like an athlete on a huge trampoline. He was sure he could find a place to put in on the north side, where the granite offered little rooting space for anything flammable. But they were safe where they were, drifting in the middle of the lake.

"I'll call him." He reached for the canteen on his utility belt. "Your throat's raw from the smoke," he said as he unscrewed the cap. He held the container to her lips and watched her wince when she swallowed. "Hurts, huh? I use this to cover my mouth, but sometimes nothing helps." He spoke of the blue bandanna he was untying at the back of his neck. He capped the canteen and dipped the cloth into the lake. "It'll help with the ashes and tears, though. You look like the kid who lost the fight." Smiling, he smoothed her tangled hair back and began washing the streaky soot from her face. "Does that feel cool?"

She nodded and made a thin attempt to smile.

"I don't want us to be tromping through the woods in the dark, anyway. We'll just stay out here for a while, and

I'll give a whistle now and then. If he hears us and comes paddling out here, we're in trouble. Deep water trouble."

"Critter goes canoeing with me all the time. Here, let me return the favor." He let her take the bandanna. She dipped and squeezed several times, as though she were doing the laundry by hand. Finally she turned to him and started with his forehead, where his hat had matted his thick hair. She combed through it with her fingers as she bathed him. "You look like the boy who *won* the fight. How did you know I was in trouble?"

"I heard the fire had gotten out of control up here. I was coming off my shift, and I heard about the evacuation, so I thought I'd check on you."

"I'm glad you did."

"This is a hell of a big mess, you know, when you've got wildland interfacing with residential. You've got people worried about their property, and you've got tourists who just won't give up and go somewhere else..." He was talking simply to ease the tension. He didn't know whether she even heard him. "Smoke jumpers don't usually have to contend with a lot of people."

She looked a little dazed, but when he tried to take the cloth from her hand, she kept it from him. "I'm not finished," she said as she dipped the bandanna over the side, then squeezed the water out. "Lift your chin. You have rings around your neck. Have you been playing in the dirt?" She undid the top button on his fire fighter's yellow shirt and swished the cloth over his chest.

"I wish I had time to play," he said wistfully. "I'd play with you."

He finally had to stop her before she washed off his two-day stubble. Not that he would have missed it, nor that he minded the attention, but he couldn't stand watching her try so damned hard to concentrate on the task so she wouldn't start crying again. Every once in a while her chin would quiver, and it nearly broke his heart.

Sundown streaked the sky to complement the fire. Lumpy pillows of smoke drifted overhead. Race propped Hannah's bundle against the bench for a backrest and settled himself in the bottom of the craft. He stretched out, thinking it was probably just as well that the second seat and most of the cross braces had been taken out. "Anything in here I might break?"

"No, just your mo—" She seemed to gain a sudden awareness of herself, as if the connection to her possessions somehow brought her back to reality. She scooted into the V his legs made and prodded him to sit up. Reaching over his shoulder, she extracted a small willow basket from the canvas bag. "Just your ordinary keepsakes and a little clothing. This is the only thing that might break."

She laid her hand on his shoulder, signaling that he should make himself comfortable again.

"Did Nettie make this?" He took the lidded basket from her and examined it, turning it over in his hand. "I'll bet it takes a lot of patience to do this."

"It's almost a lost art, really."

"I'll put it in my field pack." He thought of taking his fire shelter out to put under him, but he decided to save it in case Hannah got chilled.

He pulled her into his lap, centering her weight on his right thigh, and she cooperated by snuggling under his arm. "You rest, and I'll whistle."

His whistle echoed across the lake and into the fiery trees. They watched the shore, but both of them knew that the hope of seeing the yellow Lab bound into the water at this point was dim. Maybe he was out hunting. Maybe he'd deserted his post to chase a rabbit. Maybe he'd had the good sense to get the hell out of the area.

Flames lapped the south shore. Erratic wind gusts had spread this fire in unpredictable directions. Race imagined the kind of no-win situation it would have taken to force the crew to retreat from their attempts to save homes on the lake. Maybe there'd been a break-over on the fire line, and the commander had to hope the road would be enough of a barrier to hold it while he moved his crews to a safer position. A sudden blow-up, though, would have forced the teams to pull back. Another break-over had probably put the fire across the road, and there it was—in Hannah's backyard.

"Everything's burning up," she said distantly.

He held her close, gently kneading her upper arm to reassure himself as much as comfort her. Again he thanked his lucky stars that she wasn't a part of everything. "That stuff can be replaced," he said, and then he realized he was probably talking about everything she owned. "Most of it can. I know it's easy for me to say because it's not my stuff, but…" He stared hard into the trees. "Anyway, *you* can't be, and that's what matters."

She looked up at him to see whether he'd meant it the way it sounded. The expectancy in those huge blue eyes startled him, and he realized that he had. Exactly the way it sounded. She had made a place for herself in his life, and if he lost her, there would be an empty hole, bigger than any of those he'd learned to live with.

But he couldn't tell her anything as pathetic as all that. Instead he kissed her forehead lightly and promised, "I'll help you look for a place to stay and a new car. And if your insurance excludes natural disasters, hell, I've got money."

"Thank you," she said softly. She sounded disappointed with his offer. "But I'll be fine. I don't need a lot of things. I'm a missionary's daughter, remember?"

"Yeah, I remember."

She turned enough so that she could see the fire. "It's almost pretty, isn't it? The color of fire is so vibrant, and the way it billows and flutters is mesmerizing if you forget about the damage it's doing."

"Fire is part of the natural cycle. You get a mature forest with a lot of underbrush, a lot of fuel, dry conditions, maybe some lightning and poof! It all goes up in flames. But it starts reseeding almost as soon as the fire's out, and the cycle starts all over again. Wildlands are supposed to burn when they get overgrown."

He watched the fire, too. It was true, everything he'd learned in his years with the Forest Service. "Trouble is," he added, "we've got so little wildland left, we can't afford to let nature take its course anymore. Besides that, it all interfaces somewhere with places where people live."

"Will the trees be killed?"

"This area will look pretty bad for a while, but you'll be surprised at how fast the replanting takes hold." He gave her a friendly squeeze. "Just like you, it doesn't need much help. This is God's country."

"It feels like it even now, doesn't it? With all the fire and fury. If He notices the fall of a sparrow, surely He'll watch out for..."

"I'm sure He will, one way or another." The water rocked them gently. Maybe it was that reassuring motion, or maybe the solace of her physical presence in his arms was enough to make him speak of things he normally wouldn't. Like God. Like the people with whom he felt a new kinship.

"Some of the guys on my crew are Sioux. To them this is sacred land. The Black Hills rightfully belong to them, you know, by treaty. Even the Supreme Court says so. The government stole the whole works, including the part where your cabin was. The Sioux really believe it's God's country."

She was looking at him, listening intently. He was treading in her field now, and he wasn't too sure of himself, except for one thing. "They're a terrific fire fighting crew, and it's like this is a war, and they're fighting on home ground. What do you think? Maybe God meant for them to have it?"

"I think I'm renting from the wrong person." She smiled warmly, and he felt good for having said something to bring that about. "What about the Chippewa?" she asked. "What's your land like?"

"My land?" He shrugged. "I don't have any land. I've heard that the Turtle Mountains are pretty. If somebody sets them on fire, maybe I'll get up that way."

"You don't have to wait for a fire."

"Hey, I could open up a casino, huh? Wonder what the tourist trade is like. I could open up the Plugged Penny. Use an Indian head penny for the—"

She shook her head. "You should pay a visit first, Race."

"I think I should stick to the ground rules. I can feel a lecture coming on."

"I don't feel up to giving you one."

And so they drifted for a while and said little as nightfall tamed the wind and shifted its direction once again. Smaller fires glowed in the forest now, with little left to burn. The moon's luminescence shone through a smoky shroud. Finger fires crept up a distant ridge, and red-blue billows of smoke glowed against the night sky. Race took his silver fire shelter from his field pack and spread it over them as the canoe rocked gently from side to side.

"Am I getting heavy?" Hannah asked.

"I've got a cramp in this thigh." He started to move her, and she sat up quickly, as though she thought she'd offended him. "Slide over carefully or we'll flip over, honey. That's it." He chuckled, easing her into place as he tried to flex his stiff leg.

"You're not in the mood for a moonlight swim, are you?"

She shook her head.

The inevitable charley horse grabbed him. "I'm not, either, so take it easy." He felt for the offending muscle, but Hannah pushed his hand aside and clutched the hard mass, moving her fingers experimentally. He looked down at her, surprise superceding his pain.

"Here?"

"Close." He put his hand over hers and pressed down, then moved it up a scant half inch. "There."

Her fingers began kneading, loosening the tension in his leg but building it elsewhere. "Is this okay?" she asked. "Is it helping?"

"If it's okay with you, it plumb tickles the hell out of me."

"You see, I *am* heavy. I squashed your poor..."

He touched her cheek with the backs of his fingers, then tipped her chin up. "You didn't squash anything important. God, that feels good. This is the best cramp I ever—" he lowered his head as he muttered "—had."

He took the back of her head in his hand to steady her for his kiss. The joy and relief he'd felt when he first saw her pounding on the canoe came flooding back. His kiss was a homecoming, hers full of welcome. So intent was she on greeting his tongue with hers that she forgot to massage his leg. He put his hand over hers and made the motion to remind her. She massaged him more. He pressed to tell her *harder,* and she did it harder. He wasn't sure where the pain was now.

He tore his mouth away. ''Promise me you won't stop. If you stop, I could seize up and be miserable for the rest of...'' Quickly, deftly, he unbuttoned her blouse and unfastened the hook between her breasts, freeing them to fall softly into the palm of his hand. He nuzzled her ear. ''On the other hand, neither one of us has to be miserable tonight.''

Her hoarse voice sounded sexy. ''Race, we're in a *canoe.*''

''I know.'' He managed to tease her with a smile. ''Don't get too wild, okay?''

He covered her mouth with his, teasing the sensitive recess with his tongue, exploring and tasting while he drew circles around her nipple with his thumb, closing in on the center. When he reached it, she gasped, taking his breath away. He trailed hot kisses down her neck while he moved his hand over her other breast to touch and titillate until her nipples made a matching pair of round beads.

She whispered his name so softly in his ear it made his mouth go dry. Her small hand stirred, no longer kneading but caressing his thigh. The cramp had given way to a more insistent throbbing between his legs. She drew a long, unsteady breath, and the lovely, moonwashed mound that was her breast rose and fell beneath his lips. Of its own volition his hand slid lower, over her hip, along her thigh, and then to the button on her slacks.

She groaned, and he wasn't sure whether it was a protest or a plea. It didn't matter. Neither was necessary. He only wanted to please her. He wanted to touch her with a slow, soothing hand and make her forget all she'd lost to-day. She hadn't lost him.

But he could make her lose herself. Her slacks loosened now, he tucked his hand between her thighs and stroked them into relaxing and letting him touch the soft, slippery cloth that shielded her most secret place. Cradling her in the crook of his arm, he answered her next moan with a kiss as he slipped his hand inside to touch her intimately.

She wanted him now. Her giving body dampened his fingers with the proof. And she had to know exactly how badly he wanted her, for her hand rested on his own prominent proof. He let his tongue parry with hers, play-ing with her because he knew if he took his mouth away from hers, he would plead with her in his own behalf. He would ask her to free him, to touch him, to hold him the way he was holding her and to bring him ease.

The canoe rocked as she shifted in his lap, lifting her-self into the palm of his hand. His fingers stirred, and she whimpered, and the thousand ways he wanted to pleasure her jostled his brain.

But this was not a good time to rock the boat.

In his hand was a miniature canoe, and sitting in the bow was a small, sensitive lady who waited to be touched, only slightly. He knew exactly where, exactly how slightly. In response to his skillful handling Hannah broke open like cracked candy. So sweet. So deliciously his. He held her with a possessive hand, a protective arm, and he enjoyed her pleasure.

"Don't, please," she begged when he nudged her for a kiss. She clung to him and hid her face. "I'm embar-rassed to look at you."

Her small voice shook him deeply. "Why? What have I done?"

"It's more like...what I've done, and it's different when we're both doing it."

"If we were anyplace else, we'd both be doing it. Look—" She burrowed deeper, as if she would find a way into his shirt pocket, but he would have none of it. "No, look at me, Hannah." Slowly, she did. "It gives me pleasure just to touch you. I had a bad scare a little while ago. I was afraid you were..."

He closed his eyes and touched his forehead to hers, his favorite way to share secrets with her. "I want to feel you, alive and safe and close to me. I don't ever want to let you out of my sight again after today."

In the quiet silence that followed he knew he'd said too much. Then she whispered bravely, "I was ready to put the boat into the water. Maybe *I* rescued *you*. Or maybe we rescued each other."

"Maybe we did." He lifted his head in the hope of seeing some sentiment in her moonlit face. "You said you loved me." She avoided his eyes. Her face was shadowed, like the sooty-faced moon. "Hannah, look at me. You said you loved me."

"I do."

"Then let me know you in ways no one else has ever known you." He lifted her chin and forced her to look at him. "Don't turn away from me like you're ashamed of something we shared . . . something I thought was good."

A small, sorrowful sound escaped her throat as she touched his lips with loving fingertips and sought forgiveness in his eyes. He wanted her to tell him he hadn't shamed her, but she didn't say the words. Instead she kissed him, like the princess bestowing her favor on a frog, and then she simply snuggled into his arms. He leaned back and held her to his chest, stroking her hair until he knew she'd fallen asleep.

· He watched the smoke float across the fire's reflections in the water. Her misgivings disturbed him. He didn't understand them. He understood fire better than he understood women, especially this one. The burning was scattered now. A mop-up crew would be along soon. He wondered where the new fire line was and whether it was holding. At least the wind had died down.

Mentally he accounted for the conditions, the lay of the land, the fuel types he knew to be in the area, and he counted the options for suppressing the fire. And thus he drifted and finally slept.

Chapter 10

Hannah wasn't sure whether she was really awake when she heard barking. She was fairly certain, however, that the all-over stiffness in her body was no dream. She felt like a mummy in an updated aluminum-foil wrapping—her limbs weren't about to budge. Then came the distant barking again, harmonizing with its own echo. The body beneath Hannah's stirred, and she lifted her head to peek out from the fire shelter.

"Hi, there, ladybug," said a smiling voice. When she pushed the crisp fabric back further, she saw the actual smile. "Guess your child didn't burn after all."

"My child?"

"I think that canine kid who's barking his head off over there belongs to you."

"Critter?" Hannah pushed sleep's cobwebs away along with the covers as she rose to peer over the side of the canoe. "Critter! Oh, Race, it *is* Critter."

He grunted when she sat on his abdomen. She glanced down, and he squinted up, visibly pained. "I told you he'd come back," she prattled, easing herself down into the boat. "I *knew* he wasn't . . ."

Critter continued to bark crazily and paw the sandy shoreline. Hannah hardly noticed the blackened devastation behind him. The sun was about to rise on a brand new day, and her good friend was alive. "Will you look at that? He's showing us where to put in."

"He's picked a good place, all right. Oh, God, I'm stiff." Race extended his torso one vertebra at a time, then lifted his long arms over his head and gave another two-fisted stretch. Once he was done he reached behind his shoulder, as though he was pulling an arrow from a quiver. "Here, have a paddle."

Hannah took to the chore more eagerly than she had the night before. Critter was howling, telling her to get a move on. "Stay there, boy! We're coming!"

"Like *stay* is actually part of his vocabulary. I'm the one taught him to lie down."

"Didn't I tell you he'd come?" The sky was an energetic shade of pink, and it felt like Christmas morning. But there was no ice blocking Critter's leap into the lake. Hannah laughed. "Yes, sir, that's my doggie!"

"I don't know. Sure swims like a froggie."

"Oh, you." Her hair whipped about her face as she turned to deliver a happy scolding. "That's a very personal song. Not meant for human ears."

"Sorta like one of those screechy dog whistles, huh?" Squealing, she splashed him with her paddle. "Ah, that feels great." He scooped up a floating stick and hurled it toward the shore. "Go get it, fella!"

"Look at him go. The fire didn't hurt him a bit."

"Bet you anything some fire fighter picked him up. He must've gotten away this morning and come back."

They were nearing the shore, but the dog easily beat them. Executing a flying U-turn as he snatched up the stick, he bounded over gravel and grass and vaulted back into the water.

"Oh, no!"

Race saw it coming in time to grab his field pack and Hannah's canvas bag and hop out of the rolling canoe into thigh-deep water. But Hannah tumbled headlong into the drink. Critter was all over her. She sputtered and gasped, struggled to her feet and squealed his name, half in protest, half in praise.

"Come on, Critter, let the woman up." Race dropped the bundles on dry land. He slapped his thigh and chirped to the dog, who immediately popped out of the water, tongue lolling.

"'Atta boy. Look at her, now, you got her all wet." Critter stood at Race's feet and shook himself thoroughly to even things up. Hannah came slogging out of the water, pushing her soggy hair back and giggling.

Race grinned. "I don't know what you're laughing about. I've got dry clothes somewhere. I hope you've got something to wear in that bag."

"Socks, underwear, nightgown," she ticked off.

"That's all you need." He draped his arm around her shoulders. "I say, make a bonfire of all the extraneous stuff and get down to basics. We can find a lot of uses for that white flannel nightgown. Your basic pillow. Basic blanket." Her shoulders became an accordion under his arm as he confided close to her ear, "Basic surrender signal."

"I'm afraid we're past that." She felt as though some of the wind had been squeezed out of her sails by the word "surrender."

"I'm afraid you don't understand." He craned his neck to get her to look at him. She allowed him only a glimpse of her eyes. "I don't think I got any signals crossed last night, did I?"

If she said yes, she'd be lying, so she said nothing.

"If I do something you don't like, you tell me, and vice versa."

She nodded as she reached down to pet Critter's square head. She couldn't tell him that she *had* liked it, and that was the problem. Her dog had been lost, her house had been burning down, and the man had only touched her and she'd lost her mind. It was crazy, she told herself. Another inner voice kept trying to tell her it wasn't just crazy. But she shook her head and refused to hear the part about what else it was.

"Is that a yes, you'll tell me, or a no way, you'll keep me guessing?"

"Haven't I told you before when I didn't like something?" she evaded.

"My skinny-dipping and my blackjack tables." He took her shoulders in his hands and turned her to face him. "If I'm going to bring you nothing but embarrassment, even when we're—"

She covered his lips with three small fingers, then extended herself on tiptoe and kissed him. "I love you," she said, because that much she did understand. "I'm not embarrassed to say it or to feel it."

"—even when we're making love. You're embarrassed about that."

"No, I'm—"

He drew a deep breath and pulled her flush against him, groaning, "Aw, honey, you and me…it's like putting a cat in a cage with a canary."

Closing her eyes, she eased her nose into the V of his shirt and inhaled the smoky scent that covered them both. "You don't belong in a cage."

"Neither do you." But he meant not with him, and she meant not at all. He kissed her hair. "Wanna perch on my shoulder? I'll carry you out of the woods."

She put her arms around his neck and grabbed two handfuls of shirt collar. "Maybe if I held tight to the scruff of your neck I could fly us out."

"Lil' ol' bird like you? We'd never get off the ground."

"I hate to—" She caught his unhappy expression and quickly revised, "I'm *delighted* to remind you that we already have."

Once they got moving, it was like picking among the bones of a great, charred skeleton. Charcoaled pine duff covered the ground, and the smell of ash hung in the air. Race put his hat on Hannah's head and guided them clear of the dead trees he called "snags," which were still burning and could fall without warning. He pointed out patches of white ash and swarms of gnats, close to the ground. "Hot spot," he'd say, and they would walk around it. "Hate to leave it like that," he'd mutter.

But they soon ran into a mop-up crew, and Race was visibly relieved. He spotted the man whose hard hat, like his own, bore the words Crew Boss in large red letters.

"Hey, Jack!" Race called. "Got a civilian here whose cabin went up last night. Hannah, this is Jack Harvey."

Hannah exchanged nods with the gloved man, but a sudden awareness of herself as the person Race had just described left her feeling detached. She heard the distant bellow of a bulldozer and the whine of a chainsaw. This was no longer her woods. It belonged to these fire fighters, who were tearing the smoky remnants down. They spoke too easily of the normal and the extraordinary in the same breath.

"Is my pickup still sitting up there about half a mile from the roadblock?"

"Which roadblock?" Jack asked. "We had to move it twice, this thing spread so fast. Yesterday's fire was spotting distances of up to half a mile."

"What about the Fishtail Fire?"

"Contained, pretty much, but now we got a new one. Strawberry Hill." The man glanced at the smoke-filled skies to the north and shook his head. "Damn thing's looking at all them old wooden buildings in Deadwood and lickin' its chops. Sure hope the Deadwood Fire Department has enough manpower to hose everything down, just in case."

"It's mostly volunteers," Hannah said. Her house was gone, but she could take comfort in the fact that the New Moon Center was still standing. "What do we have to do, wet down the outside walls?"

"Most important thing is the roof," Race explained. Then, to his counterpart, "They bringing in more heavy equipment?"

"They've got some engines from Rapid City and some extra tractors, couple of choppers from the air base. The governor's declared a state of emergency, so they'll be rounding up more help. I guess nobody thought it would move this fast."

"Hell, it's just as dry here as it is in the Rockies, and we've been busy up there this summer. All it takes is a little wind." Race motioned to Hannah. "We'll start walking, see if we can hitch a ride."

Trees on both sides of the road were burned, and there were patches of brush still aflame, but Race's pickup was unscathed. He'd left the keys in it, and someone had moved it to the side of the road. They loaded Critter in the back and drove to Deadwood.

The plywood cutout of a dance hall girl that towered over Main Street appeared to have its head in the clouds. But the clouds were billows of smoke, as outrageously puffy as the only three-dimensional aspect of the howdy-there-big-boy sign—the lady's foam rubber breasts. The fire wasn't visible yet, but the roiling smoke left no doubt that the flames were on their way. People were preparing for the worst. Some were covering outside walls with silver sheets of fireproofing material similar to the fire shelter Race carried with his field pack. Others were hosing down roofs and sidewalk porticos.

Race took Hannah to the New Moon Center. Finding a place to park was a challenge.

"We've taken in a lot of people who had to leave their homes," Hannah explained. Deadwood never had wasted much acreage on parking. "From the looks of it, we've increased our numbers since last evening."

Race left the pickup blocking two cars he decided wouldn't have anyplace to go, anyway.

"You're coming in with me?" Hannah asked.

He took his hat back, pulling the brim down over his forehead. "Not without protection."

Myriad voices echoed beyond the big double doors. Because it housed confidential case files, Hannah's office was the only space that was not open to those who had been displaced by the fire. The day-care room was burgeoning with toddlers. In the chapel, those who sought refuge spoke in whispers. The craft room was full of cots, sleeping bags and crying, coughing babies.

"More evacuees," Tasha announced with a sweeping gesture as she met Hannah, Race and Critter at the craft room door. "More like refugees. This is the tourist season, so everything in Rapid City, Sturgis, even Sundance and Casper is booked. And we don't have enough toilets. We've got one little stove."

"Can you cook, Tasha?" Race asked. Hannah gave him a puzzled look much like Tasha's, but without the scorn. "I know you can stew pretty good, but can you cook?"

Tasha punched her fists to her hips. "Of course, I can cook, but we're running out of—"

"Everybody likes hamburgers and fries." His hat proclaimed him Crew Boss, and he waved Tasha toward the door with all the authority of the role. "Come with me. You're a hell of a good organizer, lady, and I have a feeling you're about to rise to the occasion."

"Race." Hannah stopped at the threshold of the door he held open for her. "I think I know what you have in mind, but your partner—"

"Is about to meet her match. Right, Tasha?" Before Tasha had a chance to answer, he managed to usher both women into the hallway, making plans as he went along. "Hannah, you'll have to coordinate this alliance, because I need to get back to my crew. This may be your chance to bring both sides to the peace table. Besides, you need clothes."

Clothes? "Mine are dry now. Except . . . underneath."

"I think I've got just the thing."

Hannah wasn't sure how she should interpret that mischievous look in his eyes, but she was glad he was willing to help her take care of all these people. She crooked her finger at a ten-year-old girl who was lurking in the doorway of the day-care room. "Do you like dogs?"

"Does he like kids?"

"He's like a kid, himself. You're in charge of him, okay?" She watched the dog nuzzle the child's hand. The little girl giggled, then grinned proudly at the three adults. Hannah was satisfied that a small measure of peace had been achieved already. "Be good. I'll bring each of you a hamburger."

The Plugged Nickel had only two customers. Even in the forenoon, that was unusual. When Race walked in Vicki hit him, with what she considered to be the major issue of the day: no help. He came back at her with his philanthropic plan.

Vicki's jaw dropped. "We're going to feed *how many?*"

"No more than five thousand," Hannah said sweetly, and she gave Tasha a wink.

Race knew he had to do some fast talking to keep all the pearly white teeth in the room from turning into fangs. He laid a friendly hand on his partner's back and directed the unlikely team of three to the door at the far end of the bar. "We're a community-minded business, Vicki."

"The hell we are." Even as she was mounting her argument, Vicki was following Race's lead. "We're a profit-minded business, and you'd better get yourself up on that roof and start soaking it down, Race Latimer, or we could be up the creek."

"The creek may be our best hope. Now, I don't have a whole lot of time, Vicki, so I want you to open up the kitchen to the New Moon ladies."

"Daughters of the New Moon," Tasha corrected.

"Since when is a lady not a daughter?" Race raised both hands in immediate surrender. "Forget I asked." Without missing a beat he turned to Vicki and reversed his palms in supplication. "They've got a lot of people over there who may lose their homes. They don't know what's happening out there. All they really know is that they're tired and hungry.''

"What if they evacuate us?" Vicki demanded as she assumed a folded-armed stance in front of the kitchen door.

"We'll cross that bridge when we come to it. The fire's not that close yet," he said quickly. He was beginning to feel the effects of being outnumbered as three women faced him with that arms-folded, man-assessing attitude.

What are you going to do now, Race? You've got two waiting for the next move, one standing in front of the door.

"Oh, yeah." He snapped his fingers and strode for Vicki's favorite cabinet behind the bar. "I need a few souvenirs."

Vicki was right behind him. "Souvenirs?"

"Plugged Nickel souvenirs. Small ladies' sweatshirt, pants, and one of those satin jackets." Hunkering down between the open doors, he sorted through the merchandise on the shelves, checking the tags for sizes. "Hannah's going to be a walking billboard for the Plugged Nickel."

"These are for *her?*" Vicki eyed Hannah up and down, pointedly considering the bedraggled condition of her shirt and slacks. "What happened? Was the creek your only hope, too?"

"I guess you haven't heard," Race put in as he reached for the box marked Women's. "Hannah's cabin burned down, which means yours probably did, too."

"Oh." It took only a moment for Vicki to digest this news and turn to Hannah. "I'm sorry to hear that. I wasn't living out there, so I...so, you know, if you need anything else..." She glanced down at Race, who was fumbling in the box and obviously needed some help. "Sure, give her some of those," she said, a new lilt of generosity brightening her voice. "What size underwear would you—"

Hannah was hesitant, and her answer came softly. "Four."

"She wears a *four*, Vicki." Grinning to himself, he plucked pair after pair from the box. "I think we've got plenty of fours."

Tasha turned to Hannah. "Are we really going through with this?"

"I think, if it's all right with both partners, it's a solution to our immediate problem."

Vicki threw up her hands. "Go ahead, take over the kitchen."

Tasha moved to do just that. The door swung shut behind her as Race slid a pile of souvenirs along the bar toward Hannah. But Vicki grabbed his arm. "Everyone's gone home, Race. I don't have any help here."

"This fire's enough gamble for anybody, Vicki."

"Well, should I sell drinks?"

"No." He glanced toward the table where the two customers sat nursing their beers and taking in the whole show. "Drink up, guys. We're closed."

"We just stopped in for a short one," one of the pair said amiably.

Race lowered his voice and formed a huddle with the two women even as he filled Hannah's arms with the pile of folded clothes. "It's not easy to evacuate drunks. Vicki, I suggest you get up there on the roof with that hose, and just pray that roofing outfit we hired last fall knew what the hell they were doing." He turned to Hannah. "You got everything you need?"

The kitchen door opened, and Tasha poked her head out. "Looks like there's plenty of food here," she reported. "And plenty of people over at the Center to help transport it."

"'Atta girl." He put his Crew Boss hat on Tasha's head, took Hannah by the elbow and ushered her around the bar.

"Don't you need this?" Tasha asked, smiling Race's way for the first time ever.

"I've got another one in my pickup. You wear that hat, you get no back talk." He noticed how different Tasha's face looked when she was smiling. Younger. "I guess you don't get much anyway."

"You'd be surprised," she said with a laugh. "Don't burn yourself, now."

Moving the length of the bar on his way to the door, Race shoved his hand into his pocket. When he looked up at Hannah, he saw the smile he loved. Warm and approving. He was doing just fine.

"I've gotta go. Listen, if they tell you to evacuate, here are the keys to my pickup, and here's—" he reached for a cocktail napkin and grabbed a pen from the cash register "—my sister Lannie's phone number. I'll get hold of her if I can't find you." He tucked the napkin and the keys in Hannah's pocket and glanced behind the bar, avoiding her eyes so she wouldn't see just how little he liked that last thought. "Take my painting, will you? It's an original."

"That?" She obliged him with the laugh he was looking for.

"Up and coming young artist, working her way through college. That's a self-portrait." She grimaced incredulously, shook her head and smiled for him. She was clutching his gift of sweats and Plugged Nickel panties to her breast, and he wanted to take her in his arms right there and kiss her, just for accepting it all and letting him feel as though he'd done something good.

But there were patrons at the table, an old girlfriend at the other end of the bar and an old enemy about to take over his kitchen. So he just smiled and touched Hannah's shoulder, taking a bit of her hair between two fingers. "I'll check back whenever I can to make sure you're all getting along okay."

Hannah's eyes shone overbright. He stepped back, reluctantly taking his hand away. "You got that, Vicki? Getting along *nicely*."

Vicki stepped up beside him, looking at him as though she'd missed the whole exchange. "I just had an idea. I Survived the Deadwood Fire T-shirts. What do you think?"

Race laughed. "I think you'll land on your feet no matter what, partner."

"And I'm always nice."

"Put me down for a couple dozen at least. Peace offering for the Daughters of the New Moon, and of course—" he looked at each of the three women in turn and grinned as he made for the front door "—for this amazing hotshot crew."

Tasha had the last word. "Fire sure makes strange bedfellows."

The Plugged Nickel became an auxiliary kitchen for the makeshift shelter at the New Moon Center. Nettie was in charge of the serving line, and Celia supervised cleanup. Vicki was generous with her supplies and equipment. She followed Race's advice and locked up the liquor, even though beer sales were good in some of the other establishments. The town was getting pretty parched, conditions being what they were. But nobody had time to overindulge.

People pulled together, and swapped jokes along with lengths of garden hose. Old Carver Jenks drew a crowd when he scaled one of the many available ladders, reverently removed the plywood saloon girl's bosoms and wrapped the rest of her in fireproof sheeting. Only Carver knew why he elected to stash the rubber bust in the sanctuary of Mount Moriah Church for safekeeping.

Sleeping quarters at the Center were close, and anyone who wasn't coughing seemed to be snoring. At Hannah's request, the sheriff evacuated two senior citizens and an asthmatic child as the air became heavier with smoke. After a day and a half, news came that the fire was near containment. Within hours word came that it had gotten out of control again.

That night, Race showed up at the Center. He needed rest and could have done with a shower, but he had no time for either. He pulled Hannah into the privacy of her office, closed the door behind them and kissed her until both of them came up gasping for air. She touched his face, his shoulders, his hair, making sure he was all there. It nearly drove him mad, since the thought of touching her while she touched him had kept him going long hours with little sleep. He arrested her hands in his, held them, kissed them, and drank in the welcoming look in her eyes.

"I'm taking a helitack team up one of the back slopes," he told her finally. "Unless we get a crew up there, the fire's sure to run that slope tonight, and we'll be looking at total evacuation by morning."

"You're going to jump?"

"No, we'll rappel from a helicopter. They get close to the ground, throw out a rope, and you slide down. Nothing to it." She wasn't buying into his lack of concern, so he didn't try to sell her any more. "They've been dropping water, but it hasn't been effective. The water just buys some time for the hand crews to get in there to dig fire lines. But this fire's running in the crowns late at night, and everything's so damned dry that by early morning we've already got spot fires way the hell out in front of the main fire."

"What are you going to do?"

"They'll drop some retardant." He pointed at the ceiling, indicating that "they" were air tankers. "We'll burn out a firebreak, and then we'll take care of the hot spots when the damn thing tries to slop over."

"What if the main fire catches up to the backfire?"

"Then we'll get the hell out of the way before the whole thing runs over us." He'd alarmed her half on purpose, wanting to see her eyes widen in fear for him.

But seeing it, he needed to take it away again, and he soothed her forehead with his fingertips and traced her eyebrows with his thumbs. "It won't. Smoke jumpers dig fire lines that hold. My survival is assured, and I've already ordered the T-shirts to prove it."

"How long before—"

"I've gotta go." Holding her face in his hands, he kissed her tenderly and smiled. "I keep saying that, don't I? I was close by, and I had a short break before—"

"You were probably supposed to get some rest before you did this helitack thing. Isn't that what the breaks are for?"

"I wanted to rest my eyes on you. This'll be a long shift. Everything going okay?"

"Critter's a hit with the kids. Vicki and Tasha make a good team." Her enthusiasm was constrained by the fact that he was pulling away. Her hand slid along his arm and found brief mooring in his grip. "Put the fire out and come back to us, okay?"

"Those are the first two things on my list." He pressed the back of her hand to his lips before he let it go. "Tell you about the third later."

The following day Hannah busied herself with the problem of finding places for people to shower. Most had brought extra clothes, but some hadn't, having assumed they were just getting out of the fire fighters' way for a few hours. Like Hannah, many of the adults who had become the Center's charges found that pitching in for the good of the shelter helped them keep their minds off whatever might be burning. Others, who were either obsessed with worry or simply numb, required patient ministry. For the children, the whole affair was an adventure.

By afternoon the talk in Deadwood concerned evacuation. Most people claimed they weren't going, no matter who held a gun to their heads. Some tried to figure out who might take them in. A few bets were made at four-to-one odds against the town going up in smoke.

By evening rumor had it that Strawberry Hill fire was under control. Several vehicles ventured out and returned to confirm the rumor. The helitack team's fire line was holding. Hannah assumed that the crew would be relieved and that Race would probably fall into a camp cot or bedroll somewhere and show up at the Center in another twelve hours.

She didn't anticipate the phone call from a Rapid City hospital.

The sterile-sounding voice belonged to a woman. "Basically it's smoke inhalation, but I really can't tell you much over the phone. You were the only person he asked us to notify, and what he said was, 'Tell her I'm okay.' Which isn't exactly true."

"*Will* he be okay?"

"Is he important to you? If he is, I suspect that your presence would enhance his chances."

Chances.

On her way out the door she ran into Nettie, who knew instinctively that something was wrong. Hannah hedged. She was the only person he'd asked the hospital staff to notify, but standing right in front of her was his mother. Race could notify his sister if he wanted to. His mother was someone he could not choose to notify.

Whether he *would* choose to if he could was a matter Hannah elected not to wrestle with as she blurted, "Race is in the hospital."

Nettie pressed her fingers to her lips and said nothing.

"They won't tell me much over the phone, but they said if he meant anything to me I should—" Those weren't exactly the words the nurse had used, but they would do. "He left me his pickup," she said as she started toward the door. "Are you coming?"

The drive was not a long one, but the tension was thick in the cab of Race's pickup. The two women had dashed out the door in a panic. Now there was time to consider how little they knew and what they might find.

"I think you have to tell him, Nettie."

Nettie fingered the button on the cuff of her long-sleeved blue dress. "We don't know what condition he's in. This isn't the time."

"All these weeks you could have told him, and 'now isn't the time.'" Hannah hadn't pressed before because she'd told herself the truth would come, in time. Now time had become the operative word, and she knew well how deceptive it could be. "Last chances don't always identify themselves, Nettie. The last time I saw my mother, I surely didn't know—"

"Why do you speak of last chances? The hospital called you because his life is with you now. You should be speaking of his life. Not his death." The older woman stared at the road ahead. "And he's known no life with me."

"He deserves to know his mother." Suddenly Hannah found herself blinking back tears. She didn't know why she'd thought of her mother's death, or why she felt so desperate now. Desperate to see him. Desperate to "enhance his chances." She ignored the speedometer as she pressed her toes against the pedal and wished for longer legs.

"I didn't mean to say...I don't want to think that he might die," Hannah explained. She took a deep breath to steady herself and tried for a little cockiness. "How bad can smoke inhalation be? The man's as strong as a horse, even though he smokes too many cigarettes."

"I don't know how bad it can be." Nettie touched her arm. "But I know seeing you will be good. It will help."

It felt like a healing touch. A mother's reassurance. Hannah reached eagerly for Nettie's leathery hand, and she repeated with bleary-eyed conviction, "He deserves to know his mother."

The tent around him was not a fire shelter. It was transparent, and beyond it, he saw Hannah's pretty face. He thought it was a mirage, and he drifted back to sleep. But when he woke again, the tent was gone, and Hannah was still there. She smiled and moved closer to the bed.

"How do you feel?"

"Hung over." The voice was too husky to be his. "Wish I could remember what great fun I had."

"Apparently what you had was a faulty fire shelter. Was it the same one we used?"

"Yeah. I should have picked up a new one." Her hand felt cool against his face. "What was my CO level, do you know?"

"The doctor said you came in at fifty percent, which means—"

"Means it was even higher out in the field, and I should be dead. Gotta quit smoking. That'd give me back five or six percent right there."

"The doctor said you had convulsions but no loss of consciousness." She brushed his hair off his forehead, smiled like an angel and touched his cheek again. He knew by her cool touch that he was feverish, and he figured he must look like hell. "You've been sleeping. You're exhausted, which is hardly surprising."

"You've been watching me sleep." Her lips parted for some kind of a serious answer, but he wanted more of that smile. "Don't deny it. I caught you at it."

"Guilty." No smile, but she touched her lips briefly to his; that was even better. "You're the most beautiful man I've ever seen. Even when you're sleeping."

"Especially when I'm sleeping. That's when I'm harmless."

"Sleep some more. It's what you need now."

"I need you."

"I'm here."

He drifted off under the sweet comfort of her lips sweeping his eyelids closed, and when he awoke a third time, after what seemed like only a quick sofa nap, he felt as though a great weight had been lifted from his chest. Carbon monoxide and smoke weighed a ton.

His throat was raw, his head still throbbed and he knew his eyes had to be bloodshot as hell, the way they burned. But he also knew that once his body had gotten the oxygen it had been starving for, it had naturally reversed the effects of the carbon monoxide in a matter of hours.

He remembered being in the safety zone—the area his crew had back-burned—when the wind had kicked up and whistled down the canyon. The main fire line had held but he and two other fire fighters had gotten themselves trapped in a low place when the fire had jumped over their heads and started burning up the hill. "Shake and bake time!" he had ordered, and out had come the fire shelters. Black smoke had a way of turning a day into night, and fist-sized embers had rained around them as they took cover.

Nothing more stupid than using a shake and bake bag that had already been deployed in another service, he told himself as he experimented with sitting up. His head swam. He was just about to call for a nurse and ask after Hannah when the old Indian woman appeared in the doorway. He hoped Hannah hadn't brought the whole sisterhood with her. He was in no mood for protests.

"What's up, Nettie? Is Hannah still around?"

"Yes. She went to get coffee. I think she's trying too hard to stay awake."

The woman didn't seem to know whether to step inside the room or stay out. She was a nice lady. He decided he didn't mind if she came in, but the damn nightgown he was wearing didn't cover much butt. He pointed toward the chair near the foot of the bed. "Could you hand me that robe?"

She offered it gingerly, as though she expected him to snap it out of her hand.

He tried a conciliatory smile, even though he couldn't imagine what she could possibly find menacing about him. His starch had definitely been sapped.

"I was just thinking I ought to find my clothes and check out, but this might be the only vacancy in town." He gestured as he tried to untangle the string tie that was supposed to hold the flimsy robe closed. "Think we could get Hannah to use this extra bed?" No answer. "Maybe if I told her I was real sick and needed a sleep-in nurse."

He looked up at the woman. Her dark eyes were filled with such anxiety that he fully expected her to tell him he had two weeks to live. "What's on your mind, Nettie?"

"A good time to tell you...is never going to come. So...I have decided to tell you now." She squared her shoulders and lifted her chin. "I am your mother."

He stared at her, trying to make sense of the words. "My mother?" No, they made no sense. He laughed and shook his head. "All I know about my mother is her name. Annette LaFrambois."

"That was my name before I married."

"You?" He studied her. All his life, he'd tried to imagine the woman who'd given him birth. There were no photographs, so he'd invented a face, and this wasn't it. "Look, I'm feeling a little weak in the head right now, and this—"

"I gave you to your father when you were two years old. I thought you would be better off." Her lower lip trembled, and she pursed her mouth for a moment to steady it. "You *were* better off."

Hearing that cool claim made something snap inside him. It intensified the dull pain he was already contending with in his chest. He stared fiercely at the woman. He could be as hard as she was. A shadow filled the doorway, and he didn't have to look to see who it was.

But eventually, he did look. Hannah her eyes glistening, had the good grace to exhibit some timidity. But he felt no sympathy for anyone now. "How long have you known about this?"

"Since shortly after we met."

"And you didn't tell me?"

"I couldn't." She stepped just inside the door. "It was something Nettie had to tell you."

"Oh, yeah?" He glanced from one to the other. Hannah was wearing his sweat shirt and a pair of jeans. He'd never seen her in jeans before. "So, what, the two of you have been playing some kind of a game?"

"Hannah had nothing to do with—"

He focused on Nettie. "Okay, then let's leave her out of it for just a minute while I tell you that *you* have nothing to do with *me*, old woman. I don't know who you are."

He left the bed and strode between them ignoring the dizziness as he looked for his clothes. The first door he opened turned out to be the john. He slammed it shut and tried the drawers underneath the TV. Bingo. He stood up feeling a little dizzy, but he was on a roll.

"I don't know a thing about you. My mother, whoever the hell *she* is, has had nothing to do with me for thirty years, so if you're that person . . ." He pulled his jeans on, snapped them closed, then stripped off the mortifying nightgown and flimsy robe while the two women just stood there and watched. He didn't care. He was getting out. "I liked you, Nettie. I don't want you to be that person."

"Nettie is a good person, Race. If you'd just—"

"Then she is not my mother. My mother left me." He sat down to pull on his socks and boots. "And she never came back. So let's just leave it at that." If he was going to make his exit without passing out in front of them, he had to do it fast. He looked up at Hannah. "You've got my pickup?"

"Yes, it was the only—"

"That's fine. Take it and get back to the Center. Those people need your services."

"Race, you have to let the doctor check you over before you—"

"I'm gettin' outta here *now*. I've been checked over enough." He inspected the drawer again, wondering who had his billfold. "Probably talked over, too, right? Sure as hell *worked* over."

"You need your pickup, Race, otherwise how will you—"

"Always the voice of reason, this one. Always the pure and innocent." He shook off the keys she was trying to hand him on his way out the door. "I don't feel like driving."

"I'll drive." There was an eager-to-please look in her eyes that was hard to walk away from. But he was walking. Her hand shot out with his billfold, which he accepted and shoved into his back pocket.

"I'll take a cab. I'm goin' places you don't wanna be, Miss Hannah. Guaranteed." He turned to Nettie, looking her straight in the eye. "You stay away from me."

Chapter 11

"I stayed away from him for a long time," Nettie told Hannah as they exited Interstate 90. They were headed for Deadwood through beautiful, unburned Boulder Canyon. "I should have kept it that way."

"I'm sorry, Nettie."

"No, you were right. The lie was unspoken, but it was there. He looked at me just innocent, expecting me to be what I was supposed to be the way he did when he was a little boy. I was supposed to be his mother then."

The evening light was waning. In the shadows of the pickup cab the creases in Nettie's face seemed less pronounced. She spoke as though she, too, were fading. "And now I was supposed to be just some old woman who hung around the New Moon Center and made baskets." She shook her head. "I should have stayed away from him. Miles away."

Hannah felt sick. It was hard to drive. Harder still to respond to Nettie without giving in to tears. Her stomach cramped up as though there were some kind of rodent gnawing on her from the inside. And she knew she was responsible for bringing this sorrow and sickness down on both their heads.

"I think it was the shock, Nettie. I think when he calms down—"

"He should know everything. Now that he knows who I am, he might go searching and find out where I've been."

"There was always that chance."

"I know." Nettie's voice drifted, defeated. "I wanted to be able to see him once in a while. To look at him and take a little pride in the man my son has become. Even though I gave him nothing."

"You gave him life." Fighting the constrictions in her belly, Hannah made an effort to assume the old buck-up demeanor her mother had always demanded of her. "And you gave him up, but that must have been hard for you."

"It was easy. I said, 'Phillip, you take him.'" Nettie turned to the side window and told the pine saplings on the side of the road, "It was easy."

"I don't believe that. You're always being too hard on yourself. In thirty years, it's never been easy."

"He has a right to hate me for it."

"He regrets his losses, too. Yes, he has that right. But you gave him to a man who provided him with a home and a brother and sister, both of whom he loves very much."

"Sooner or later, he'll find out that I was in prison. I don't want it to be part of a bad joke someone tells him."

"The story should come from you, Nettie."

"I've had my chance. It's over and gone." Nettie turned her whole body on the bench seat and faced Hannah with an incredible demand. "I want you to tell him. I want it to come from you."

* * *

It wasn't the easiest charge she'd ever had. Once she would have been more than happy to try to fix things up. But now she wanted to see Race on her own behalf, and she didn't want this added missive messing up her chances.

Only she had been the one to persuade Nettie to reveal herself, for whatever good that had done. She owed her this favor.

It had been two days since the debacle at the hospital, and Race had not reclaimed his pickup. Hannah's work at the Center had kept her busy. There were fewer people to feed, but more agencies to deal with as neighboring community services offered to share the load. Tasha was still providing meals out of the Plugged Nickel's kitchen. Hannah resisted asking whether she had seen Race there. Tasha didn't mention him.

She decided to venture over there early in the morning, before the casino was open for what little business there was. The gambling trade was hardly back in full swing, but Vicki would be ready for it. Hannah caught her cleaning the mirror behind the bar. She was dressed as the perfect Western hostess—in her black cowboy hat and her fringed white leather vest.

"Most of the help is sort of on emergency leave," Vicki explained, sparing Hannah a quick glance as she sprayed more blue cleaning solution. "You know, you look cute in that sweatshirt. How 'bout if I give you a spare, so you can wash that one?"

"I have washed it. I have two other tops now. But thank you."

Vicki set the spray bottle and paper toweling aside and squatted next to the cabinet where she kept her souvenir stock. A blue shirt flopped on the bar, followed by a pink one. "Here, this one's a cotton polo. And here's a little midriff T." The black hat and the brown eyes rose over the polished hardwood horizon. "Think you'd wear something like that?"

"Oo-oh, I don't know..."

"Well, take it anyway." She slid the two folded shirts across the bar as she stood. "I think I'll have a fire sale on these and get in some new styles."

"Vicki, do you know where Race is?" Hannah stared at the Plugged Nickel logo on the pink shirt. "The last time I saw him was at the hospital. His fire shelter—"

"I know what happened."

Hannah's eyes met Vicki's. "Then you've seen him?"

"I know he's okay." Almost sympathetically she added, "I also know he doesn't want to see you right now."

"Did he tell you why?"

"You know Race. He never tells you much about what he's thinking."

The Race Hannah knew had told her all kinds of things, and she'd longed to do the same. Since she couldn't, she'd pretended ignorance. And many times she'd squirmed, pinched by confidences she couldn't reciprocate and knowledge she could not pass on. It was an awful situation to be in.

But, then, coming to Vicki to ask where he was wasn't exactly comfortable, either.

"Would you tell him... Would you just ask him if he would—" she ran her hand over the top shirt, as though she were ironing the imprint "—please not go off to another fire somewhere without..." Another thought sparked some hope. "Or maybe he's already gone back to work?"

"No, I wouldn't say he's been working too hard."

"I see." Hannah's heart sank. She realized that the only way to save her self-respect would be to say goodbye and leave.

But she took a deep breath anyway, and tried to achieve a modicum of dignity with measured words. "I would appreciate it if he would call me. I would like to hear his voice. It sounded so raspy and painful when I last—"

"It's back to normal."

Hannah turned and looked up to the loft. There he stood on the landing, both arms braced on the rail. His chest was bare, and sleep had made a tousled mop of his thick black hair. The black-trimmed red door stood open behind him, and Hannah wondered how she'd missed hearing him open it. "Come on up," he said.

"Oh, no, that's all right, I..." It was Vicki's room. Hannah wasn't interested in seeing what kind of sheets she had on her bed, or imagining how many heads had slept on her pillows. "I was hoping we could talk."

"We can talk up here." He leaned away from the rail and stared down his nose. "Right, Vicki?"

"Sure. You can do whatever you want up there." Vicki turned to Hannah. "I'm staying out to my sister's. This man hasn't been fit company for anybody but rattlesnakes the past two days, so just be warned. He got so drunk the other night—"

"Vicki."

Vicki ignored her partner's admonishing tone and turned her volume up. "—That I was lucky to get him upstairs before he passed out."

"I was tired," Race reminded her.

"And you've been sleeping like a baby, and you haven't eaten a thing." To Hannah, as if the information took on new meaning between women, she repeated, "He hasn't eaten a thing."

"You comin' upstairs, Miss Hannah, or you wanna hear more of this?"

"Wait a minute." Vicki ducked into the kitchen and returned presently with a mug of steaming black coffee. "Take him this. You drink coffee?"

"Thank you, no."

Vicki tucked the shirts under Hannah's arm. "These are yours."

Hannah felt as though she'd been summoned, but it seemed hypocritical to chafe at the idea of mounting the steps bearing his coffee when she'd just made a bald-faced plea for news of him. Most of which he'd probably heard. He looked like the Colossus of Rhodes, standing there shirtless and humorless at the top of the stairs. She ascended the last steps quickly, anxious to put her feet on par with his.

He took the hot mug from her hand and sipped noisily as he gestured toward the door. "Damn stuff's hot," he muttered as he followed her.

The sheets were red satin, and the bed had a big brass headboard. Race's workboots sat on the floor next to a tufted velvet chair. His yellow shirt was draped over the chair's arm. A pack of his brand of cigarettes lay on the night table.

Hannah watched him take a seat on the bed, sipping his coffee dutifully, as though it might fuel him. He still looked tired. "How are you feeling?"

"She made it sound like I'm in really bad shape, and I'm not. I had no business drinking that night. Hell, the smell of the stuff was enough to put me away."

"You were completely exhausted."

"I don't often..." He looked up at her warily, as though he expected her to doubt him. "I used to. I used to party around a lot. Get drunk. Get mean. Punch out anybody who got in my way. My sister..." He smiled, remembering. "Lannie used to give me hell for it. Everybody thought she was this scared little mouse, and she pretty much was when our dad was around, but she's the one who raised me. She wasn't afraid to tell me I was screwin' up royally."

Hannah swept his shirt up and sat in the velvet chair, draping the shirt over her knees. "I'd like to meet her."

"Oh, she'd like to meet you, too," he said on his way to another sip of coffee. He pressed his lips together briefly and nodded. "You're two of a kind. Damned reformers."

"I've never seen you in the condition Vicki described, so I hardly think it fair—"

"You don't want to." He set the mug on the night table and rubbed his hands over his face, drawing a deep breath. He looked at her for a moment, trying to decide whether to tell her why. She waited.

"A while back, when I was still living at the house in Mobridge, my sister fell for this Indian guy. George Tracker. My brother, Trey, is married to his sister." He gestured off-handedly. "It gets kinda complicated. But I knew George from way back, and he'd always had a bad reputation for carousing around the countryside. So I told Lannie what a loser this guy was, told her stuff I never should have told her. Because she's a lady, you know?"

He looked to Hannah for the kind of affirmation only another lady could give. She nodded, encouraging him.

"Anyway, I told George to stay away from my sister, even tried to fight him one time when I was half shot. He was sober. In fact, he'd quit drinking altogether, and he wouldn't fight me. But he got beat up real bad that night by some other guys, and he nearly died. Left him blind in one eye and crippled on one side. Lannie stuck by him.

"See, most guys didn't know how good she was because all they saw was this kind of a plain Jane. Matter of fact, I heard a guy call her a 'dog' once. He only said it once. I beat the livin'—" His eyes brightened with the memory, and he checked to see that Hannah got the picture, too. She smiled knowingly.

"So she never went out much before George. Anyway, he recovered and they got married, and she's trying to get pregnant even though she's way past her prime."

"People aren't as persnickety about 'prime time' as they used to be, thank the Lord."

"Yeah, thank the Lord." Echoing the words gave Race pause. "You think it's okay to—" he lowered his voice, as though the walls might have ears "—kinda pray for something like that to happen?"

"For your sister to have a baby?" He nodded, and she wanted to hug him. "I think—"

"She'd make a hell of a good mother. I can personally vouch for that. Even when she was just a kid herself..." He heaved himself off the bed and snatched his cigarettes off the night table as he searched the front pocket of his jeans for matches. "What did I need the ol' basket lady for, with a sister like Lannie?"

Hannah rubbed his shirt collar between her fingers. She'd almost hoped they wouldn't get to this. "What did your father tell you? Did he explain anything about his relationship with your mother, or why—"

"He didn't have to tell me anything. I knew he had a wife and kids, and then there was me. And I didn't look anything like the other two." The cigarette bobbed in the corner of his mouth, unlit. He plucked it out of the way. "He told me I was his kid, and he was responsible for me. He told me what her name was—Annette LaFrambois. 'Course, I knew I was half Indian, and I knew that embarrassed my father. He didn't like to talk about it, so I never brought it up." His face tightened. "And he told me she wasn't coming back. Ever."

"She asked me to tell you more about her."

"There's nothing I want to know about her." Impatiently he stuck the cigarette back in his mouth, lit it and turned his head to send a stream of smoke toward the well-equipped wet bar in the corner.

Thus fortified, he faced her again. "The only thing I want to know is why you introduced me to her. Did you know then?"

She gave a guilt-ridden sigh and nodded.

"We talked about her—like a fool I'd stand there talking *to* her—and you never *once* hinted—"

"I couldn't tell you, Race. You know that. I'm not even sure why she told me, since I wasn't counseling her anymore. Except that she still comes to the Center, and we're...friends." Hannah tried to maintain a sensible tone. When she spoke of her professional commitment, it came naturally, but now she spoke of her commitment to Race.

"Once you and I started seeing each other, there were so many times I wished she hadn't told me. But I couldn't change the fact that I knew. I wanted her to tell you." He met her claim with a vacant stare, and she sprang from the chair in protest. In supplication. The sensible tone was gone. "I *wanted* to tell you myself. But I couldn't."

"I feel like I've been lied to." Before she could object, he added, "Maybe technically it isn't true, but it sure as hell rides in the chest like a lie."

He inhaled another lungful of smoke as he moved toward an ashtray. Hannah followed, her pulse racing as she watched him dispose of a large chunk of cigarette.

"I'm sorry. I probably didn't handle it right. I probably should have distanced myself, extricated myself." He caught her arms as though he were afraid she might do it now. The gesture pleased her, and she spoke softly. "Right from the beginning, probably, but I think I loved you too soon."

His smile came slowly. "When did you love me?"

"When I first saw you swimming in the lake, I remember thinking..."

"The *first* time?"

"Well, that visual moment is etched forever in my memory. Maybe I loved you even then."

"I doubt it. You tried to drive me away at gunpoint."

"But since you had no trouble disarming me, I think it must have started happening right away." She aligned her arms with his, remembering her mission. "I want to tell you about your mother, Race. Now that you know who she is, she thinks you should know—"

"I need a shower." He broke away quickly, giving them both a reprieve. "See if there's anything in that little refrigerator, huh? I could eat a sow and nine pigs."

There were eggs and bacon in the kitchen downstairs, and by the time Race had cleaned up, Hannah had breakfast ready for him. She served it to him on a TV tray, and they sat side by side in a pair of Vicki's boudoir chairs while he ate. They spoke little, and when they did, it was on neutral non-threatening topics. She had brought him the change of clothing for the day—a souvenir Plugged Nickel T-shirt. He chuckled when she told him about Vicki's fire sale plan.

"All right." He set the tray aside, crumpled the paper napkin and dropped it in the middle of his empty plate. "I really don't give a damn, you understand, but I know you're not going to give up until you tell me what you've got to say. Lay it on me."

It seemed best to plunge in headlong. "Your mother spent fifteen years in prison."

"Terrific." Race's reaction was not what Hannah had expected. He slapped his knee, as if to say that was that. "My mother's an ex-con. What did she do, kill somebody?"

"She killed her husband in self-defense. She was charged with murder instead of manslaughter."

For a moment he was motionless, but he recovered quickly and spoke with the voice of reason. "If it was self-defense, she shouldn't have been charged with either one."

"Well, there was no way to prove that he was attacking her at the time she killed him, and apparently she didn't have a very good lawyer. But her husband had abused her for years, and she was terrified of him. In my mind, it was self-defense." Already, Hannah had supplied more details than she felt she had leave to give. "An Indian attorney found out about her case and petitioned for a new trial. She was convicted of manslaughter, and the judge said she'd served her time."

"And then some."

"That's right. But I think you should ask her—"

"I'm not interested. Why does she think I need to know all this?"

"Now that you know that Annette LaFrambois is Nettie Couteau, she thought you might hear the rest sooner or later. She didn't want it to take you by surprise."

He laughed sardonically and shook his head. "Honey, I've had my surprise. She handed it to me at the hospital. I don't care if she spent the last thirty years living in a convent or a whorehouse." But then he softened his tone, seemingly in spite of himself. "This guy Couteau... treated her really bad?"

"He broke several bones. Caused her to have a miscarriage." At the mention of the first offense, he glanced away. A muscle in his jaw twitched on the second. He'd gotten the idea.

"She has her share of scars, Race, but the details are hers to share, or…I suspect she'd prefer to spare you." He looked up from his study of the pattern in the Oriental rug. "Actually, I think that's the decision she made thirty years ago."

"She wasn't with him then, was she?"

"I think she knew him then. But she was a woman with few options. She was looking for a way to give you more."

"I was probably in the way of the options she had."

"Maybe so." She knew he was angling for her to disagree, which she couldn't do, not flat out. "I don't know, Race. I've never been there. And since you're not a woman, you haven't either."

"I was a kid, Hannah. I had no choice about where they put me, and nobody ever told me why." He leaned back, rested his neck on the top of the chair and complained absently to the ceiling. "No matter what I did for him, it was never good enough. *I* was never good enough."

"But he did take his responsibility for you seriously." He rolled his head and gave her a wearied look. It was a characteristic he didn't appreciate, but one he'd inherited himself. She wondered if he realized it. "That's something good," she assured him.

"After all these years, why now?"

"She's her own person now. A kind, gentle woman. A wonderful friend to me." She thought better of adding *like a mother.* "Give her a chance, Race."

"I'll stay out of her way, and she can stay out of mine." He stood up. "That's the same chance she gave me, and it turned out just fine, didn't it?"

He took his plate across the room to the wet bar and deposited it in the small sink.

Hannah followed, carrying the shirts Vicki had given her over her arm like a waiter's towel. She'd done her best, she decided with a sigh. "I should go try on my new midriff T and see whether I have the nerve to wear it out in public."

"You can do that right here. I'll give you an honest opinion." She laughed and turned to leave, but his hands were on her shoulders and his voice close to her ear. "If we leave here now, we have to deal with a lot of dead wood, Hannah. A lot of burned up stuff for us to come to terms with." He turned her around. "Stay a while."

"But this is Vicki's room."

"Nobody's been sleeping in that bed these past couple of nights but me." His smile was most seductive. "And I've been dreaming about you."

"Race, you are so disarming." The gleam in his eyes made her mouth go dry. "And so charming."

"You bring out the best in me."

And he took her in his arms and gave her his best. Her arms, souvenir shirts and all, went around his neck, and she moved close, planting her feet between his. Kissing her deeply, stroking her tongue with his, he slipped his hands beneath her sweatshirt and measured her small waist. The fragile feel of her rib cage gave him pause. He wanted to wrap his arms around her and hold her tight, breath-stealing tight against him. Too delicate, he thought. His hands found softness everywhere.

He reached behind his neck for the new shirts, dropped the polo and held the short T-shirt aloft. "Let's try this on."

She smiled dreamily and groaned, but he ignored her, pulling her sweatshirt over her head and dropping it atop the polo. Then he smiled and hooked his forefinger over the fastener between her breasts.

"But we're trying the shirt—"

"We want the natural look." With a flick of his thumb, her bra went slack, and he slid the straps over her shoulders. He admired her pale, soft breasts with their rosy nipples, but he postponed his touching. "Naturally, you look great," he told her. Her eyes were closed, and he thought about turning out the lamp in deference to her modesty. But then he wouldn't be able to see her.

"You always look great," he said as he slipped the shirt over her head.

It pleased him to know that no one else would see her this way, the soft curves of her unbound breasts covered by a single layer of cotton. Such sensuality mocked the innocence in her eyes. She was the embodiment of both, but that would remain his secret.

He kissed her again as he subtly unsnapped and unzipped her jeans. He let his fingers linger against her belly, and he wondered when she would release the tenuous breath she'd taken—and held—seconds ago. "You okay?" he whispered against the side of her neck.

She nodded quickly, and he could feel her breathing again.

He knelt slowly, taking her jeans down with him. When her hip was eye level, he smiled. She was wearing her Plugged Nickel panties. "First time I've seen them on anybody."

She giggled bravely. "That's good news."

"Best part is, I get to take them off." He came up, still smiling. "Later."

And it did come later. After he had taken her to the bed with the glamorous red sheets and removed his own clothes. After he had caressed her breasts and teased her nipples until they made a tantalizing show beneath the skimpy T-shirt. After he had kissed her and touched her and made her face glow with the pleasure of being cherished by him, *then* he removed the panties and held her hips against his. He rocked himself in her pelvic cradle, adjusting when she told him without words where the pressure felt best. Finally she kissed his neck and implored him to come inside.

He felt for the packet he'd dropped discreetly next to the bed.

"I have to take care of this first," he said as he tore into the foil. It was awkward, he fumbling, she waiting. His lips brushed her forehead, and he spoke with a hint of humor. "The better to take care of you. You don't mind if it's another souvenir of the Plugged Nickel, do you?"

She groaned. "Don't tell me it's printed on the—"

"Right on the wrapper."

"Oh, my." Her smile was his invitation. When he was ready, he nudged her thighs apart with his knee and found his way home. "Oh myy-yyy."

It was his turn to groan. "That's right, honey, exclusively yours." He stroked inside her slowly. Her eyelashes drooped to half-mast. "Available to you at the Plugged Nickel..." Her eyes requested another choice. "...Or in the privacy of your own home...your own canoe." He felt her growing pleasure almost as keenly as his own. "Wherever you want me, Hannah."

"For a limited time only?"

"*Whenever* you want me." He slid his hands beneath her knees and lifted them to give her more of himself, and, ah, she gave him more passage. Sweet, slick, loving welcome. "I'm taking you past the limits now. Way past the limits."

The rhythm redoubled, and the sensation soared, set records and shattered. It left them both feeling utterly boneless, completely content as they lay in each other's arms.

After a while he turned to her, smoothed the swatch of hair that covered her shoulder and asked gently, "No regrets this time?"

Her smile was wistful. "I've never had any regrets with you."

"Second thoughts, then."

"None that you need to worry about." She comforted him with the touch of her hand against his cheek. He felt favored. "I'm a minister's daughter," she explained. "What am I saying? I'm my *mother's* daughter. I grew up with a whole list of shalts and shalt nots, and they niggle in my brain just a little bit."

"Just a little bit?"

"A little tiny bit, but I don't worry about it."

He believed she was trying hard not to.

"I'm worried about you, though," she said, and she kissed his shoulder, then pressed her cheek to the place she'd kissed. "I was so scared when they called from the hospital. I thought about my mother."

"Why?"

"She died three years ago in Guatemala. I should have gone down there when I'd heard she'd gotten sick. It had been four years since I'd seen her. I was too busy with school, trying to get a job—excuses like that." She leaned back and sought his eyes. "I didn't want to go back there. I'd lived in those places as a child, and I'd had enough."

With a sigh she laid her head back against the pillow. "But not Mother. She kept at it until it killed her." She paused before she told him, "It was never a good time to come back. I had no guests at my college commencement."

"You should have sent me an announcement."

"You should have given me your address." She brushed a lock of dark hair back from his forehead. "I got to the hospital, and you were in intensive care. The nurse said you were sleeping, but I didn't believe her at first. You lay there so still. Then you opened your eyes, just for a few seconds, but I could've sworn you were trying to smile for me."

"I was." He smiled for her now, then took her in his arms and settled back against the pillow. She cuddled against his chest. His back felt clammy, and he remembered what he'd always hated about satin sheets.

"Carbon monoxide is a funny thing," he told her. "It has a half life of about four hours, so one minute it looks like you've bought it, yet a few hours later you can be back on your feet. That's if you were in good shape to begin with."

"Which you were," she said, hugging his waist.

"I carried your name and phone number in my pocket. I couldn't talk. I just showed it to the guys in the white coats."

"They wouldn't tell me anything over the phone. Just that if you were important to me, I'd better get down there." She looked up at him, and there was a sense of urgency in her eyes. "You're very important to me. Please believe that."

"I do. But you have to be honest with me, Hannah."

"Without Nettie's permission, I couldn't—"

That again. He wanted a promise, not a disclaimer. He sighed. "I know. You were in a bind. But I felt like a chump, can you understand that? It was like finding out that my girl had something going with somebody else."

"And the somebody else was your mother." She gave him a tentative smile. "Am I your girl?"

"I sure hope so." He heard the schoolboy in his answer, and he laughed. "I *should* hope so, considering how generous I've been with all my Plugged Nickel souvenirs. This is like wearing my football shirt for all my friends to see."

She looked down at the little T-shirt as though she were surprised to be wearing it.

"But those other souvenirs," he assured her, "are just between us."

Chapter 12

The red and white rectangular basket was a thing of beauty. Crafted of scrub willow, which most people would dismiss as good for very little, it was tightly woven and perfectly shaped to serve a function. The square lid fit firmly to make a container for Hannah's collection of recipes, and Hannah was a good cook. But Nettie?

Race knew nothing about his mother's cooking. He had no idea what color she would choose for a new dress, or whether she ever had headaches, or how good she was at playing cards. But the basket he had tucked in his field pack for safekeeping told him something. It had taken a lot of painstaking work to produce it. If she'd had no patience thirty years ago with a two-year-old's bellyaches and sticky fingers, she had found a measure of it since then. At least, for her craft.

He turned the basket over in his hands and wondered whether she had learned to do this in prison. It was a Chippewa craft. Maybe she'd learned it from another

Chippewa inmate. Or maybe her mother had taught her. Or her grandmother.

Who were those people? Race's father's parents had been dead a long time, but Trey and Lannie had known their mother's father. A small man with white hair and a farmer tan, he'd said, "Call me Grandpa Klein." But Race never had.

Years ago he'd left home thinking family ties meant mostly trouble. He sure as hell felt troubled by them now. There was no need to get mixed up with this woman who said she was his mother. Okay, so now he knew. He was a big enough man to say hello to her if he passed her on the street, but the best thing was to leave it at that. He was definitely going to leave it at that.

But first, there was one question he had to ask. What was wrong with her back then, or with him, that she would want to be rid of him? There was a damn fool kid inside him that wouldn't be still until he had the answer.

He left the basket on the seat of the pickup. He had spent the afternoon running Hannah around Rapid City, picking up food and clothing donations, placing people in temporary housing. She was staying at the Center tonight, but after he was done with this little chore, he was going to make sure Hannah had a place to stay before he reported back for fire duty. He already had the place picked out. A nice place, too. One way or another, Hannah would be living there soon.

The door to Nettie's basement apartment was at the bottom of a flight of cement steps at the rear of an old house on the outskirts of town. Race rapped on the windowless door, and Nettie answered. She looked at him strangely, and he couldn't tell whether she was surprised or pleased to see him. Wordlessly she stepped back and widened the space for him to go inside.

"I know it's late," he began, walking in hesitantly. She closed the door, and he felt as though the walls had just closed in on him.

"It doesn't matter. Most of the time I'm up late."

It was only a little after ten, but he figured that must be late for an older lady. He glanced around. Her apartment wasn't much more than a sleeping room. It was sparsely furnished and poorly lit, but it was clean except for the pile of willow sticks lying next to the small table. There was also a mess of peelings and shavings under the table and a large, shoe-shaped basket on top.

"What are you making there?"

"It's a baby's bed." Nettie moved toward the table, and Race followed her. "For a small baby. A newborn."

He wondered whether he'd ever lain in such a thing. He tested the bed part with the flat of his hand, then examined the arching bonnet.

"You have to wrap the little baby up in blankets, bundle him up tight so he can't wave his arms around. That's the way Indians do." She appeared to be looking at something in the small bed that wasn't there. "He sleeps better that way, all bundled up like he's still inside his mother's womb."

"You sell a lot of these?"

"Not too many. It's a big-ticket item, as they say." She bent to pick a slender stick from the pile. Race thought it was the kind of thing a person would dread if one had ever been used on his butt. But he felt only curiosity as he watched her pull at a loose strip of bark. "Hannah told you about me," she said.

"Yeah, she told me."

She seemed driven to make certain. "I killed a man. I went to prison for it."

"Sounds to me like you got railroaded. A man who beats up on a woman like that deserves what he gets." He couldn't tell whether the statement pleased her. He couldn't tell much of anything yet. "My father never hit you, did he?"

"No, he never did."

"I didn't think so. He's cold, but he's not..." Not what? Cruel? "He doesn't approve of fighting, making a scene."

"He was good to you, then?" She dropped the peeling on the floor and laid the stick next to the baby basket.

"He never hit me." Race shrugged. "He never touched me at all."

"But he took care of you," she insisted. "You lived in a nice house, and you stayed in school."

"I finished high school, yeah. I've had a lot of different jobs. I like to try things."

"You like to fight forest fires."

"I like keeping the damage to a minimum. It's kind of a challenge. Mainly I like jumping out of..." This wasn't getting him the information he wanted. He met her eyes head-on. "So how did it work? Did you just decide one day that you didn't want me around anymore?"

"No. Not one day." She sidestepped, putting the table between them, and stared at the basket as she spoke. "He wasn't seeing me anymore. He offered money, but I didn't want his money. There were other men by then. I could have taken you to Turtle Mountain, but being a Latimer would have meant nothing there, and you were his son, just as much as the other boy was." Her voice softened now. "I knew Phillip. He always knew what was right. I never did."

"What's right is whatever he says is right. Did he tell you you were making a mistake?"

"He told me I was a poor excuse for a mother, and that was right." She looked at him, her eyes bleak. "I was no good for you. I couldn't seem to get myself turned around. I belonged in prison. Not for killing Brady Couteau—he needed killing—but for giving up my son."

"I don't know why I'm not anxious to agree with you. Maybe I truly don't give a damn about it anymore." He shoved his hands into his pockets and stood there studying the basket with her as though they were judging it for flaws. "Hannah likes you," he said finally, knowing it was significant to both of them. "None of this stuff bothers her."

"She knows Nettie Couteau."

The name jarred him, now that it carried new meaning. "Yeah, but she knows about . . . the other."

"I've told her about Annette LaFrambois. She knows what I've done, but she knows I've toned down a lot." She chuckled dryly. "Kinda had no choice. But that Hannah, she's a real good woman."

"I know. Too good for me."

"I don't see her acting good." It was the first defensive tone he'd heard her use.

"She doesn't have to act. Like you said, she really is. And . . . I guess, like you, I haven't exactly been a saint."

"Maybe she isn't looking for a saint." She eyed him cautiously. "Are you?"

"I wasn't looking for anybody. She just came along." He smiled, recalling those first run-ins. "Funny how she came along. We're two opposites who sure do attract." Nettie nodded and almost smiled. It felt a little like approval. "What do you think of the casinos in Deadwood?" he asked. "You think they do more harm than good?"

"People do the harm to themselves."

"That's what I say. Hannah says they can't help it sometimes." His head had been buzzing the last few weeks, and he wanted a sounding board. "This town needs the New Moon Center, too. I've got some ideas..."

"Have you told Hannah about them?"

"Haven't had time." Hannah was the intended sounding board, but for some reason it was the old woman getting an earful. "I've got the money. I can give her more money. Hell, what am I gonna do with it?"

"The church board might want your money, but it's not what Hannah wants from you."

"I don't know what else to give her."

"Yes, you do." She squared her shoulders, and he detected a smile in her eyes. "Don't play dumb with me, Race. I know you're a smart boy."

"This does look pretty dumb, doesn't it? I tell you to stay away from me, and I'm the one knocking on your door."

"It's all right."

"I can be pretty hotheaded sometimes. I get over it quicker than I used to." He glanced away. "People change."

"Sure. They have to if they want to keep living."

"You hope it's for the better, right?" She nodded gratefully. "But sometimes you make a choice, and you're thinking, what the hell, it can't get any worse. Might as well go this way. And maybe it turns out okay, maybe it doesn't." Tears stood in her eyes now. He reached across the table and touched her shoulder. "I guess everybody makes some bad calls."

"You turned out just fine, though."

"You got some rose-colored glasses on you?"

Tentatively they shared some laughter as she wiped at her eyes with the backs of her hands. He rested his hand on the bonnet of the baby basket and wondered how a person could be small enough to sleep inside. Maybe he should buy this from her and give it to Hannah.

"Did you pick out my name?"

Still blinking furiously, she laughed more readily this time. "You were in such a hurry to be born, you beat out the doctor. By the time he popped his head through the doors of that delivery room, the nurse said, 'Sorry, Doctor. Baby wins the race.'"

He chuckled. "I've done a lot of running since then," he told her honestly. He wasn't looking for sympathy, just telling the truth. "Never felt like I really belonged anywhere."

"Get yourself a place to live. That's what you need." She jerked her chin in the now-familiar Indian way, indicating her front door. "This is a good place. I can unlock it from the inside."

"That's a plus." He looked at her and she returned the look expectantly. "It's good to finally meet you."

She nodded once. Her eyes seemed younger now. "You're a man with fine strong shoulders. I should have been able to see that."

He wasn't sure what to make of the meeting as he slid behind the wheel of his pickup and shoved the key into the ignition. He couldn't account for the sudden weightlessness he felt. Some kind of burden seemed to have fallen by the wayside. He hadn't known what to call the woman, so he hadn't called her anything. *Mom* didn't feel right, but *Nettie* didn't, either. He needed some time to think about it.

He needed to do a lot of thinking. About a lot of things.

Pastor Mike had told Hannah about an elderly woman who had a spare room to rent. Marta Turnbull's brother had a vacancy in a duplex in Rapid City. Neither prospect thrilled her, but she was trying to decide which one to check out first when Race popped his head around her office door.

"You got a lunch break coming soon?" She started to check her watch, but he was already dragging her out of her chair. "I've gotta take off for Yellowstone this afternoon, but I've found something I think you might like."

"A place to live?"

"It would be a longer drive for you." He smiled like a man bearing gifts. "Pactola Lake."

"Pactola! Oh, it's beautiful there. And the fire—"

"Didn't touch it."

They had to drive through burned-out areas to get there, though, and Hannah felt as though she were venturing into a war zone. Acres of blackened lodgepole pines lined the winding road. Sections of untouched greenery offered relief, but then came more blackened trunks and mounds of ash.

Race seemed not to notice. He was too full of plans. "I've been thinking about the New Moon program, Hannah. The town appreciates the way the Center pitched in, and there's an after-burning of community spirit now. I'm thinking we can get a new lease at the old rate if we act now."

"How would you manage that?"

"Part of all the gambling profits goes to the city. Some goes to charity. We ask the city to subsidize the lease on that building. We get the casinos to kick in."

"Do you think the other owners would go along with that?"

"We won my partner over, didn't we? The rest are easy pickin's compared to Vicki." He grinned at her across the cab of the pickup, and she decided to take his word for it.

At this point, she would believe he could conquer the world. She'd visited with Nettie that morning, had seen the change in her. The truth had set them both free, and Race's enthusiasm was impossible to resist.

"The other thing is, we take out the shop and use the space for day care. Then we put the shop in my restaurant."

"What restaurant?"

"The one I'm opening in Lead." He anticipated her protest, and he waved it away. "Look, it's practically the same town—two miles away—without the gambling halls. And not a decent steakhouse in either town, far as I'm concerned. Vicki wants in on it, so we'll probably have to put up with red velvet drapes, but we will need a gift shop."

"To sell Plugged Nickel souvenirs?"

"No, but I may have to do some fast talking to keep those in Deadwood," he confided as he turned off the main highway at the Pactola sign. "The space for the shop is rent-free, Hannah. It's a tax write-off."

"You make it sound like a done deal. Are you thinking of getting elected to the church board? They'd have the final word on all of this."

"I'm thinking the church board isn't about to look a gift horse in the mouth. And I'm also thinking of people coming together on this like they did when they had a fire breathing down their necks..." They'd reached a fork in the road, and Race chose the narrower gravel tine as he went on explaining his plan. "We don't want Deadwood to go soft on us, but we don't want to run all the women and kids out, either."

"It sounds magnificently crazy."

"Crazy enough to work," he claimed as he parked the pickup in a copse of cottonwoods. He slammed his door, and she opened hers with less certainty. She didn't see a house anywhere.

He took her by the hand and led her to the edge of the bright water. She had to skip along to keep up with his eager stride.

"There it is, across the lake. I'll take you over there, but I wanted you to see it from—"

She could see it quite clearly from here. It was a log home with acres of glass and wraparound decks. "Race, that's a big house. I can't rent a house that size."

"I thought we'd share it."

"Share..." Here it was. The suggestion she'd dreaded. *"Live together?"*

"Unless you don't want to." His sails drooped. There was less energy in his voice as he offered an alternative. "You could take that one, and I could easily rent something close by in the winter. Summer's when it's hard to find—"

"Race, that's too much house for me, and I'm sure I couldn't afford it, and the idea of living together..."

"Doesn't appeal to you?"

"I know it's perfectly acceptable to most people, but for me..." She permitted herself another look at the house across the water. Surrounded by birches and pines, its plate glass winked at her in the midday sun. She could live there with the man she loved if she but said the word.

He had asked for honesty.

"I want to be married to the man I live with. Does that sound too old-fashioned?"

"No." It was his turn to scan the lake. The breeze ruffled his dark hair. "I own a casino, Hannah. I run around chasing fires all summer long. I play cards, I smoke, I drink, I cuss, and I don't remember when I last stepped inside a church."

"That sounds awfully depraved."

"It is." He said it seriously. Then he gave her that look of dancing-eyed mischief. "The ultimate challenge, isn't it?"

"My only problem is—" he wanted to tease her into yielding, and she had to look away from those eyes or she would "—that I'm just plain boring."

"Says who?"

"Says me. I don't do any of those things." She did others, though. The cottonwood leaves rattled overhead, mocking her. "Every time we make love, I wish we were married. I wish we could just dispense with the 'souvenirs' and have a baby." She risked a glance at him. "Boring, huh?"

He nodded, but he was having trouble suppressing a grin. "So how come I love you so much?"

She didn't know where her laughter came from. Maybe from the outrageous joy he spawned in her as they stood there in the sunshine, he demanding "Can you answer me that?" and she claiming "*I'm* the one loving *you*."

Nor did she know who reached for whom first, or how they came into each other's arms, laughing and exchanging kisses. "I saw you first," she said. To which he replied, "But I came through hellfire for you."

"I already bought the house, Hannah."

"Bought?"

"Well, made an offer. I couldn't stand the idea of you sleeping on the floor at the Center. And I wouldn't expect to live in sin with Hannah Quinn." The laughter drifted around them like the echoes of children's voices as he took her face in his hands. "Wouldn't want to. I want a real home, with you as my wife, but if you had any sense at all, woman, you'd turn me down."

"I have no sense at all," she promised.

"You think if we got married in a church, lightning would strike me?"

"I think the sun would stand still until you said, 'I do.'"

He smiled, approving of the idea, then snapped to attention. "Oh, here." He leaned back and produced, not cigarettes, but a small blue box from his shirt pocket. "Since we're doing this the old-fashioned way..."

She held out her hand. On the top of the box, embossed in gold letters, were the words Souvenir of the Plugged Nickel, Deadwood, S.D.

Hannah read it twice. She looked up at Race, incredulous.

"Open it up," he urged.

"You can't really sell..." Inside was a nickel with a hole in the middle.

"We don't. I took that off a keychain." Grinning broadly, he took her under his arm as he punched his finger at the box. "That's my marker. Until we can get to a jewelry store and get a ring on your finger, that says you're promised."

"Promised" sounded *very* old-fashioned. Hannah smiled. "Can you show me the house now?"

"You're gonna love it, Hannah," Race assured her as he walked her back to the pickup. "You can sit in the window seat in the master bedroom and watch Critter and me swim."

"Mmm, that could be sinfully stimulating."

"How about if I teach you a couple of card games?"

"But then I'd have to learn to cuss, too. Don't you have to cuss when you play cards?"

From the lily-of-the-valley to the crowns of the pines, his laughter rang with hers.

*   *   *   *   *

TAKE A WALK ON THE DARK SIDE OF LOVE

October is the shivery season, when chill winds blow and shadows walk the night. Come along with us into a haunting world where love and danger go hand in hand, where passions will thrill you and dangers will chill you. Come with us to

In this newest short story collection from Sihouette Books, three of your favorite authors tell tales just perfect for a spooky autumn night. Let Anne Stuart introduce you to "The Monster in the Closet," Helen R. Myers bewitch you with "Seawitch," and Heather Graham Pozzessere entice you with "Wilde Imaginings."

Silhouette Shadows™
Haunting a store near you this October.

In the spirit of Christmas, Silhouette invites you to share the joy of the holiday season.

Silhouette
CHRISTMAS
Stories
1992

Experience the beauty of Yuletide romance with Silhouette Christmas Stories 1992—a collection of heartwarming stories by favorite Silhouette authors.

JONI'S MAGIC by Mary Lynn Baxter
HEARTS OF HOPE by Sondra Stanford
THE NIGHT SANTA CLAUS RETURNED by Marie Ferrarella
BASKET OF LOVE by Jeanne Stephens

This Christmas you can also receive a FREE keepsake Christmas ornament. Look for details in all November and December Silhouette books.

Also available this year are three popular early editions of Silhouette Christmas Stories—1986, 1987 and 1988. Look for these and you'll be well on your way to a complete collection of the best in holiday romance.

Share in the celebration—with Silhouette's Christmas gift of love.

Get them while they're hot—and sweet!
Look for

ELIZABETH
LOWELL

Too Hot To Handle
Sweet Wind, Wild Wind

You won't want to miss these favorite sizzling
love stories by award-winning author
Elizabeth Lowell. Look for them in September
and October at your favorite retail outlet.

Only from  *Silhouette*®

NORA ROBERTS

Love has a language all its own, and for centuries flowers have symbolized love's finest expression. Discover the language of flowers—and love—in this romantic collection of 48 favorite books by bestselling author Nora Roberts.

Two titles are available each month at your favorite retail outlet.

In October, look for:

One Man's Art, **Volume #17**
Rules of the Game, **Volume #18**

In November, look for:

For Now, Forever, **Volume #19**
Her Mother's Keeper, **Volume #20**

THE **LANGUAGE** of **LOVE**

Collect all 48 titles
and become fluent in

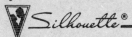
Silhouette®
™

Take 4 bestselling love stories FREE

Plus get a FREE surprise gift!

Special Limited-time Offer

Mail to Silhouette Reader Service™

In the U.S.	In Canada
3010 Walden Avenue	P.O. Box 609
P.O. Box 1867	Fort Erie, Ontario
Buffalo, N.Y. 14269-1867	L2A 5X3

YES! Please send me 4 free Silhouette Intimate Moments® novels and my free surprise gift. Then send me 6 brand-new novels every month, which I will receive months before they appear in bookstores. Bill me at the low price of $2.96* each— a savings of 43¢ apiece off the cover prices. There are no shipping, handling or other hidden costs. I understand that accepting the books and gift places me under no obligation ever to buy any books. I can always return a shipment and cancel at any time. Even if I never buy another book from Silhouette, the 4 free books and the surprise gift are mine to keep forever.

*Offer slightly different in Canada—$2.96 per book plus 69¢ per shipment for delivery. Canadian residents add applicable federal and provincial sales tax. Sales tax applicable in N.Y.

245 BPA AGNP   345 BPA AGNQ

Name	(PLEASE PRINT)

Address	Apt. No.

City	State/Prov.	Zip/Postal Code.

This offer is limited to one order per household and not valid to present Silhouette Intimate Moments® subscribers. Terms and prices are subject to change.

MOM-92R   © 1990 Harlequin Enterprises Limited

It's Opening Night in October—
and you're invited!
Take a look at romance with a
brand-new twist, as the stars
of tomorrow make their
debut today!
It's LOVE:
an age-old story—
now, with
*WORLD PREMIERE
APPEARANCES* by:

Patricia Thayer—Silhouette Romance #895
JUST MAGGIE—Meet the Texas rancher who wins this pretty
teacher's heart…and lose your own heart, too!

Anne Marie Winston—Silhouette Desire #742
BEST KEPT SECRETS—Join old lovers reunited and see what
secret wonders have been hiding…beneath the flames!

Sierra Rydell—Silhouette Special Edition #772
ON MIDDLE GROUND—Drift toward Twilight, Alaska, with this
widowed mother and collide—heart first—into body heat
enough to melt the frozen tundra!

Kate Carlton—Silhouette Intimate Moments #454
KIDNAPPED!—Dare to look on as a timid wallflower blos-
soms and falls in fearless love—with her gruff, mysterious
kidnapper!

**Don't miss the classics of tomorrow—
premiering today—only from**

TM   *Silhouette* ®

PREM